"Keep moving."

A door appeared in front of her so quickly that she almost ran into it. The last thing she wanted to do was push it open and see what was on the other side.

He gripped her arm. "Wait. Don't go out there."

Ha! No chance of that.

He released her and moved around to push through the doorway. A loud whirring sound filled the space as the door opened, and Callie hung back for a second. He didn't let her stall for long. "Cavalry's coming and we don't want to miss the party. Let's go."

She squinted up as a large military helicopter passed low overhead. The man beside her waved his arms and the aircraft banked to the right, heading back their way. When it reached their location, it hovered above them. A door opened and a ladder unfurled, stopping within inches of their position.

Just as suddenly, there was a whistling sound. A flare of light appeared over the roof's horizon.

"Get down!"

Callie's body crumpled like a rag doll as something heavy fell on top of her.

TINA BECKETT

A Harlequin® Medical™ Romance author and three-time Golden Heart Award finalist, Tina Beckett is the product of a navy upbringing. She was always on the move, and her travels eventually took her outside the United States, where English reading material was scarce. Her supply of books finally ran out, and she started writing her own stories, fashioned after the romance novels she'd loved through the years. She finished that first book and moved on to the next. After the fourth manuscript, she realized there was no going back...she was officially a writer.

When not in the middle of her latest book, Tina enjoys crafting stained-glass panels, riding horses and hiking with her family. Fluent in Portuguese, she divides her time between Brazil and the United States and loves to use exotic locales as the backdrop for many of her stories. You can learn more about Tina at her website, www.tinabeckett.com, or find her hanging out on Facebook or Twitter.

IN HIS SIGHTS

TINA BECKETT

**CARINA
PRESS™**

CARINA
PRESS™

Recycling programs
for this product may
not exist in your area.

ISBN-13: 978-0-373-06284-3

IN HIS SIGHTS

IN HIS SIGHTS

To my fabulous critique partners,
who looked over everything I threw at them.
Thank you guys so much!

ONE

COLE'S BACK ITCHED.

A normal person would simply reach behind him and fix the problem. But keeping his sniper rifle trained on the bad guy required two hands. And one eye.

He shifted his body a millimeter to the right, holding his finger steady on the trigger. Maybe his black shirt would blot the slow-rolling drop of sweat before it drove him over the edge. Unless the voice dribbling through his earpiece like the incessant drip of a leaky faucet sent him over first. What was that hostage negotiator doing anyway?

When your bosses told you to clear an American embassy—*now*—that didn't mean to sit around and shoot the breeze. It meant something bad was headed your way.

Moss threw him a warning glance from the roof of the building fifteen yards to his left. Leave it to his buddy's sharp eyes to catch the restless movement. His Special Forces chum could sit in one spot for hours on end. Cole could too, but the effort ate away at him. He craved action. Lived for it. Maybe that's why no one woman could ever hold him in place long enough to get a proposal out of him.

Short attention span.

ADHD they'd called it in elementary school. They'd drugged him up, slapped a "normal" label on him and sent him on his way.

But he'd proven them all wrong. Cole was anything but normal. Why else would his knees be glued to the roof of a sixteen-floor apartment building in a sweltering third world country? Could it be that it took one madman to take out another before said crazy person took out any of Cole's countrymen? Or country*woman,* in this case.

ADHD. Yeah. Channeled in the right direction, that label had become an asset in his line of work rather than a liability. It allowed his brain to rapidly switch tracks when the need arose. He took situations apart, analyzed them and solved them. Fast.

The military called it "thinking on his feet." Cole called it pulling his thumb out of his ass.

Then why couldn't he figure out how to make the skin on his back stop doing the hokey pokey? Because he wasn't getting any action. That's why.

If they'd inserted *him* in the middle of the situation, instead of that Washington bureau-I-don't-give-a-crat, they might have already put this baby to bed with no casualties. As it was, the only one talking was the schmuck with the bomb strapped to his chest. The so-called hostage negotiator who'd been embedded with them hadn't gotten so much as a complete sentence in edgewise. What was the use of psycho-bullshit if you didn't even try to use it? Not that Cole put much faith in that kind of thing. He was convinced the whole psychological community had been put on earth for the sole purpose of bringing him grief. It worked. He didn't trust any of those sniveling, mind-melding types. Not one of them. He trusted his gut and not much else.

Unfortunately Cole's gut wasn't getting the chance to prove itself. Bomb guy had anchored that pregnant woman to his chest as tightly as his explosive pack and kept her there for the last ten minutes. Cole could get a clean head shot and take the guy out, but he couldn't guarantee the hand holding the switch wouldn't trip it in a reflexive jerk as he went down.

He moved his telescopic sight down an inch and took in

the condition of the hostage. Large, calm eyes seemed to stare up toward his position. Cole frowned. Could she see him?

Doubtful. He was hidden in the shadows and sixteen floors up. Still, it gave him a moment's pause. And threatened his icy detachment. Not good. He moved the sights a bit lower.

The woman was barely showing. In fact, Cole hadn't realized she was pregnant until her hands had gone to her abdomen in the age-old stance of a mother protecting life in the womb. It was then he'd seen the tiny bulge. It was possible the kidnapper didn't know what he had in his clutches. It would only give the rebel that much more ammunition if he figured it out. Better if Cole kept this little secret to himself. Besides, his colleagues would bend over backward to keep a pregnant chick from getting blown into the afterlife.

Cole bent over backward for no one. He did his job and moved on. No hesitation. No regrets. At least that's what he told himself. Forcing his rifle sight away from the vulnerable slope of the woman's abdomen and back to the spot just over the kidnapper's right eye, his finger tensed.

Just one shot. That's all he needed. But first he had to make sure the suicidal little shit's hand was far away from the red button, or whatever he was using for a trigger.

He glanced at Moss and raised his brows. *Got anything?*

Moss's thumb took a downward dive. *Nothing. You?*

Cole shook his head.

A quiet female voice came through the earpiece, startling him.

What the hell?

He moved his sight down, hoping that voice wasn't coming from who he thought it was.

Shit and double shit. The hostage was speaking in slow measured tones. In flawless Portuguese.

What did she think she was doing?

She brushed her hands over her stomach. *"Você tem filhos, senhor?"*

Do you have kids?

No, no, no. Do not tell him.

The directional listening device picked up her voice just as easily as it had the kidnapper's.

"Cala a boca," the rebel screamed, warning her to shut her mouth.

"I'm sorry." The woman leaned her head back against the crazed man's chest. Cole recognized what she was trying to do. Initiate physical contact and make herself human in the man's eyes.

It didn't always work, though, and she was risking a hell of a lot. Especially when there were already people on the ground trying to get her out.

The man glanced down at her, surprise flickering across his face as her hands continued to travel in slow soothing strokes across her abdomen.

Fuck.

Cole's cuss-meter was blinking a red warning light, threatening to overload if he hurled one more word at it.

"You are with child?" the kidnapper asked, shifting his weight to his left foot. Any movement made him a harder target, but it also showed he was getting nervous.

The woman gave a contented sigh. "Yes. A boy."

Cole threw a questioning scowl at Moss and tilted his head.

Moss answered with a slight shrug. He didn't know what was going on, either.

"Cole…Moss," a hurried voice came through the earpiece, drowning out the woman's, "can either of you get a clean shot?"

"I can," said Cole. "But I can't see the target's trigger hand."

"Doesn't matter. As soon as you can take the shot, do it.

That contingent of approaching rebels is closing in. E.T.A currently stands at ten minutes. If we're going to evacuate the embassy, it has to be now, which means we need past that target."

"And the woman?" Cole tried to blot out the image forming in his mind.

There was a slight pause. "Take the shot."

What had been one droplet of sweat turned into a steady stream as he squinted through the sight and tried to ignore the woman's soft, mellow voice as she said all the right things. If they'd had the time, she might've turned this around on her own. As it was, fifty embassy employees were at stake, not just one woman.

Before he could talk himself out of it, he lined up the shot and squeezed the trigger. Blood sprayed even before the muffled *thwap* of impact made it back to his ears. The woman's face, still tilted up at the dead man, caught some of the spatter before she had a chance to look away. She flinched.

He expected a shrill scream to pierce his eardrums, but got nothing. The kidnapper fell away from his victim, his hand still clutching some kind of string. The trigger. And, instead of running for her life, the woman went down on her haunches and felt the target's neck for a pulse. Cole could see the reflexive death twitches as the man's nervous system began to implode. One hard convulsive movement and the device would go off.

"Get out of there." Cole stood up, shouting.

The hell with this. He was going in.

Cole detached his gun from its support and slung the strap over his shoulder. The rappelling ropes he'd secured earlier were coiled at the edge of the rooftop, ready to go.

"Cole," Moss yelled through the earpiece, as if reading his mind. "Wait for orders."

Cole hooked the pulley system to his harness. All he heard was "Fuck!" before he pushed away and headed down the side of the building.

He fed the rope through as fast as he dared, but the descent seemed to take forever. In reality, he was at ground level in less than a minute.

Releasing the clip, he sprinted for the woman, who was still crouched beside the kidnapper.

"He's dead. Let's go." Cole wrapped a hand around her upper arm and hauled her to her feet, turning toward a bank of graffiti-scrawled apartment buildings to his left.

Instead of following, she planted her feet. "Who are you?" The look in her eyes sent a chill crawling down his spine. It was the same expression she'd turned on the kidnapper. Eerie calm with a tinge of dread.

"Who am I? I'm the man who just saved your ass."

Her glance went to the rifle. "You! You murdered him."

He ignored the insult and dragged her away from the body, making for the safety of one of the apartment buildings. The embassy was too obvious a target. The rebels were itching to teach Washington a lesson for supporting the newly elected Angolan president—who'd conveniently fled the capital an hour ago. If those forces made it before the extraction team arrived, Cole needed to get the woman to cover. There was no time to argue.

So why did he feel the need to justify his actions as they made their way across the rough pavement? He jerked his head toward the bloody corpse behind them. "The bomb strapped to his chest said he was going to die anyway. I kept you from joining him."

"All I needed was a few more minutes." Her voice rattled in time with her jarring steps. "No one had to die."

In his line of work, someone always died.

"Lady, you don't know what the hell you're talking about."

"And you do?"

"Yeah. Me and nineteen others like me who are here to get you and the embassy officials out."

"Why does the military always think force is the answer to everything?" Her gasping breaths were growing louder by the minute.

They reached the shadow of a building four blocks from the embassy. Cole ducked into the doorway, pulling her next to him and out of the line of fire.

Anger went through him. He'd just busted his ass to save her life—possibly risking a formal reprimand—and she was complaining? "And your solution would be what?"

"The best solution would have been to appeal to his humanity."

"He had no humanity."

"Yes, he did. The same way you do. The same way I do."

The fury behind the soft tone was unmistakable. Cole had no idea what she was so worked up about. The man had just tried to kill her and she was defending him. "What are you a shrink or something?"

She jerked away from his hold. "I'm a psychiatrist."

Oh shit. A mind melder. He should have let someone else go in after her. Anyone else. This was the last thing he needed on his hands today. Someone who thought she could save the whole fucking world single-handedly. "Well, whose method would you say was more effective in this case? Yours or mine?"

Her eyes flashed up at him. "Yours was certainly faster. But that doesn't make it right."

"Well, you can tell that to my commanding officer… ma'am." He started to usher her away from the doorway when the sound of machine gun fire ripped through the air.

Too late. The rebels were here. And Cole and the woman were sitting ducks.

THE UGLY SOUND OF GUNFIRE peppered the air a short distance away, stopping Callie's reply in its tracks. The soldier next to her was right. If he hadn't gotten her out when he did, she'd probably be dead. She and Micah both.

He thrust her behind him. "Don't move."

Without another word of warning, he whipped his rifle around, firing at the plate glass window of the apartment building. The whole sheet of glass shattered and collapsed into the building with enough force to send a gust of air rushing past her cheek. The soldier's body had protected her from any flying glass particles, but what about him?

He stepped through the opening he'd created and motioned her to follow. She did, glancing at the security window to the right and expecting a guard to run out at any moment brandishing a gun of his own. But if there was a *porteiro,* he'd evidently abandoned his post, because all remained silent inside. What about the people living here? By breaking the glass, the soldier had left them vulnerable to looters, or worse.

But wouldn't the men with the machine guns just shoot out the glass barrier anyway? Besides, Callie had her baby to think about, and most of the city dwellers had already fled. Like she should have.

It wasn't as if she hadn't *tried* to leave once reports of rebel forces converging on the city began flooding the news channels. Even the local police had scattered during the chaos that ensued. She'd been at the embassy, hoping to secure a flight out of the country when the man standing in line behind her grabbed her and dragged her outside.

She'd never had a chance to find out who he was or what he wanted. And now he was dead.

Recriminations and finger pointing would have to wait until later. All she could do at the moment was try to keep up with the man in front of her as he bypassed the elevator and pushed open the door of the stairwell. The electricity was still on, so Callie wasn't sure why he hadn't punched the button and taken the easy way up.

The sound of rifle fire came closer and she realized the elevator would tick down the floors as it went up, a dead giveaway that someone was inside the building.

Where was the soldier taking her? She wasn't stupid enough to think the rebels wouldn't search these buildings. They had all the time in the world now, unless an outside country stepped in and cut them off. Not likely at this point. Especially if the United States was evacuating its embassy personnel rather than sending in reinforcements to protect them. Callie and her grim companion had no place to hide. Even if they broke into one of the apartments and found it empty, someone would eventually hunt them down and kill them. Or use them as bargaining chips. Or rape Callie and kill her. Fear rose high and fast, a tornadolike force that sent a burst of adrenaline whipping through her system.

If she died, Micah died with her. And she couldn't bear to do that to her sister's memory. She had to live. She'd do anything it took. Even survive a rape. The baby's father deserved it. Her sister, who'd desperately longed for a child, deserved it.

By the fourth floor, she was panting and sweat dripped from her chin. The stairwell was airless, and the oppressive heat pressed in on her from all directions. A wave of nausea washed over her, and her hand went to her throat in an effort to hold it back. She stumbled up a few more steps, then had to stop.

"Wait."

He halted immediately. "What is it?"

"I…I just need to stop…just for a second." She sucked down several deep, careful breaths, hoping to slow the gyrations within her stomach.

His brows drew together. Without warning his fingers went to her wrist and pressed.

She yanked her hand away. "What are you doing?"

"Checking for shock."

She focused on his narrow-eyed gaze. Brown eyes. Deep. Unblinking. "I'm not going into shock. It's just so hot in here. It's making me feel sick. And seeing that man die…" She touched her face, the dried blood she found there making the bile rise even higher. He stood there waiting, his expression blank. How could he just go on as if nothing had happened?

"We'll stop," he said, "but just for a minute. The sooner we arrive at our destination, the faster we'll get out of the heat."

His rifle came over his shoulder and he lounged against the wall, still watching her. He drew a cigarette from his pocket and she frowned at him. "You've got to be kidding."

"I'm not going to smoke it."

Maybe he was one of those nervous types who just held the thing between his lips. But that theory went down the tube when he broke the cigarette and re-pocketed both halves.

"What are you doing?"

"Tobacco can help with motion sickness. It's also a stimulant. You're paler than—"

"I'm pregnant." She put all the outrage she felt into those two words. "I'm not going to smoke a cigarette."

"Of course not."

She blinked at him. "Then what's all the talk about tobacco?"

"If I think you need it, you'll put a wad of it in your mouth and hold it there. Your gums will absorb the drug."

She knew from her medical training it was true. Still, if he thought she was doing that, he had another think coming. "I'll be fine."

The muffled sound of gunfire reached into the enclosed

space and grabbed her by the throat. The shooters weren't inside yet, but they were getting closer.

"Time to go," he said.

The man pushed her up the stairs…ahead of him, this time. Suddenly it dawned on Callie that she didn't even know the soldier's name. And he didn't know hers. And yet he was still trying to save her.

That didn't sit well.

He was a soldier. An automaton, like her stepfather, who'd demanded discipline at home, while sucking down beers and bragging to his military buddies about how many Vietnamese he'd taken out during the war. Would this soldier do the same—brag to his friends? He'd already proven he could kill without hesitation. But instead of leaving her there to her fate, he'd dragged her away from the scene, risking his own life.

Probably under orders. She hurried upward, instinctively trusting his decisions.

That also went against the grain. Her profession craved knowledge as an insight into the human spirit—or soul, if that's what you wanted to call it. She knew nothing about him, other than what she'd gleaned through his actions.

One thing was for sure, he was jumpy as hell. Not able to sit still for long.

Machine guns tended to do that to a person. As if on cue, the vicious sounds kicked to life again.

An additional shot of adrenaline spurted through her system and her steps hurried. She gripped the hand-rail tighter.

"You okay?"

"Yes," she gasped. A stabbing pain gripped her right side. Muscle cramp from pushing herself so hard. At least she prayed that's what it was.

Please let the baby be safe.

"Not much farther," he said. "I think this building's around eighteen floors tall. We should hit the roof any second."

"The roof?" She stopped so fast that he bumped into her from behind, his arms going around her waist to steady her.

This had to be some kind of sick joke. Surely God couldn't mean to test each and every one of her weaknesses right here, right now. That was why she'd gone into psychology in the first place, to deal with her fears and her past, and to help others deal with theirs.

"It's the safest place."

Safest for whom?

"Maybe we can just hide inside one of the apartments."

"No. We'll be trapped. We need to keep our options open."

"Options?" The sound came out as a squeak.

His hands moved to her hips and urged her to start climbing again. Under normal circumstances, she would consider his touch inappropriate, but these weren't normal circumstances. And somehow, Callie doubted he was copping a feel. Besides, she was pregnant. For most men, a strange pregnant woman shouted "hands off" the way nothing else could.

"We can see what's going on from the rooftop. See where they're headed."

"And if *they* head our way?" She threw a look backward.

His hard mouth quirked up. "Then we make like Spider-Man."

He couldn't mean what she thought he meant.

"Spider-Man?"

"Yeah. We spin a thread and drop out of sight."

The only thread Callie was spinning was the noose she planned on dropping over the soldier's head.

"No way."

"Keep moving."

A door appeared in front of her so quickly that she almost ran into it. The last thing she wanted to do was push it open and see what was on the other side.

He gripped her arm. "Wait. Don't go out there."

Ha! No chance of that.

He released her and moved around to push through the doorway. A loud whirring sound filled the space as the door opened, and Callie hung back for a second. He didn't let her stall for long. "Cavalry's coming and we don't want to miss the party. Let's go."

She squinted up as a large military helicopter passed low overhead. The man beside her waved his arms and the aircraft banked to the right, heading back their way. When it reached their location, it hovered above them. A door opened and a ladder unfurled, stopping within inches of their position.

Just as suddenly, there was a whistling sound. A flare of light appeared over the roof's horizon.

"Get down!"

Callie's body crumpled like a rag doll as something heavy fell on top of her.

A huge flash and a burst of heat enveloped her from all sides.

Pain speared through her eardrums and they popped just when she thought they might explode from the pressure.

An agonizing screech of metal against concrete grew until it became a mountain of sound. The apartment complex seemed to tremble on its very foundations.

Then…everything stopped. Time itself hung suspended with an abruptness that was even more frightening than the chaotic activity of the past few minutes.

The only thing left was the silent, unmoving weight on top of her. And the steady splash of hot liquid on her right cheek.

Callie swallowed. She'd felt the same horrible wet sensation less than a half hour earlier. She knew what it signaled. And why.

TWO

COLE WINCED AS THE FIRST fingers of pain tunneled into his skull. The soft, fragrant form beneath him tempted him to drift back to sleep. But he couldn't. Not yet. He had a job to do. One that the warm fuzzies in his head were trying to keep him from remembering.

He reached a hand to the source of the pain and felt something over his right eyebrow.

Funny, hadn't he shot someone in that same spot recently? He recalled the spurt of blood, the falling…

Shot.

Lurching to a sitting position he opened his eyes and heard a soft groan.

Shit. His memory came rushing back. The woman. Was she hurt?

Something dripped into his eye. He dashed the moisture away and looked down. She was on her side, curled up tight. Still calm despite what she'd just been through. The baby?

"Hey." His voice croaked and he cleared his throat. "You okay?"

"Y-yes." She blinked a couple of times, moisture glittering across the dark fringe of lashes. "But I thought you were…"

He frowned. Maybe that steady calm he'd thought so remarkable was only on the surface. A façade. That was something Cole could relate to.

"No. Not yet anyway." He brushed a strand of hair from her eyes, his fingers pausing as he spied the dark blood on her cheek and a small pool of the stuff on the ground beside her head. Fresh blood. Not from the kidnapper. He touched the wet stickiness on her face and held his fingers up for her to see. "You're hurt. Let me see."

She shook her head and sat up. "The blood's not mine. It's yours."

"Mine." Puzzled, his hand went back to his forehead and found the shard again. *Great.* He braced himself to pull it out. "Turn your head for a second."

"Let me look at it." The woman brushed away his hands. "I'm a psychiatrist, remember? I have a medical degree."

She wasn't squeamish. Of course she wouldn't be. She'd peered into minds far worse than his. He asked himself for the millionth time how he'd managed to get saddled with a shrink.

Hide the evidence. Don't let them see.

The mantra from his childhood came back to haunt him. The paralyzing fear that someone would make him swallow pills. Would turn him into a zombie without a soul. The punishment for misbehaving, for being different from the other kids.

Before he could stop her, the woman reached up and yanked the shrapnel free. Either that or she'd just cleaved his head in half. *Damn, that hurt.* A trickle of liquid ran across his forehead, much like the sweat that had run down his back earlier. He lifted his hand to swipe away the blood, but the woman pushed his arm away. "Stop it. The wound's contaminated enough as it is."

He watched her untie something at the back of her shirt and yank it loose from the garment. Half a belt or a tie or something.

"Sorry, it's not sterile."

Sterile. Hell, someone had just shot down their ride, killed some good men, and she was worried about germs?

They had a lot more serious things to contend with at the moment.

"We need to get out of here."

"In a minute." Placing gentle fingertips on his forehead, she pushed. His head stung like hell as she did. He guessed she was closing the wound the best she could.

"Here, put your fingers over mine and hold them in this position," she said.

He did as she asked, groping until he found the icy tops of her hands, then slid down her fingers until he reached the sweaty skin of his brow.

The woman placed the strip of fabric on his forehead and tied it tightly at the back of his head. He gritted his teeth until she was done.

Getting on her knees in front of him, she lifted the hem of her shirt and used it to swab his face. Cole got a peek of the creamy skin of her stomach in the process. Definitely a small bump there. Sexy as hell.

Something flipped in his chest. Just what did he think he was doing? "Okay, okay, that's good enough." He levered his body up until he was standing, fighting the wave of dizziness as he glanced toward the edge of the roof. He measured the distance to the next building. Looking back at her, he said, "Are you into jumping?"

She glanced at the space between the buildings and her eyes widened. "Not particularly." She drew in a deep breath and her hand went to her stomach. She paused, then pulled her shirt lower and straightened her back. "But I'll do whatever I have to."

Admiration for her gutsiness made him blink. The same begrudging admiration he'd felt when she'd talked to her kidnapper. She had somehow tugged at whatever small amount of humanity the guy had left. With more time would she have succeeded?

Cole doubted it, but the woman didn't.

She could jump, but he didn't trust his balance enough at the moment to risk her life on it. If he'd been alone, maybe. Moss would be looking for him. There was still the possibility of a rescue, no matter how remote.

As if reading his mind, she asked, "How long do we have before the rebels realize we're here?"

"They already know. Once they saw that chopper hovering and the ladder drop, they knew there were people up here. Right now, they're just not sure how valuable we are. They're after hostages they can use to negotiate with their government. Americans."

"Us."

"Yeah. Us."

"Any chance some more good guys are going to fly overhead anytime soon?"

Cole glanced at her and thought of the helicopter-load of men who'd just fallen to a fiery grave. "I hope not."

She blinked at him, but showed no fear.

He adjusted the tie she'd laced around the back of his head. At least it kept blood from running into his eyes. Remembering her sudden stop in the stairwell of the building, he turned toward her. "Still feeling sick?"

"No. Just tell me what to do."

That was the problem. They were trapped on a rooftop and Cole didn't have the slightest clue what his next step should be. He hated being in charge of civilians. The guys on his team knew the stakes and were willing to make their wagers. Civvies were dead weight. You had their back…and front… and side—without the luxury of getting anything in return.

Making his way to the edge of the building, he motioned to her to stay back. He crouched and peered over the edge. The wreckage of the helicopter was still smoking, but evidently the explosion had sent the bad guys scurrying to whatever roach holes they'd found to hide in. But once they realized it was safe, they'd be back. And they'd head toward the chopper's last stopping point.

Cole needed to have the woman, and hopefully himself, out of here by the time the bad guys reached the roof.

He took a look over the other three sides of the building. Rebel activity was heavy around the perimeter of the embassy, but the rest of the streets seemed empty. Periodic snaps of gunfire told him that wasn't necessarily true. He spied the rooftop where he'd gotten off the shot at the kidnapper. Empty. So was the adjoining one where Moss had been stationed.

Where was his friend?

Safe. Cole was sure of it. Had the team gotten the embassy personnel out before the rebels swarmed the place?

No telling. That wasn't his problem at the moment. The only problem he had was the one three yards behind him.

He remembered his earpiece and fumbled with the wire until he located it and punched the transmit button. "Moss. You out there?"

Nothing but silence met his question. Had the rebels taken out the satellite link? Cole hoped not, because his team needed to be able to communicate to get out.

"Moss, anyone. Do you read?"

A moment of dead airspace met his question, then someone spoke. "*Sim, senhor, estamos te ouvindo perfeitamente.*" The sneered boast told him it wasn't Moss who had his ear.

He switched to the native tongue. "Who is this?"

A low chuckle came through his earpiece. "Who? Someone very interested in knowing what the Americans are doing meddling in the business of Angola."

"We're not meddling. We're simply trying to evacuate our own people."

"You, maybe, but your government continues to lie and manipulate. So no one leaves unless *we* give permission."

Callie came up next to him, her brows raised. He'd forgotten she could understand Portuguese. She couldn't hear what came through the earpiece, however. He held his index finger to his lips, signaling her to keep quiet. He didn't want whoever was on this frequency to know she was with him. "Then give the permission."

"All in good time. All in good time. Where are you, *senhor?* Inside your embassy building?"

He glanced down at the front gates of the U.S. building. They were spread wide and armed guards stood in front of it. Rebel guards.

"Possibly."

"Wrong. If you were inside, *senhor,* I would know it by now."

Cole didn't want to give this bastard anything, but he needed as much information as he could get. "Your people are all over the embassy, then."

"Hmm. Yes. I also have several members of your team with me. But I don't have you. And you, in turn, have something I want."

He couldn't imagine what the hell the rebel was talking about. Nor did he think for a second that this group of pissants was intelligent enough to round up nineteen of the best men the United States military had to offer.

"What could I possibly have that you want?"

There was silence for a good ten seconds. Sweat pooled under Cole's arms and ran in streams down his back.

"I think you know, *senhor.* After all, you took her away from us. *That* I will not forgive."

Cole's gaze swung to the woman beside him.

Rough breathing came through the wire. The bastard was angry. Not good. The voice continued, not bothering to switch to English. "If you want to make things easy on your-self, you must give her up. And yourself. Because if I have to take her back by force…you will die. Slowly. But first, you will watch her die, the way she was meant to."

The way she was meant to.

It dawned on him in an instant. This whole situation had been a setup from the beginning.

Why?

To make it look like a lone act of terrorism? A suicide bomber? If so, someone had gone through an awful lot of trouble. What had Cole gotten himself into?

"All we want is one person," the voice continued in a more reasonable tone. "Dr. Calista Nascimento. Give her to us now, and you will live. If not, you die. Along with your men. We will give you five minutes."

Cole switched off his earpiece and gripped the woman's arm. Looking into her white, pinched face, he said, "Okay, Dr. Nascimento, you've got exactly one minute to tell me who you are and what you're doing in Angola."

CALLIE STARED INTO the angry face of her rescuer and realized something had gone horribly wrong with her plan.

How did he know her name?

"I—I told you. I'm a psychiatrist."

His lips tightened. "Yes. But you're a little far away from your practice, aren't you?"

Why she was here was none of his business. "I'm here for personal reasons."

He ripped the earpiece out of his ear and held it up at her. "I just had some rebel lord use your name over a government line. He suggested I hand you over. Or die."

"What?" He had to be wrong. No one knew she was here. Or why. Not even Gary. "That's impossible. You must have misunderstood him."

"I don't think so." The soldier jammed the earpiece back in place. "You want to try that again, before I tell this lunatic whether or not I'm willing to pass you over to them?"

Her teeth dug into her lower lip. Would he really do that? "I don't understand."

"You wound up on some crazy bastard's Most Wanted list. It seems it's you or me, babe."

The matter-of-fact declaration sent a flash of panic racing through her chest. Her hand instinctively went to her belly, until she caught his eyes following the movement. She lowered her arm, keeping her fingers loose and slightly curled. She didn't want him to see just how frightened his words made her. The baby had to live, no matter what the cost. She decided to call his bluff.

"Then I guess you have a decision to make." Her chin went up. If he thought she was going to beg him not to choose his life over hers, he was wrong. Although, why anyone would believe she was important enough to be used as a captive, she had no idea. She had no money, and her sister was…

Her eyes closed and she forced her brain not to go down that dark path.

Warm fingers trailed across her cheek and her lids sprang apart. "Don't look so scared, doc. I'm not handing you over to anyone. But I need to understand what we're up against."

His touch did what her mind couldn't: blot out her grief and make her focus on the present. "I don't know how they got my name. I told you the truth. I'm a psychiatrist from New York."

"Again, you're a long way from home. I want to know why."

"My sister was killed in a small plane crash a little over a month ago. Here, in Angola." She focused on the slight jog in the otherwise straight bridge of the soldier's nose and wondered how he'd broken it. "I needed to see for myself where it happened. And maybe get a sense of why. I needed closure." Her words were true enough. The rest of the story had nothing to do with their current situation.

"Was your sister famous?"

She shook her head.

"We're running out of time, so let's try a simpler question. Why was your sister flying through Africa? Why specifically Angola?"

"She was here with Doctors Without Borders. She's been helping treat and relocate some of the refugees that the Angolan government ejected from their homes."

His gaze left hers and went to the edge of the building, his fingers touching the device in his ear again. "*Não tenho mais ninguém aqui comigo, senhor.*"

His Portuguese was heavily accented but understandable. She was impressed. Not many Americans bothered learning other languages. Not in depth anyway.

Callie's Brazilian father had insisted she and Sara speak to him in his native tongue. They'd learned Portuguese from the cradle. Their two years in a Brazilian elementary school had guaranteed a flawless accent. She considered herself lucky to have had the benefit of two unique cultures.

The soldier turned back toward her, cutting her thoughts short. "I don't think he believes there's no one else up here with me. That's our cue to get out of Dodge while we still can."

She knew practically nothing about this man, but he seemed to be her only hope. So, for now, she was willing to follow his lead. Until it became impossible to go any farther.

She stuck out her hand. "I'm Callie Nascimento. But then, you—and everyone else around here—already seem to know that."

A slight flash of teeth met her statement. He took her proffered hand and glanced down at it. "Pleased to meet you, Callie Nascimento. I'm Cole Scalini."

The sound of more shattering glass made them both pause. Someone was coming.

Cole removed a thick metal rod from his belt. Twisting the handle, multiple sets of arms unsheathed and curled, forming what appeared to be large vicious-looking fishhooks. He attached a clip from the other end of the device to his harness and pulled out a length of rope.

"Spider-Man," she murmured, remembering his earlier words.

He grinned at her. "One and the same." Putting an arm around her, he guided her toward the far side of the building.

She tried to smile back, but her face suddenly felt frozen as they neared the edge. He reached down and hooked the device around a large piece of metal sticking up from the rooftop, testing it a time or two. Would that thing hold the both of them? She could only assume he hadn't been joking about spinning a thread and dropping…and dropping.

Don't look down, don't look down…

Her breath began rattling in her chest as she tried to obey her edict. Before she could stop herself, her glance plummeted sixteen floors and smacked the concrete below. A low moan escaped as the distant vision seemed to reach up and grab at her, trying to pull her over the side.

The soldier drew her closer and his black eyes bored into hers. "I want you to get behind me and put your arms around my neck as tightly as you can without choking me. And wrap your legs around my waist." He grinned again, a bit strained this time. "Just pretend I'm your husband."

Her teeth chattered. "I—I d-don't have a h-husband."

He pulled her against him, her stomach bumping intimately against his. "Then pretend I'm the one who did that to you."

Oh God, if he only knew, he wouldn't say that.

He released her and turned his back. She did as he asked and wrapped her arms around his neck, trying not to let panic charge through her system and ruin what he was trying to do.

Cole turned his head. "I won't be able to hold onto you as we go down, I'll need to feed the rope and control our descent." He paused. "The ride'll be a little bumpy. It's important for you to grip tight and stay flat against my body. I don't want you in any danger."

Although she appreciated him relaying the process, one word stuck in her mind. Danger.

"What about gunfire from below?"

"The rebels are probably expecting me to hang out on the rooftop or come charging back down the stairs. They won't expect us to rappel down. Besides, I haven't seen anyone on this side of the building. We'll go down fast, hopefully before anyone spots us. Just remember to hang on tight, okay?"

"Don't worry," she said with a shiver. "I'm your new best friend."

He gave a pained laugh, but didn't say anything, except, "Ready?"

Swallowing, she said, "Yes."

"Remember. Arms and legs tight as soon as we go over."

"Arms and legs." She shut her eyes. "I'll just keep my eyes closed until we reach the bottom."

"No, don't close your eyes. Keep them open at all times."

Callie pried her lids apart, just as he started to lean his weight against the rope.

"You need to see what's going on, especially as we get close to the bottom." He nodded. "Okay. We're going over. Hop up and wrap your legs around me. Now."

Callie did as he said, thankful her stomach was still small enough to allow her to press close. She swallowed a scream as their bodies swung over the side of the building into space.

Within a matter of seconds, they were on the sheer vertical face of the wall.

And despite his dire admonition, she shut her eyes tight and waited for the plunge that would send them crashing back to earth.

THREE

FOR THE SECOND TIME in a little over an hour, Cole fed rope through his gloved hands. The grappling hook didn't feel nearly as secure as the bolt anchors he'd pounded into the roof of the other apartment building. His descent was slower as well, in concession to the woman clinging to his back. The hot gusts of air rasping against the side of his neck had nothing to do with great sex, and everything to do with sheer terror.

"Ditto, babe." He muttered the words like a prayer, under his breath.

He kept track of the floors as they dropped past banks of dust-streaked windows. He couldn't risk craning his neck to look toward the ground below for fear of jarring the woman's hold and losing her. Even as he thought it, her legs seemed to loosen their grip.

"Hold tight," he said, willing her to obey. She did, her limbs tightening until he thought she would strangle him. But he didn't tell her to let up. He preferred fighting for oxygen to having her drop to her death.

Twelfth floor.

Rounded eyes peered from the window directly in front of him, startling the hell out of him. For a second, the hand controlling the rope's brake faltered, and they dropped a yard or two, before he was able to halt their free fall. His passenger gave a gasp that was just short of a whimper when the quick stop tested the line's tensile strength, bouncing them a time or two.

"Shit."

He wasn't going to let his demon suck away his powers of concentration. Not this time. He paused to gather himself and to make sure the woman was still firmly attached.

Wouldn't she be thrilled to learn what a defective screwup she'd gotten stuck with? A man who acted first and didn't use his brain until after the fact. Somehow he didn't think so.

He rested his chin against her clinging forearm for a second, more to reassure himself than anything. "It's okay, doc, just hang on and try to stay calm."

Stay calm. Yeah. Good advice. He should try it sometime.

He eased up on the brake and started back down.

Ninth floor.

His glance strayed to the receding roofline. No sign of rebel fighters. Maybe they were still searching the apartments inside.

If he could just make it to the ground…

Sixth floor.

"Not much farther." He pushed off the wall harder than he meant to and the woman gave another soft gasp.

Hell, he wasn't cut out for rescue missions.

But at least the good doc seemed to be keeping it together. She kept her face pressed hard against his neck and left the worrying to him.

Third floor.

Almost home. He glanced up again. Someone could cut the rope at this point and they'd theoretically survive the fall, but not without some injuries. And Dr. Nascimento would be captured and…

He didn't want to think about the rebel's final words regarding her fate. Cole fed the rope faster. Just a few more yards.

First floor.

The second Cole's feet touched the ground, he surveyed

the smoky stillness of their surroundings. He'd expected the doctor to let go of him the instant they hit ground level. Instead, she clung tight. He unhooked the carabiner and freed the line from his belt.

Still she held on.

He reached up and touched her hands. As if operated by a spring-loaded trigger, she released her grip. Cole turned toward her, noting the way her hands immediately went to her stomach.

Their gazes caught. Tangled.

He wasn't staring. He was just giving her a minute or two to catch her breath before they got the hell out of there.

"I closed my eyes," she whispered, as if explaining why she'd held onto him for so long.

She'd closed her eyes...had trusted him enough to disobey orders. Cole liked that. "It's okay. So how was the ride?"

Her hands continued to explore her abdomen, moving in tiny circles. She offered up a tremulous smile. "We landed with all our parts intact. That's all I care about." She dragged in a long breath, releasing it on a relieved sigh. "So, what's next on our agenda?"

He glanced down the empty street. So far so good. "I don't know. Dinner and a movie?"

Under other circumstances, would he have been attracted to her type? Enough to ask her out on a real date?

Her type.

Just what was he referring to? The *pregnant* type? Or the *mind-melder* type? His sworn enemy.

Who the hell cared what she was? Her powers of psycho-observation were the least of his worries.

She edged a little closer, her hand touching his arm, drawing his attention back to her. "What's playing?"

"Playing?" The urge to wrap his arm around her waist came and went without incident.

"At the movies."

This he could do. Joking away his fear was something he excelled at. "They're showing *Escape From Angola*."

"My all-time favorite. I hope the ending's as good as I remember."

She was tossing off witty comebacks with ease, even while her body language screamed fear. Maybe the two of them had something in common after all. Cole's admiration crept one notch higher, before he stopped himself.

He didn't want to admire her...*or* search for common ground. He wanted to run. Get away before she discovered the truth. To steer as clear of her as he could possibly get.

He didn't have that luxury. He'd been thrust into a situation he hadn't asked for, but one he wouldn't back down from. Not even to shield his demon from discovery.

Turning away, he edged her behind his body while he tried to judge the best route out of this hellhole. His team had been positioned to the east. But to head that way would be to walk right into the devil's arms. And around the corner, to the west, was the downed chopper. He was leery of taking the doc past the charred wreckage. He could at least spare her that.

And if they had to walk out of Angola on foot? Would she be up to it?

He heard shouts above them, just before chips of concrete spat to life to the left of his leg, stinging the bare skin of his wrist as they hit. The woman behind him flinched and gripped a handful of his shirt. Without looking, he pushed backward, crowding her against the side of the building.

The bastards had evidently reached the roof—and found his damned lifeline. He kept her body pressed between him and the concrete wall as he swung his rifle from his shoulder and tried to locate the origin of the gunfire. If he'd been hoping to get off a couple of clean shots, he was mistaken.

The glare from above blinded him, making it impossible to guarantee a hit. He patted his pockets with one hand. Sunglasses were long gone.

If his luck had been heading into the toilet at the beginning of the day, it had now reached the flushing stage. But at least his focus was back where it needed to be.

On the job.

There was a brief lull in the gunfire, but Cole had no illusions. Now that he'd been discovered—*with* the girl—they'd either send in a ground contingent or come barreling down the stairwell themselves. Neither option appealed to his survival instincts.

The dangling rope next to his hip jiggled. He shielded his eyes and then cursed.

Or, the idiots could try using the same route he and the woman had taken. A man-made elevator that promised a one-way ticket.

Straight down.

Like a skinny, fully clothed version of Tarzan, a man dangled from the top of the building, his bare hands gripping Cole's rope. The fool's legs flailed as if trying to get a hold on something…maybe the line, and failed. Cole knew what was coming.

He grabbed the doctor's arm and pushed her ahead of him. "Stay against the wall. But move. Now."

As if she too sensed something awful was about to happen, she sprinted forward without a word, and he thanked his few remaining lucky stars he hadn't landed a screamer. He'd need her to stay quiet for the next several seconds, even when the shit hit the fan. Or the ground.

Which should be right about…

On cue, an unearthly shriek filled the air, sweeping toward them at a frightening rate.

The doc, still running in front of him, slowed for a second, twisting her head toward the sound.

Planting his hand in the center of her back, he used his forward momentum to keep her going. "Don't look."

She did as she was told.

The horrific *thwack* of raw meat hitting a concrete skillet reached them just as they made it to the corner of the building.

Cole grabbed her arm and stopped, forcing himself to glance back to make sure no one else attempted sliding down the same disastrous route. Or arrived from another direction. He avoided the broken figure on the ground, praying the body wasn't harboring explosives. But no explosion came. No gunfire. No pursuing rebels. No nothing.

Not good.

Before he had a chance to choose a course of action, the woman wrenched her arm free from his grasp, as if she couldn't stand his touch.

He frowned and turned to let her in on the harsh reality of their situation.

"Listen up, doc—"

Cole's hissed accusation fell on deaf ears. In reality, it fell on no ears at all.

She was gone.

SENATOR GARY PARKER paced his office, the phone in his hand damp from the hours spent on it. He clutched it tighter. "Any word on my sister-in-law, yet?"

The voice on the other end, belonging to a General Markesan—the third such general he'd been shuffled to in the last hour—gave him the same song and dance as the previous person: evacuation attempts at the embassy were still ongoing. There was no specific news he could relay about any of the evacuees at this time.

Evacuees.

Hell, he didn't give a rat's ass about the embassy personnel or about what the military was or wasn't trying to do. The only person he wanted to know about was Callie and the baby she was carrying. And if someone didn't feed him some useful information soon, he was flying to that godforsaken place himself.

And if that happened, General Markesan, along with all his tight-lipped cronies, were going to be dealing with a lot more than gun-slinging rebels and military evacuations.

They'd have to contend with him.

FOUR

She had known it would come.

Her time on the roof had been a short reprieve. In the end, her soldier's skill hadn't been enough to save her, despite her hopes.

Callie didn't struggle, knowing it would do no good. She could only pray the man let her talk. Both her hands went to her captor's forearm, but he was strong—the hand covering her mouth, a vise. She settled for pulling in a quick breath through her nose, expected a fetid odor to burn her nostrils, like the stench of so many unwashed bodies.

Like her earlier captor. The dead one.

Instead, this man's scent was raw and masculine. His sweat, clean and earthy. It gave her a false sense of security, but one she latched onto with all her might.

A low voice came from somewhere nearby. "I don't know what the hell you thought you were doing, but you can take your hand off her mouth, Moss. She's not a screamer."

Callie's eyes swiveled to the left. She could hear Cole, but she couldn't see him.

"Oh no?" Her captor's breath whistled across her cheek, the hand remaining plastered across her mouth. "And just how would you know that?"

"From experience." Her soldier materialized without a sound. When he flicked the other man's hand away from her mouth, her captor let her go immediately. "Dr. Nascimento's specialty is talking people down from rooftops, right, doc?"

He gave her a reassuring grin. Callie scooted sideways and sagged against the hard brick wall of the building in relief.

The second man, probably another soldier, studied her with narrowed eyes. "Yeah? Well if that mess decorating the pavement around the corner is any indication of her expertise, count me out."

Outrage filled her chest, replacing the stabbing fear. She took it from the exchange that these two men knew each other. And were apparently in sync as to their opinion of her career choice.

She straightened her spine. "That wasn't my work. I didn't get a chance to talk to him. If I had, he might have walked away. I happen to be very good at what I do."

It was true. Callie had made sure of it. She didn't want anyone to go through what she had without a support system for recovery.

The second man's brows flicked up, but he said nothing.

Cole's mouth twisted. "Yeah, she's good. You saw the bastard who had her earlier. He turned out a whole lot better than Boneless Wonder back there."

What was his problem?

"That wasn't my work, either." She punched him in the shoulder with her index finger, almost yelping when the digit bounced off a solid mass of muscle. "It was yours. And if talking people off rooftops is my specialty, then what's yours? Killing whoever stands in your way?"

Like her stepfather had?

His shoulders stiffened. "No, right now it's keeping you alive. Unfortunately for you, I tend to suck at it."

Something strange flashed through his eyes at his last words.

She blinked, disbelief rolling over her along with an unexpected wave of compassion.

He actually believed what he'd said. The man who'd yanked her out of the jaws of death—more than once—thought he sucked at it. He wasn't so indestructible after all.

Callie's mind whirled and she opened her mouth to say something, before snapping it shut again when she realized he'd already turned away to survey the area. The one who'd jerked her away from Cole now had his rifle in hand and was stalking down the alley toward the far corner of the building. The street was empty. Still no sign of the people who'd shot at them. But they were there. And if someone didn't intervene, she, Micah and these two soldiers were probably going to be killed by rogue extremists.

Something made her look up. Cole stared into the distance, his jaw rigid with something more than tension. What was he thinking?

His words came back to haunt her, and she heard again the harsh recrimination of his tone. *"I seem to suck at it."*

Callie swallowed back a wave of emotion and firmed her resolve.

She wasn't going to die. She was going to live. She was going to get Micah out of Angola and let Gary know what she'd discovered about her sister's death.

But most of all, if it was the last thing she ever did on this earth, she was going make sure this soldier knew one thing.

He didn't "suck."

"How do I know you're telling the truth? You have a propensity for lying which surpasses even my own."

Pro-pen-sity.

José Coelho rolled the word around in his mind. He didn't like being talked down to, even for money. These gringos were all alike. They wanted his help, but refused to show him the respect he deserved. Glancing at his translator, he raised his brows.

Rosa covered the phone's mouthpiece with a delicate hand. *"Tendência."*

His grip tightened around the receiver. Being called a clever liar was acceptable. Being called a habitual one was not. But his cause needed the shot of money this gringo could provide.

All this for one woman. Men were fools.

He let the silence over the line draw out, imagining the gringo on the other end squirming in his high-powered business suit. He knew just how far to push.

Resting his hip against the desk, he took control of the conversation, just to show he could. "And if this phone call is intercepted? Then you will do what?"

"I already told you. The signal encrypts as it goes out."

José hated the Americans, but he loved their toys. He stroked his fingers over the black box's sleek lines. "I want two more of these devices when we're done."

"That wasn't part of the original deal." The man's tone changed. Lowered to a soft growl.

José wasn't fooled. He'd heard the trace of fear in the man's voice during their very first conversation. It was too late for him to play the aggressor now. "Neither was chasing the woman through the jungle. Deals must change to match the circumstances."

The woman hadn't made it to the jungle; she was still in the city. But the American didn't need to know that. The more difficult he thought the job was, the more willingly he'd agree to added conditions.

"Her escape was your doing," the voice on the other end of the line said.

"No, it was your government's. The soldiers you sent." How quickly they forgot.

There was a pause. "I had no choice."

"There is always a choice, my friend." The niggling idea that the troops had been sent to kill him once the woman was out of the way made him angry. Angrier than even the American's attitude. His rage sought an outlet and found none.

He glanced toward his translator.

So lovely.

"Is she with the troops, then?" The voice drew him back to the current subject.

"One. One troop. I've spoken with him."

"What?" The first hint of panic came through. "I told you no contact. With anyone."

José flipped through the pages of a large three-ringed binder sitting on the embassy warden's desk. He came across his own picture with a graphic description of suspected terrorist acts. He smiled. At least the *Embaixada Americana* knew who they were dealing with. At least *they* treated him with respect. "Don't worry. There will be no one left to carry tales back to your country."

"You can finish the job, then?"

"I always finish them."

"How long?"

"One week. Maybe two."

"Let me know when it's done."

"But I cannot. You have my number, but I do not yet have yours. Our partnership is not equal."

"I'll call you." The answer came fast, too fast. José paused, wondering if he should remind the gringo that panic had a tendency—no, a pro-*pen*-sity—to be followed by discovery.

Propensity. He mouthed the syllables. Another smile rose. Yes, he could learn to like the new word.

Still perched on the desk, he finished the conversation and hung up. He turned his head to study the embassy's translator. His own little mole. Paid for by the American government.

He stood to his feet. "Rosa, come here."

The fear that sprang into the woman's liquid brown eyes was quickly extinguished, but he hadn't missed it. She edged toward him, keeping one hand tucked behind her back.

José glanced at the desk and noted what was missing.

So she hadn't forgotten their last little encounter after all. What a pity.

He waited until she reached him. He slid his arms around her, gently kissed her. Before she could react, he brought her wrist, the one with the letter opener, to the front and held it up for her to see.

"How disappointing, Rosa, that you would choose this path." He trailed his lips across her cheek.

"Do you know what I have a pro-pen-sity for, *minha linda?*"

He drew the knifelike object, still imprisoned in their joined hands, slowly down the length of his own chest, watching her face.

Desire was etched there. And hatred.

So much hatred.

In one fluid motion he turned the letter opener and pressed the object deep into her abdomen, making sure the trajectory was perfect.

Her eyes widened, and she gasped his name. He stepped back and watched as she slid to the ground. He waited until she was motionless, her beautiful eyes still open—still surprised.

José set the bloodstained object on the desk, laying it diagonally across his picture. The *polícia* would do nothing. They never did.

As he turned to leave for a meeting with his lieutenants, the image of another beautiful target came to mind.

Soon he would have a new translator.

He imagined the horror and the fear on his American

sponsor's face when the woman's voice came over the satellite phone. One last little reunion. One final goodbye.

Then José could ask what he would of the gringo. And he would get it.

Anything.

FIVE

Moss MOTIONED TO THEM from the corner of the apartment building.

"Markesan gave me two hours to reconnoiter. If I found you, I was to drag your ass back, dead or alive. I think he wanted to take care of the 'alive' portion personally." His brows went up. "You're not the teacher's pet anymore."

"I never was." And that had been one of Cole's major problems growing up. He was the antithesis of teacher's pet material.

"You're impulsive," said Moss, as if it explained everything. It probably did.

Cole grinned. "And you live up to your name." When Callie tilted her head, he explained, "You know the old saying, a rolling stone gathers no moss? Well, Moss rolls so slowly that—"

"Funny." Moss gave a quick look around the corner and then glanced at Callie. "My last name is Moss."

She laughed out loud, clapping her hand over her mouth when the sound carried.

When Cole found himself smiling back at her like a loon, he quickly straightened. "Let's come up with a plan before we end up with a houseful of company."

"Plan's already in place."

"You wanna let me in on it? Are we pulling back to our previous position?"

"Negative, they're sending a chopper to the original insertion point at the soccer stadium. They'll pick us up there.

Markesan's idea. He got orders from higher up to pull out, but he's been holding off to give me time to locate you. At the end of the two-hour limit, the chopper lands. It's up to us to be there on time." He shifted his gun. "Embassy's already been evacuated and the personnel moved out by chopper. One translator is unaccounted for, but she's an Angolan national and has family in the area."

"How long have we got?"

"Half hour. After losing a bird in the last attempt to save your ass, they don't want to lose another one by hanging around in one spot. We lost one other man. Colbert was taken out trying to get to some of the embassy personnel. By the time we got to him, his transmitter was gone, so they've got our number. Radio silence from here on out."

"Shit, a half hour. No way we'll make it in time." Not with Callie along.

"No choice."

Cole nodded, his stomach churning at the thought of the men they'd lost. A sudden eerie thought occurred to him. "The rebels want Dr. Nascimento. Dead. I think that's what they rode into town for."

Callie spoke up for the first time. "That's impossible. They couldn't have known I was here."

"They asked for you by name, remember?"

"Wait a minute," said Moss. "Maybe that's why their attempts to take the rest of our team out have seemed half-assed, as has the swarming of the embassy, despite the intel we got. Any idea why they'd want her?"

"None."

"They took out *your* rescue chopper and didn't bother with the one carrying the embassy personnel." Moss nodded toward Callie. "And if they *are* after her, don't bother trying to hitch a ride on my taxi. The rebels will be eyeing any chopper landing to see who boards. We need to split up. She has a better chance if we're not together when the chopper arrives."

Cole thought for a minute, his mind whirling in a hundred directions at once. He captured the most likely idea and held on. "There's a set of waterfalls due east."

"Calandula, but that's almost two hundred miles away." Moss's brows went up. "You sure you want to do that? There are still landmines all over the fucking place."

Was he sure? No, but since when had that ever stopped him? "We'll stick to the beaten paths. They'll expect us to head south to safety. Toward Namibia. Going east will throw them off track."

Moss picked up a device and glanced at the screen. "When can you be there?"

Cole took in Callie's clothing and studied her shoes. Ballet slipper-type things. Not very sturdy, but passable. At least she wasn't wearing heels. "We'll try to get a vehicle, but if not, can you do that kind of distance?"

She blinked, but didn't balk at the idea. "Before the pregnancy, I jogged three miles a day. I can do it." The flat determination in her voice convinced him.

Moss shouldered his weapon. "Okay. How long?"

"If we get a vehicle we can do it in two days max. Walking? If I were alone, four days. With company along for the ride? Double that."

"If you're on foot, you'll need to cover over twenty miles a day." Moss tilted his head at Callie. "You sure you're up to it?"

"Yes."

"If you get there before the allotted time, what then?"

"We'll hang out. Relax." Dodge terrorists. But Cole left that part unsaid.

Moss glanced at his watch. "Sixteen hundred hours, eight days from now. Make sure you don't stand me up."

"Don't worry." Cole would be there. *With* Callie. Whatever it took. "Now get your ass in gear and move."

"I'm going to make myself a visible target for about five minutes. Use it to your advantage."

Thinking of the men already lost, Cole clapped Moss on the shoulder. "Not too visible."

"Don't worry. I don't plan on painting a target on my back—even for you."

With that he slipped around the corner. After two minutes, Cole heard the renewed sounds of firing. He tensed. The rebels would assume Moss was the one who had Callie. His friend would draw off the fire…but at what cost?

"Okay, doc. Our turn."

"I'm right behind you. Just tell me what to do."

"How familiar are you with Angola?"

"Not at all. My father's Brazilian, though, so I'm fluent in the language."

"I know. I heard you."

She tilted her head at him and frowned.

He clarified, "When you were talking to your terrorist friend on the ground."

"You heard me? How?"

"Not important. We need to get moving while Moss has their attention all to himself."

She hesitated and took a deep breath.

"What is it?" he asked.

Gnawing on her lip, she stared at him. "If we're going to be traveling for the next several days, we need to pick up some antibiotics for that wound."

"Wound?"

She motioned toward his head.

He reached to adjust the cloth. The thing ached like a sonofabitch, but it could wait. "Time enough for that later."

She licked her lips. "I'm serious. We need to find a pharmacy. Before we get out of the city."

Where the hell did she think they were, Shangri-La?

Her hands going to her hips in a show of stubborn defiance sent him over the edge.

He threw his arms out wide and leaned closer. "Does it *look* like there's an open pharmacy around here, lady? When I say I'll be fine, I mean exactly that."

CALLIE FLINCHED, HER eyes watering at his reaction, but she stood her ground. Soldier or not, she would not let him intimate her. If it wasn't for Micah, she wouldn't insist. But she couldn't risk Cole getting an infection…or worse before they reached their destination. Without him, she and the baby were goners.

She certainly hadn't expected him to flip out about it. Although from what she'd seen of her stepfather's band of buddies, it was pretty much par for the course for these guys. They were cold and unfeeling—until they blew wide open. Then woe to anyone who stood in their path.

Swiping at her cheeks, she heard him curse softly.

"Shit, not tears." He put his arm around her shoulders and pulled her close. "You'll find I'm a pretty tough bastard, but I promise we'll stop if we come across one, okay? Right now, we need to move to a safer location. Stick close, and don't move out from behind me, unless I tell you to. Got it?"

"Yes." A sliver of panic pushed through her, but she worked past it. She focused on her initial impression of Cole instead. He'd defend the baby to the death. She was sure of it.

WITH HIS GUN POINTED forward, Cole peeked around the corner. Moss had done his job well. No rebels in sight. He turned back to give Callie the all-clear signal, before remembering she'd have no idea what he was doing. Cole wasn't used to having a woman along for the ride…at least not this particular kind of ride.

He headed left down a neighboring alley and tried to scope out the area while keeping an eye on his companion's progress behind him. His interactions with women were normally short and to the point. No complications, no strings and definitely no commitments.

And here he'd committed himself to one for the next eight days.

Without any of the normal fun.

This was getting way more complicated than he'd bargained for. He was responsible for not just the woman, but for the budding life inside of her. The weight of duty pulled on him like a ball and chain.

They ducked down another alley, and Cole kept his internal compass going. *Keep heading out of town in an erratic path.*

Erratic he could do.

He glanced behind him. He was going at a decent clip, and she looked like she was keeping up. She'd held up well for all she'd been through. Hardly a peep, even when rappelling down that building.

He rolled his eyes and turned back toward the front. Yeah, she'd been fine until he'd worked his own special brand of magic. A few careless words and he'd had her in tears in no time flat.

That seemed to be his specialty. Making women cry. First his mom, and now Callie.

It was why he preferred to keep his activity with women wordless…and between the sheets.

Ducking into the doorway of a building, he stopped to let her catch her breath.

"You okay?"

She looked up at him uncertainly, maybe expecting him to snap at her again.

"You're doing fine."

"I'm sorry for making you deal with all this."

He shrugged. "My choice, not yours."

"Still, you didn't have to come after me, not after you shot that man."

Why had he anyway? Cole still wasn't sure what urge had propelled him to charge down the side of the building and drag her out of the path of danger.

Time to change the subject. "Sure you don't want a smoke?"

She frowned up at him, but when he waggled his brows to show her he was joking, she smiled. "No, but I could do with a big ol' hunk of chocolate. Dark, preferably."

There it was again. That uncanny ability to block out her surroundings and concentrate on the moment at hand.

He envied her that. While his thoughts scattered like machine gun fire, hers seemed to collect like droplets of molten lead, sliding together until they became a cohesive whole. What would it be like to have those amazing powers of concentration? Better yet, to have them focused completely on him?

Swallowing hard, he dragged his thoughts back from the gutter. This woman was pregnant. She wasn't married, but she still might be involved with someone. His thoughts were inappropriate at best, obscene at worst.

She touched his arm. "How about you? Are you okay?"

He laughed. "Yeah. Great." Sliding out of his hiding place, he checked the surroundings. "Let's get moving."

Around the next corner, Cole stopped dead.

Farmácia.

Here was their chance.

Callie pulled up beside him. "A pharmacy," she whispered.

Touching the security grate covering the plate glass windows, she glanced at him. "How are we going to get in?"

He pulled out a small metal container.

"You're going to pry the grating open with a pocket knife? It doesn't look strong enough."

Neither do you, he wanted to say, but he held his tongue. Instead, he opened the set of picks and, working quickly, felt inside the lock until the mechanism gave way. Then he slid the accordion-style grating to one side. The door itself was easier. When the lock clicked open, he stepped inside, motioning to her to follow.

She touched his sleeve. "Normally these buildings have an—"

A siren went off, finishing her sentence.

He ignored the blaring alarm and gestured toward the shelves of medicines. "What's the name of the antibiotic?" He had to shout to be heard.

"You grab some Band-Aids and I'll find it."

Cole quickly found a package of butterfly bandages, shoving them in the pocket of his pants just as Callie called out that she'd found what she was looking for.

Conscious of the still-screaming siren, he wrapped his hand around her upper arm and tugged. "Let's go, before the wrong people hear that thing and come to see who's here."

He watched her lift her shirt and tuck the boxes of medicine beneath the waistband of her pants, fitting them against the smooth skin of her stomach. She dropped her blouse back over the top of it, cutting off his view.

Don't think. Just move.

Following him past the cash register, Callie stopped again.

He shook his head. "I draw the line at stealing money." Even as he said it, he grabbed some candy bars and stuffed them into his already-bulging pockets.

"No, not money, the phone." Callie gestured at the object

behind the counter. "I need to get word to my brother-in-law that I'm okay."

It was always something with this woman.

"Now's not exactly the time. Besides, you said no one knew you were here."

"They don't." Her chin went up. "I still need to call him."

"Why?"

"To let him know I'm okay. That the baby's okay."

He frowned at her. "Why not call the baby's father?"

"Gary *is* the baby's father."

Cole's mouth popped open and he gaped at her. Surely she couldn't mean what he thought she meant. Disappointment mixed with some other indefinable emotion and spurted through his system. He'd never be able to look at her the same way again.

"No," she blurted, evidently gauging his reaction. "It's not what you're thinking."

"Hell, lady, I doubt you have a clue what I'm thinking right now."

"I'm pretty sure I do, but you'd be wrong."

With the alarm still blaring in the background, she looked into his face. "Yes, Gary's the father. But my *sister* is the baby's mother, not me."

Before her meaning had time to register, she touched his arm. "I'm a surrogate."

SIX

COLE DIDN'T KNOW what he'd expected her to say. Maybe for her to justify an affair or to claim her brother-in-law had forced himself on her. The last thing he expected Callie to say was that she was carrying her dead sister's baby.

He'd have to sort through his feelings on that subject later. Right now, they needed to get out of there.

"We don't have time for phone calls. Maybe later. Or better yet, you can call when we make it out of Angola."

Pushing through the door, he waited for her to follow and then shut it behind him. He pulled the grating back across and secured it. Someone looking at the shop wouldn't know there'd been an intruder. Maybe they'd think the alarm was malfunctioning. Cole glanced at his watch. He figured they'd spent about five to seven minutes inside.

"The farther we get from this street, the better."

Even as he spoke, he heard a vehicle approaching from the west. Fast.

Grabbing Callie's hand, they took off down the street and dashed into a smaller side street. Cole searched for any place to hide.

There.

Among the clothing dangling from spindly clotheslines on the side of the apartment building was a dingy quilted bedspread. The bottom of the fabric almost brushed the ground. And the space behind it was just about right...

"Get behind that bedspread." He began pulling at the clothespins, struggling with the unfamiliar catches.

She pushed his hands away, unhooking each pin with deft precision and lowering the fabric until it dragged the ground, providing the perfect camouflage.

They ducked behind it, Cole making sure his body was angled in a way that hid hers. Using the tips of his fingers, he turned the edge of the spread so it almost touched the side of the building, leaving a sliver to peek through.

Within two minutes, a military-style jeep crept down the street perpendicular to theirs and paused at the entrance to the alley. The familiar trickle of sweat coursed down his back. The vehicle seemed to wait for long minutes, when in reality it was probably a matter of seconds. In fact, the wheels were still creeping forward. A pause, not an actual stop. He was thankful for the other clotheslines, which held various pieces of laundry. It made their hiding place less conspicuous.

Still, he expected the vehicle to stop…for someone to jump out and snatch the protective shield from his hand and shoot them on the spot. He held his breath. Callie seemed to shrink closer to him in the silence, her arms slipping around his waist, and her cheek pressing between his shoulder blades. The waiting had to be worse for her, since she couldn't see what was going on. He didn't dare reach back and give her a reassuring touch, because the rebels might see the movement under the spread.

A reassuring touch? *Dammit.* Since when did he think in those terms? The less personal he made this, the better. It didn't matter that the baby she carried wasn't a boyfriend's or a husband's. She was still just a mission.

A self-assigned mission.

He shouldn't even be here in the first place. Markesan was probably going to have his ass when he rejoined the team. He could only imagine the man's reaction when Moss made it back and relayed the news.

If he'd even made it back.

He had.

Cole hadn't put his best friend's life in danger for nothing. An innocent woman's life was at stake. He concentrated on the arms around him. Hell, Moss would have done the same thing if Cole hadn't jumped into the fire with both feet before anyone else could react.

Impulsiveness strikes again.

His eyes glued to the still-crawling tires, he clenched his teeth as the rotation picked up a tiny bit of momentum. He willed them to move faster.

Yes. Nobody's here. Go find another mouse to play with.

The vehicle jumped to life and surged forward with a suddenness that made his muscles twitch. Callie's arms tightened convulsively around him. He'd scared her.

He reached back and squeezed her leg. At least he hoped it was her leg. "I think they're gone," he whispered. "Let's just wait another minute or two to make sure they're not going to double back."

Her head moved back and forth between his shoulder blades. He hoped that was simply a nod and not her wiping away new tears.

Cole didn't think he could handle them twice in one day.

Three minutes went by. He saw no movement. No sign that anyone was out there. He checked the rooftops for signs of snipers or lookouts. Nothing. The pharmacy's siren had cut off. He had no idea when it had happened, but he didn't care. Silence was his friend right now. Callie was still snugged tight against him and the temptation to wait longer than necessary hovered in the air.

He frowned and shifted his body, and her arms dropped away immediately. Turning toward her, he searched her face, trying to tamp down his own strange reactions.

"You okay?"

"Yes."

He nodded toward the far side of the bedspread. "Let's go out on that side, away from the road. The spread will shield us for about half a block if we stay tight against the wall."

She didn't question him, just turned and slipped from under the fabric and waited for him.

A few feet down the street, Callie stopped and stared up.

"What is it?" he asked.

"Boost me up."

"What?"

"Give me a boost, I want to get some clothes off that line."

Cole looked up and saw some old clothing on a neighboring clothesline. Unlike the bedspread, these were just out of reach. They were also cheaper and less conspicuous looking than their current attire.

"Good thinking." She was smart, he'd give her that.

"Give me some money, while you're at it."

"Money?"

She gestured at the line. "Do the owners look like they can afford to replace them?"

Great. Just what he needed. A bleeding heart.

Without a word he sifted through what money he had and handed over two bills.

She glared at him. "Twenty Kwanzas. That's less than fifty cents."

"Most of those clothes aren't worth half that. Besides, I need to hold some funds aside for us to travel on."

Callie shook her head, but didn't argue. "Boost me."

He formed his hands into a sling. "Okay."

"No, I won't be able to reach like that. Boost me onto your shoulders."

Cole gave another glance down the street. No sign of anyone yet.

He squatted on the ground, trying not to think about how

uncomfortable the idea of having her legs wrapped around his neck made him. Scratch that. The thought didn't make him uncomfortable. It made him something altogether worse.

Once she was in place, he pushed to his feet and Callie stretched to reach the clothes. To change the direction of his thoughts, he called up, "Be sure to pick out something nice."

She laughed, but the sound was as strained as Cole's nerves. Slinging several articles over her shoulder, she started to hang the money on the line with one of the clothespins.

"No," he said. "Don't hang it in the open. Someone will either steal it, or it'll alert the rebels that we were here. We don't want them questioning the residents if they're home."

She held the bills in her hand. "I *am* leaving them money."

Why did she assume the worst about him? Irritated, he snapped, "Pin it behind some of the other clothes so it can't be seen from the street."

"Oh." A beat went by. "Right. Sorry." She did as he'd suggested.

He gave a mental sigh when she climbed off, relieving him of his burden...and his thoughts.

Callie faced him and handed him his share of the clothing. "Here. Hurry up and put these on, while I get out of my old things."

His face heated as thoughts he'd banished just seconds earlier came rushing back.

The horrified question spewed out before he could stop it. "You're going to change in front of me?"

"I'LL OVERLOOK THE insulting tone of that remark and pretend pregnant women don't remind you of slow-moving blimps." Callie nodded at the hanging bedspread. "I was planning on using that as a shield while undressing, lucky for you."

Red seeped up Cole's neck and flooded his face. "I didn't mean it as an insult."

"I was kidding." This man was way too serious. Part and parcel of his profession. At least, judging from her experience with military men.

No, don't think about that now.

Hurrying behind the bedspread, she stripped off her old clothes and yanked the elastic waist of the long cotton skirt over her hips and tummy. Next she pulled on the rough muslin blouse, thankful that its loose, peasant style successfully hid the baby's presence.

She was sweaty and filthy, yet it had only been three hours since she'd stood in line in the air-conditioned embassy building. It already seemed like a lifetime ago.

Peeking from behind the bedspread, she noted that Cole was already dressed, but facing away from her, his gun at the ready. Her gaze trailed over him, taking in the cheap navy t-shirt that strained to contain his powerful shoulders…the thick bulge of his biceps. The beige drawstring pants, on the other hand, were painfully casual—and totally at odds with her image of the sniper who'd shot and killed a man.

The military boots were still in place, reminding her of who he was. She shivered. Shades of her stepfather. Someone who wouldn't hesitate to kill.

But there'd be no more killing if Callie could help it. Cole turned before she could avert her eyes. The chain around his neck glinted, and she had to force herself not to imagine the metal dog tags hidden under his shirt, against the warm skin of his chest. Clearing her throat, she pretended she'd just come out from behind the screen.

"Let me see your head." The tie from her discarded shirt was still wrapped around his wound.

He touched his hand to it. "This needs to come off so it doesn't attract attention."

"Let me check to make sure it's stopped bleeding first."

She held up her old clothes. "And I'm not sure what you want me to do with these."

"There's a pile of garbage in that niche over there. I buried my clothes underneath the stack."

"Okay." She dropped her garments at her feet and reached up to gently push away the tied fabric around his head. The wound was no longer bleeding, but it was puffed and ugly. The edges of the wound parted as soon as she released the skin. Callie was doubly glad they'd stopped at the pharmacy. Now if she could only get him to take the antibiotics.

"We'll use Band-Aids to hold it shut. You need stitches, but I probably can't talk you into—"

"No. You can't." He handed her the package of bandages and held still while she smeared antibiotic ointment across it and re-closed the wound, taping it shut. He took the blood-stained strip of fabric from her hand, gathered up the rest of her clothes and carried them to the garbage pile.

Lifting stacks of soggy-looking cardboard, he pushed her clothing underneath, then carefully pulled everything back in place.

"Are you sure they won't find them?"

He stood and glanced at the stack. "Pretty sure. They're not going to want to mess with some of the stuff underneath the cardboard."

She nodded, trying not to think about what would be disgusting enough to keep out scavengers. Instead, she rooted around in the pocket of her skirt until her fingers closed over a small bottle.

"Ready?" he asked.

"Yes. But hold out your hands first."

He tilted his head and stayed where he was.

"I'm not going to hurt you." She smiled. "Promise."

Slinging the gun over his shoulder he held out his hands.

She squeezed a small portion of hand sanitizer on his right palm and backed away to watch his reaction.

He blinked—stared at his hand for a long second and then looked up at her. Out of nowhere came a rumble of sound. Low and quick, but she definitely recognized it as a laugh.

Cole rubbed his hands together, spreading the clear gel. "Lady, you are something else."

"If rebels aren't going to want to touch what's under there, then why should you have to?" She couldn't shake the thought of how much he was giving up to help her. He could be safe in his chopper by now. With the soldier named Moss and his other colleagues.

So even if he thought she was silly...crazy...and any number of other things, she would do her part. Even if it was something as simple as making sure he didn't die of some noxious bacterial infection.

"If you're done making sure I don't contaminate you, can we get moving now? We have a lot of territory to cover in a short amount of time."

"I wasn't trying to protect myself, I was..."

He was already moving down the alley, leaving her no choice but to follow.

From time to time during the next hour, they saw other residents scurrying down the streets, evidently as scared of the rebels as she was. But they'd seen no more signs of the prowling jeep. At this point, it seemed they'd succeeded in losing their pursuers.

She hoped.

With one less thing to worry about, Callie's bladder began to remind her of its presence. She'd already held on for far longer than usual. But how did you tell a man who was hell-bent on getting out of the city as fast as possible that he had to stop? Again.

He didn't seem to feel hunger or tiredness or any natural urges at all.

"Cole, can you hold up for a sec?"

He turned around, his brown eyes meeting her own.

"You used my name."

"Ye-es…" She'd been calling him Cole inside her head for quite some time now. Had she committed some kind of faux pas by saying it aloud? Maybe she was supposed to call him by an official title or something. "Oh, I'm sorry, am I supposed to use your rank?"

"No, Cole's fine." He looked past her. "So, what's going on?"

Heat flooded her face. "I need to, um… The baby's pressing on my…"

He frowned, but continued to stare as if he didn't have the foggiest idea what she was getting at. So much for subtlety. She might as well just come out and say it.

"I have to pee."

If her face was warm, his had to be flaming hot, judging from the dark color that stained his skin.

He blinked at her a time or two as if unsure how to respond.

Oh, come on. They were both adults here. "Well?"

Cole scanned the area, evidently realizing she was serious and that he'd not misunderstood her bald statement.

"I'll turn my back." He proceeded to do just that.

"I'm not going in the middle of the street!"

He faced her again. "I thought you said you had to—"

"I know what I said, thank you very much, but that doesn't mean I'm going to squat in the middle of a public street."

"Your skirt's long. No one will know what you're doing."

"I'll know."

His cheeks puffed as he blew out a long exasperated-sounding breath. "What do you expect me to do about it, then?"

"I don't expect you to *do* anything. Just find me a spot where I can be discreet. Preferably behind a bush or a public bathroom."

"I doubt there are public bathrooms anywhere except the city parks, and they're too dangerous."

"Then a tree. A hedge. A trashcan. Some place I can have a little privacy." She shook her head. "Don't you have to go too?"

"I can wait."

Of course he could. Mr. Indestructible.

"Well, I can't."

His eyes skated over her stomach. "Come on, then. We need to hurry."

He took off at an impossible clip. Callie literally had to jog behind him, which did nothing to help her aching bladder.

When he turned the corner and gestured, her eyes widened. Surely not.

Oh, but it was. Vasco de Gama himself. She could only hope he didn't turn over in his grave at being used as a shield.

She wrinkled her nose. "Gee, thanks."

"No problem," he said without blinking an eye. "You have thirty seconds. I'll even turn my back."

COLE DID AS HE PROMISED, but as soon as he was sure she was hidden behind the large statue, he peeked behind him periodically to make sure no one came up on her from another direction.

Surprisingly, she was back in the prescribed time, rubbing hand sanitizer into her skin. He bit back another laugh. At this rate, that small bottle wouldn't last twelve hours, much less the eight days they might have to travel.

Cole figured they had another hour before they were out of the city and into the outskirts. The landmine situation in the surrounding countryside worried him, but he really didn't have a choice, since they were without a car. Another thing that couldn't be helped. He wasn't willing to drag Callie around the dangerous streets long enough to scrounge up a working one. Maybe in the next town. Besides, with the invasion of the rebels, most people had either fled—in their vehicles—or were holed up in their homes.

The Angolan government would eventually get its act together and send in military reinforcements to drive the rebels back to their jungle hideout, but Cole couldn't wait around until that happened. Not after what the head honcho had said about wanting Callie dead.

She interrupted his thoughts. "Are you ready to take your first antibiotic?"

"Later."

Her scowl said everything and more, but it could wait until they were less out in the open. He set off, checking her pace to make sure he wasn't moving too fast.

"The sooner you start taking them the better."

He acted as if he hadn't heard her, opting to change the subject instead. "How far along are you?"

"A little under four months."

He had no idea what that meant, but kept pushing forward, hoping that by keeping her talking, she'd continue moving as well. "What is it, do you know?"

"The baby's a boy."

A boy. Cole swallowed. He'd never wanted kids. Never felt the need for a family.

He avoided looking at her stomach. "Congratulations." He kept walking, needing to hurry all of a sudden.

"My sister chose the name Micah. It's a strong name, don't you think?"

He didn't want to think about baby names or pregnant women. He just wanted to get to Calandula Falls and pass his responsibility on to someone else. Someone more equipped to deal with people like her. "I'm sure it's a great name."

She caught up to him again and touched his arm. "What's wrong?"

"Other than trying to outrun the terrorists before they find us? One of whom is after you for reasons I've yet to discover?" He slowed his pace, but didn't turn to look at her. "Other than that, life is peachy."

"Is it? I don't think so." Her grip on his arm tightened. "Something else is bothering you."

Crap, not the mind-melding bit. Not now. He turned down a side street, trying to buy time and make sure they weren't being followed. For the millionth time, he wished there were people lining the streets. Anyone other than them and the rebels.

"Cole?"

The husky sound of his name on her lips made him do a double take. He glanced down. There was concern in her face. Professional concern. He swore a blue streak inside his head.

Time to throw her off track.

"You want to know what I'm thinking? Fine. You were taking a hell of a risk coming to Angola without a good reason."

"My sister's not a good enough reason?"

"Didn't your sister's relief organization issue a report on the crash?"

"Yes, they said the fuel tank exploded midflight. The bodies were all incinerated. They had to use the flight manifest to determine who the victims were."

Her voice quavered, but she didn't cry.

There had to be something burn-in-hell-worthy about protecting his own soul at the expense of someone else's.

He said the only thing he could think of. "I'm sorry for

your loss." He groaned. And that was supposed to make her feel better?

Cole stopped in his tracks and looked down, making sure he met her eyes. "I really am sorry."

She glanced away. "Something about the story just doesn't sit right."

"The story?"

"About the accident."

"That's why you came to Angola, isn't it?" He went from sympathetic to irritated in the space of a second. "You thought you'd do a little amateur detective work, dig up a little dirt."

"No! I just…" She bit her lip. "I just needed to know the truth."

"And do what, when you found it?"

Callie shook her head. "Get some closure, maybe." She paused. "Maybe the rebels had something to do with the crash and they're afraid I'll find out."

"How would they have known you were coming here in the first place?" He started moving again, turning down another street, surprised when it ran smack dab into a shantytown at the edge of the city.

Cole held up his hand for silence as he studied the rows of shelters. Planks of wood were nailed together helter-skelter, forming ramshackle boxlike houses. There were holes the size of fists here and there between the slats, and most of the roofs appeared to be made with black plastic tarps held down with a scattering of bricks. A few of the better-made structures had corrugated metal roofs screwed to the tops of the wooden boxes.

"A *favela,*" Callie whispered, moving closer to him.

He turned his head, his eyebrows raised. "A what?"

"In Brazil, there are huge areas like these, right on the border of cities. Lots of drugs. The entrances sometimes have armed guards. Even the police are afraid to go into them." Her fingers pressed against her closed eyelids for a second before she looked up again. "It's why Sara and her team were here. Angola has been displacing the residents of these *favelas,* sometimes bulldozing the houses right out from under whole families. Her team was helping provide medical care and find temporary housing for hundreds of thousands of these people."

If these slums were as dangerous as the ones in Brazil, he could see why the government wanted them bulldozed, but it wasn't up to him to decide. He had his mission. That's all he needed to worry about.

These streets didn't appear to be guarded. In fact, there was no activity at all. No children playing, just a couple of stray dogs sniffing odd piles of garbage. "It seems these people moved out before they had a chance to be evicted."

He checked his watch. Almost five o'clock. *Shit.* The whole afternoon wasted just getting to the edge of town. They'd probably only covered five miles. Traveling at night was stupid, though, especially with someone who wasn't used to rough conditions. Maybe they could find some-place in the shantytown to hide until morning. The more he thought about it, the more sense it made. If the residents of these towns were normally heavily armed, like Callie said, he didn't think the rebels would risk an unnecessary firefight. Rebels relied on being seen as champions of the poor. Be-sides, these particular rebels seemed to be after bigger fish.

Callie.

He needed time to figure out why.

First, he had to make sure the area really was deserted. He glanced around, looking for a place to stash Callie while he checked out their new digs.

A woodpile behind one of the crude shelters caught his

eye. Taking her arm, he spoke in low tones. "I want you to wait there, while I see if anyone's home."

"No, it's not safe. Please don't go in there."

He shifted his rifle on his shoulder to bring her attention to it without being obvious. "I'll be fine. Just wait here, okay?"

She swallowed. "Be careful."

Her tone of voice pulled him up short. He stroked his fingers across her cheek before he had time to think about what he was doing. "I will."

Moving on silent feet, he slid between two houses, peeking through holes in the boards. Crude furnishings, stale odors of old food, but no occupants. He kept moving until he'd surveyed one entire row of buildings. There were hundreds of shelters, too many to check all of them. But this particular group seemed deserted. They could just go to one on the far end and hole up until morning. He pried the door open on the last house and stepped inside, fighting to adjust his eyes to the gloom.

Empty. At least the front room. He used his rifle to push through the slatted door leading to what was probably the bedroom. A low voice and the glint of steel stopped him in his tracks.

"Eu não mexeria, se eu fosse você."

Cole's mind scrambled to translate. He figured out the meaning at about the same time he heard the safety click off the other man's gun.

I wouldn't move if I were you.

SEVEN

WHERE WAS HE?

Callie shifted behind the woodpile. She'd watched Cole creep between the rickety shacks with a stealth that sent shivers down her spine. If you wanted someone dead, this was the man to send. You'd never hear him coming.

So, then…where was he?

Her back ached a little from trying to hold still, but at least they had somewhere to spend the night. "One less thing to worry about, right, Micah?" She patted her stomach, willing the tiny life inside to feel the vast amount of love she had to give.

She swallowed. At least until she handed him off to his rightful father.

Gary would surely treasure his child even more, since the baby carried a part of Sara. Her sister had said their relationship had been strained over the past several months, but she'd hoped the pregnancy would draw them back together—might lessen some of his political ambitions. And it worked. The man had grown more loving and attentive once the implantation took hold. He'd followed the pregnancy every step of the way, his excitement almost palpable, as he held hands with his wife, listening to the heartbeat that first time.

Sadness washed over her. Yes, she owed it to her brother-in-law to make it out of Angola intact. She should have never left the States to come here in the first place.

Her coming must seem crazy to someone like Cole.

Maybe he was right. But until she placed her feet in the

spot her sister had walked—where she'd died—Callie would never know peace.

She hadn't gotten the chance to do either. And now a rebel fighter knew her name. Claimed he was after her.

But why?

She'd told her kidnapper her name as they'd stood in front of the embassy. Maybe he'd relayed it to the rebels before Cole shot him.

Could the man have been working in conjunction with them—hoping that by killing an American they could get across some kind of sick message? Blowing up a pregnant foreigner would get them plenty of media attention.

That had to be it.

The idea took root and grew. It would be too much of a stretch to believe that rebel fighters had converged on Luanda at almost the exact same time as a lone suicide bomber—unless there was a connection. And the bomber *had* been communicating with someone. She'd assumed it was Cole's band of soldiers.

But maybe he'd been talking with the rebels as well.

So, they knew her name from the man who'd held her. They knew she was pregnant. They could almost hear the gruesome headlines: Pregnant Tourist Killed by Rebel Freedom Fighters. And then that chance at stardom had been snatched away. Of course they were furious. They'd want a chance to finish what they'd started.

Cole suddenly materialized from nowhere, and she almost jumped out of her skin. She flew from her hiding place, anxious to let him know what she'd figured out. Her excitement shifted to horror when she saw the armed man following close behind.

Cole's eyes narrowed in warning.

Her knees quivered and threatened to give out, but she

held herself upright and waited for him to give her some kind of indication as to what she should do.

It came soon enough.

"Isto é a minha esposa, Calista."

Oh God, he was introducing her as his wife?

She murmured that she was pleased to meet the man, surprised at the steadiness of her voice.

"You are Brazilian?" he asked in Portuguese, studying her closely.

Her accent. "Yes, my father was Brazilian. I have dual citizenship."

The man's dark eyes glittered with anger as he waved the barrel of his gun toward Cole. "Is what this American said true? You are his wife?"

Cole looked her, and then said two words in English. "Trust me."

"Silêncio!" The other man's gun hand came down with frightening swiftness and caught Cole at the base of the skull. The force of the blow drove him to his knees, but he kept his eyes fastened on hers.

Her mouth went numb. She couldn't speak, couldn't think.

The man's hand lifted to deliver another blow, and Callie crouched beside Cole in an instant, wrapping her arms around his neck to shield his brainstem.

"I am his wife. He is my unborn child's father."

The man's gun stopped at the top of the arc. "You are with child? Show me proof."

"Don't," Cole whispered.

Ignoring him, she stood and lifted her shirt, baring her abdomen. She mounded the small bump with her left hand. "A boy. Our first child."

Callie released the hem of her shirt and glanced down at Cole. A trickle of blood curved down the side of his neck and disappeared in the collar of his dark T-shirt. Trying not to let her panic show, she lifted her face in a show of defiance.

"Would you leave my child without a father?"

"How do I know you are not part of the government plan? Corrupt. All of them. One by one they wipe out our homes. Force us to flee into the jungle."

"No." She shook her head, realizing why the man was so angry. "We have nothing to do with that. My sister was with Doctors Without Borders. They were trying to help your people. Her plane crashed and she died."

He shifted his feet. "We heard about the deaths. There is talk that the government was behind it. They want us gone. They do not want interference, especially from outside." He glanced at the rows of shacks. "This area is next on the list. Most have already left. Only a few of us remain, refusing to go."

"We are running from the government too." It wasn't quite a lie. When the man looked into her face, she gazed back without blinking. She deplored the tactics the government was using to rid the city of the *favelas*. Instead of building more government housing, it was simply easier to herd the people out so they didn't sully the landscape. After all, they could funnel more tourist dollars into local businesses if hungry faces didn't get in the way.

Callie tried another tack. "Maybe we can help. We need someplace to stay for the night. But once we get back to our own country, we can tell our own government what is happening here."

"They can do nothing for us."

"Then we'll go to the newspapers, let them know what we've seen. If the world knows, maybe they can pressure your president to make changes."

The man tilted his head. "You give your word you will do this?"

"You have my word. I'll tell everyone I can."

To Callie's surprise, he reached his free hand down to Cole, who took it and allowed himself to be hauled to his feet.

"I apologize," the stranger said, "but I have my own family to protect."

Cole nodded. "Just as I have to protect mine."

Her hands immediately went to the back of Cole's head and reached into his thick hair, searching for the source of the blood. She located a small nick where the gun had gouged him. No gaping hole or damage that she could find. But, oh, how his head must ache.

He brushed her hands away. "I'm fine."

"You may stay with us tonight. We have clean water and a little food," the man said. "My wife will prepare a meal. We have to be careful with cooking fires. We don't want to draw unwanted attention."

Cole spoke up. "We don't want to take your supplies. We have our own food."

Callie leaned forward and caught his eye. It was her turn to warn him. Turning to their host, she said, "Thank you, *senhor*. We would be happy to accept your hospitality."

"We can't afford to catch dysentery," Cole hissed under his breath.

"Can you afford to get us killed by offending him?" She kept her voice low and her words in mumbled English, in case their host had some grasp of the language.

"Same outcome either way."

AFTER THE MEAL, Callie stood alone with Cole staring at the narrow hay mats on the ground, while darkness crept through the dwelling. She glanced up at him. Community bedroom. Four family members.

That left one extra bed.

One.

For the two of them to share.

So much for the husband and wife pretense lasting just until bedtime. Maybe she should have let the proud home-owner give Cole that second whack on the head.

If he hadn't said she was his wife...

He wouldn't have said it if he thought there was any other way. No, he'd saddled himself with her when it was the last thing he'd wanted to do. How did she know this? From the glimpse of raw distaste she'd caught in his eyes when she talked about her pregnancy. Oh, he'd squelched the look fast enough, but the rapid pace he'd set had said it all.

Maybe it was because she was already round and would get rounder by the day, while he was muscular and hard-bodied...a perfect physical specimen. Well, all except for that temper of his.

And that mouth.

She bit her lip as her gaze slid sideways to the object in question. Okay, the mouth itself wasn't half bad. It was what came out of it that infuriated her.

No, that mouth was everything a...

The lips in question curved and her thoughts backed off in a rush.

He knew. *Oh gawd.* Just what the man needed. A bigger head than he already had.

Her glance veered back to the mat. What was she going to do about that? Worse, was what she wanted to do *in* it.

She mentally gave herself a slap. She wanted to sleep. Nothing more. Nada. Zilch.

"Callie?" His mouth twitched again. "Penny for your thoughts?"

Not a penny, not a dime, not a million friggin' bucks, buddy. "Just wondering how comfortable you're going to be on that hard ground next to my mat?"

He gave her an innocent blink. "Well, at least I won't have vermin pole-dancing on my sleeping body."

She flinched and glanced at the dingy coverings. Her hand reached into the pocket of her skirt and fingered her hand sanitizer. Fat lot of good it would do her when she was asleep.

"Hey, if I had to eat the food, you have to sleep in the bed."

Despite herself, she smiled. "Touché."

"Actually, we're both going to sleep in the bed."

Her heart flipped. "Huh?"

"They think we're husband and wife, remember?"

Before she could think of a suitably snide remark, Pedro, their host, stepped into the room with his wife and children.

With that the choice was made. No more arguing. Callie would be sleeping with Cole, whether she liked it or not.

COLE KICKED TOWARD the watery surface of consciousness. It was still dark, but he sensed dawn would be here soon. He had to be ready when it arrived. Fighting to get his bearings, his fingers stroked something soft.

Callie.

It all came rushing back. His arm was thrown over her waist, his hand cupping the warm swell of her left breast. And his cock...

He jerked upright as if he'd been burned.

Shit.

Frozen in place, he watched her sleep, praying she didn't realize what he'd been doing.

Unconsciously doing. A natural primitive response to having warm female flesh pressed against his sex organ.

Ah, hell. Who was he trying to kid?

He climbed quietly to his feet and glanced down. Her skirt was bunched halfway to Saturn, revealing long bronzed limbs that looked as if they could...

He reached down and jerked the fabric over her legs, hiding the enticing sight. Callie's lips pursed and she murmured something. Cole turned away, while he still could.

Going outside, he took care of business, scoping out the surroundings. Silent as a grave. Better to take off now. They could cover an hour's worth of ground before sunup.

When he returned to her side and touched her cheek, she started. He put a finger to his lips.

She nodded and got to her feet, blinking in the gloom.

Cole leaned close to whisper into her ear. "I want to be out of here by the time the family wakes."

Her glance went to the dark forms on the neighboring mats. "Were you able to sleep at all?"

"Yeah. Plenty." He left out the part about the dreams he'd had as he'd been snoozing, or how he'd been in the process of acting on one of the hotter scenes when he woke up. If she didn't already know, he wasn't about to enlighten her.

Following him into the front room, she said, "Can we leave them some money for the food?"

Money. Again. It wasn't as if he'd *wanted* to eat their damn food in the first place. She'd practically shoved the stuff down his throat. But he took out a substantial bill and waved it under her nose so she could see the amount. He didn't have time for her to jack his ass up about leaving too little.

He placed the money on a plastic table, weighing it down with a small rock. "There. Enough this time?"

Callie nodded. "Thank you."

Leaving her to do whatever women did in the morning, he consulted his GPS unit and planned their route. They should stick to the West-East highway, passing through Guanza Norte before hitting the province of Malange, where Calandula Falls was located. They might even be able to make it in less time than he'd anticipated, if they hit a lucky streak.

He paused. Dragging along a resident shrink wasn't

exactly under the heading of "lucky" in his book, but he didn't have much choice.

Pedro had said the road was riddled with potholes and missing asphalt in large stretches, but it was passable. There was even the possibility of finding a periodic vehicle or bus traveling along it. For a hefty fee, they could catch a ride.

Cole figured staying on foot was the safer bet, at least until they were well away from the capital city. He wouldn't put it past the rebels to stop all traffic heading in or out of town. Besides, it would be easier to slip off the road and out of sight if they hoofed it. Anything to keep their options open. And open options was the name of the game in Cole's neck of the woods.

Just as he started to get antsy, Callie joined him. He kept his eyes to her face, afraid if he glanced down he might find the scorched imprint of his hand branded onto her shirt.

"I'm ready, but I want you to do something for me first."

"What's that?"

"I'd like you to go ahead and take some antibiotics, prophylactically."

He stared at her, trying to work that last word around in his mind. Wasn't *prophylactic* a fancy word for condom?

She touched warm fingertips to his forehead. "Your wound from the helicopter crash, remember? I don't want infection to set in. The antibiotics will help kill any lingering bacteria."

Irritated that she'd seen his confusion, he shook off her hand. "I'll be fine."

"Please, Cole." She touched her stomach. "I need you."

His skin prickled, goose bumps actually traveling up his arms and spiraling across his chest. He might be able to shake off her hand, but he was going to have a hell of a time shaking off those three words.

I need you.

She did. But not in the way he wanted her to.

"Fine. I'll take them." A tightness in his throat gave the words a strangled sound, and he tried clearing his voice. "You're the doc. I don't want to be stuck in this hellhole any more than you do."

She opened her mouth to say something more, but he swung away from her. He didn't need her giving his brain anything else to pick apart and examine. Not after his dream, and his embarrassing behavior as he woke from it.

As they set out through row after row of pitiful-looking shacks, he tried to blot out the image of Callie's protective hand resting over her stomach. But it did no good. In his head, the film repeated time and time again. Her dark eyes on his as they drilled through to his very soul.

I. Need. You.

He pushed forward, his feet picking up the pace. But he couldn't outrun those words. They burrowed deep, their hooklike barbs piercing a place he'd always assumed was impenetrable. A fortress, free of entanglements.

His heart.

EIGHT

JOSÉ TAPPED THE LONG steel bar against the toe of his boot. The woman had slipped from his grasp over thirty-six hours ago, along with the soldier. According to his calculations, he had six more hours in which to safely inhabit the embassy building and make his political statement heard. The government troops were already gathering on the outskirts of town, gearing up for a showdown.

The government's troops?

No. *His* troops.

He gripped the metal rod until it bit into his palm. The government had stripped him of everything at the end of the war. His position. His family. Even some of his own men had betrayed him. For five long years he'd watched from the fringes and waited for this very opportunity. He was not going to let a woman and a rogue American soldier rip it from his grasp.

Anger and impatience swirled through his gut, forming small whirlpools of rage. He forced it back. They would all pay. Including the Americans. Until then, he would use their money, earning back the power and respect that had been stolen from him.

He tilted his head and studied the large, silent man held upright between two of his men. Blood oozed from various cuts on the man's face. Dripped from his chin. José slid the metal bar along the floor behind him, making sure the man watched its approach.

"I will ask you again. Where did you come by such a large Kwanza note, Pedro?"

"I stole it."

It was the third time José had asked the question and the third time he'd received the same answer. The spurt of fury that erupted at each lie was becoming harder to resist. He hated these *musseque* dwellers almost as much as he hated his country's current government. Both groups drained the nation's resources, sucking it dry like a horde of parasitic insects. It would continue until nothing was left of Angola but a dried out husk. Unless José was able to regain power and stop it before it was too late.

His American sponsor's money would help him accomplish that and more. Once he was again head of the military, he would personally take over the bulldozing of Luanda's slums. There would be no more Pedros with the courage to lie to his face.

"Where did you steal it?" he asked.

A shrug. The same defiant shrug he'd gotten twenty minutes ago.

"You know what the military does to thieves, don't you?"

That question didn't even elicit a shrug, only a cold stare. José nodded to one of the men lounging against one of the room's clean white walls.

A fist sent blood flying from Pedro's ruined nose onto one of the other soldier's jacket. The man's face contorted in disgust.

Why was this man still holding out? What could he possibly hope to gain? No matter, Pedro knew something. And José knew just the way to coax it out of him.

He took a step closer, still dragging the metal rod along the tiled floor. The clinking sound as the heavy object hit each grout line reminded him of the snapping of brittle bones. Perfect for what he had in mind.

"Care to change your story, *amigo?*"

The man's head lifted and he spat, catching José on the chin with a mixture of spittle and blood. He forced himself to neither recoil nor lash out. Instead, he kept his voice calm and friendly.

"No?" He pulled a clean handkerchief from the pocket of his uniform and dabbed at the mess on his face, before carefully folding it into a square. He deposited the soiled object into a drawer on the desk, smiling as he imagined someone unfolding it and finding Pedro's blood. "I believe I can make you change your mind."

The man's eyes fastened on him with unholy hatred. "You are as bad as the government—no, *worse*. Soon everyone will know the truth."

"Will they?" José's thoughts swung to Rosa. Poor dead Rosa. His little translator. She'd tried to stand up to him at first too. And yet, in the end, she'd done everything he asked of her. Everything. He'd only needed to find the right kind of incentive.

He had no doubt he could change Pedro's mind as well.

With the right incentive.

Pedro only *thought* his wife and children had gotten safely away. But his men had found them huddled in the woods just outside the city. The wife had soon admitted to harboring the Americans. But only Pedro knew where they were headed.

He motioned to Carlos, who stood by the door.

"Bring the woman in first."

Carlos went outside the door and the sounds of screaming pierced the air. Children's screams.

His victim's head jerked back as if struck. "No! They know nothing."

"Maybe. We'll soon find out for sure." José smiled and turned as Pedro's struggling wife was brought into the room. His smile faded. The upper portion of the woman's dress was ripped to the waist, and she struggled to cover herself with the tattered remains. Her left eye was swollen shut and dried blood smeared one portion of her mouth.

Fury swelled in his throat. He hadn't authorized the woman's rape. It would make getting information from the husband that much more difficult.

Someone would pay. Starting with Carlos, his first-in-command.

But for now, José leaned against the corner of the desk and feigned nonchalance. He turned back to Pedro, watching his reaction as Carlos dragged his wife across the floor.

Pedro's face changed, horror seeping into his expression, along with something infinitely more dangerous.

Just as José feared. The woman's usefulness was as ruined as her polluted body. She would only make his prisoner all the more unwilling to cooperate.

Time to change tactics.

"Hold her there and send for the youngest. I want them both to watch."

Carlos handed the woman to another soldier and went to the door to give the order. A uniformed man carried in a crying toddler who was maybe two years old. A girl.

The child spotted her mother and held her arms out, her cries growing desperate.

Perfect.

This time it was the woman who screamed and struggled to break free, no longer worried about protecting her lost virtue…or her modesty. José watched with interest. What would his prisoner do with this latest threat hanging over his head?

"Bring the child to me."

Setting the metal rod on the desk, he held out his hands for the child.

He cradled her in his arms and murmured to her, making sure Pedro watched his every move. Within a few seconds, the child's cries quieted, fooled by his soothing whispers. Shifting her slightly, he reached behind him and fingered the steel rod as he gauged his captive's reaction.

In a split second he saw he would triumph. The man's chin no longer jutted in defiance. Instead, his shoulders slumped, his eyes pleading in silence. He would cooperate. And maybe, just maybe, José would find it in his heart to set the woman and children free. After all, he was not without mercy.

But Pedro would pay for placing his loyalty in the hands of foreign scum, rather than remaining true to Angola. Mercy could only be extended to those who earned it. It was how power was captured and kept.

He patted the child's bony back and tried to keep down his jubilation. Now was not the time to crow. Not until he had Dr. Nascimento and her protector in his grasp. Not until he'd crushed them beneath the heel of his boot and collected his money. "Now, *amigo,* let's start from the very beginning. I want to know everything. Starting with where you got the hundred Kwanza note."

CALLIE SETTLED INTO the deep, straw-colored grass, trying to escape the baking rays of the sun. But it was hot even in the shade. The humidity had to be over ninety percent. It was as if a heavy veil of moisture hung in the air, coating her body in tiny droplets that she couldn't see, but which smothered her little by little.

"How long have we been walking?" She downed a sip of tepid water, then offered the plastic bottle to her companion.

Cole, still on his feet in the chest-high grass, seemed impervious to the sun's effects. Instead, he fidgeted as if he couldn't hold still, capping and uncapping the bottle of water several times.

Had he heard what she asked? Or was he purposely ignoring her?

Just as she opened her mouth to repeat the question, he put the bottle to his lips and swallowed with powerful movements of his throat. Callie bit her bottom lip and tried not to stare as he passed the back of his hand across his mouth.

"Six hours."

So he had heard her. She nodded, drawing her knees to her chest to rest her chin on them. Her thickening stomach made the act more difficult than it used to be.

They'd been traveling longer than she'd thought. Callie was proud of herself. She'd kept up, although she was pretty sure Cole had cranked his velocity way down to accommodate her. And from the thumb steadily drumming against his cotton pants, he was obviously anxious to be on their way. Her mouth twisted in a wry grimace. She was slowing him down and he wasn't used to it.

Well, he should be glad she wasn't so big she was waddling. Yet.

His eyes slid across her resting place. "You okay?"

"Sure. Just hot. Why?"

"I expected you to need to stop more."

She coughed on a dry laugh. "Have you forgotten so soon? I've stopped plenty, remember?"

Cole had insisted she stay well hydrated. For a pregnant woman, staying hydrated meant stopping. Lots and lots of stopping.

"No, I mean, I expected you to need to rest more." His thumb stopped its nervous tapping for a minute while he averted his eyes.

Her jaw tightened. "Because I'm a woman?" Maybe he

saw a glimmer of anger in her face, because he switched gears. "You're pregnant. This can't be easy."

She relaxed. "The stress of the last two days has been rough. But the traveling? Not so much. I've always been active. Did a lot of hiking and camping."

"If we don't find shelter before nightfall, you're not going to like the result. It won't be camping like back in Kansas."

"I grew up in Ohio, not Kansas. And my name's definitely not Dorothy. Surely there's a town somewhere along the way." She glanced at the sun, which was well overhead, thanking God for the blessing of insect repellent wipes.

"The interior of Angola is sparsely populated."

Callie thought about that for a few minutes. "Exactly how sparse?"

"Enough to make covering a lot of ground important."

She sighed. "Too bad we don't have a couple of hammocks. In Brazil, you just sling hammocks around a couple sturdy trees and let the wind rock you to sleep. It's wonderful." She plucked a blade of grass and drew the cut end past her nose, letting the fresh scent cool her from the inside.

Cole's stare caught her up short.

He thought she was crazy. Here he was hustling away from terrorists, while she lay back espousing the benefits of getting close to nature by swinging from a hammock.

She crumpled the grass blade and dropped it. Maybe she was crazy. Besides, she'd never actually slept in a hammock out in the open overnight. She'd just napped during the heat of the day at her aunt's house when there'd been a lack of beds. And there'd been hooks *inside* the house on which to hang them.

Looking up, she was dismayed to find him still staring. His thumb no longer drummed against his thigh, but was drawn up into a tight fist. The sight made her swallow.

He must think her a fool for rambling on about nothing. To draw his attention away from her blunder, she gestured at their half-empty two-liter bottle of water.

The bottle was the second of three they had with them. Cole had taken a worn backpack from their host's house, along with some empty plastic soda bottles, which he'd filled from an outside spigot. She was glad they'd left the family a decent sum of money.

Callie assumed the little tablets Cole had dropped into the bottles had somehow sterilized the contents. "What do we do when the water's gone?"

The blinking of his eyes brought him back from wherever he'd gone, and his fingers uncurled. "We find more. Towns form around water sources. One more reason to try to find one before nightfall."

Good point.

"Are we still on schedule?"

He nodded. "I'd like to go for another four or five hours, but if we find a town before that, we'll stop. I don't want to take the risk of being stuck in the open after nightfall."

"Maybe the rebels have already given up." It was something Callie had been thinking about. She wasn't worth so much that people would track her two hundred miles, right?

He reached down a hand. She accepted it and allowed him to pull her to her feet. His palm was cool and dry. She longed to press it to her cheek to absorb some of his composure. She settled for allowing her hand to linger in his.

"Did you figure out any possible reason for them wanting you in particular?" he asked.

"I told my captor my name, hoping to talk him into letting me go. He could have relayed it to someone else. Maybe that's how the rebel knew it."

He held her hand for a second longer before releasing it. "Maybe."

"You don't buy that explanation?"

"No."

"Why not?"

"The rebel talked about you dying 'like you were meant to.'"

Callie shivered, glad she hadn't heard the man's voice when he'd made that statement. "Maybe a suicide bombing involving an American citizen would have given them some kind of recognition."

"Doesn't it strike you as odd that you—a woman whose sister recently died in this country—is randomly grabbed out of line at the embassy? By a man who had every intention of blowing himself up...and taking you along with him?"

"I don't know. What else could it be other than a coincidence?"

Cole set out walking and Callie tagged along, the spring going out of her step as reality weighed down on her. She'd hoped this mad dash to safety was a farce, that there was no one actually hunting them.

Hunting *her*.

"Pedro said the government may have downed your sister's plane. Any possibility of that?"

Callie had felt there was something off about the crash, but she hadn't been able to find out anything other than whispered rumors. "I don't know. I heard a few things here and there. Doctors Without Borders seemed so sure a mechanical problem was to blame. The civil war in Angola is over, but many people still don't entirely trust the government. You've heard how corrupt some of the police officials are." She shrugged. "It's the same in Brazil. Some of the police uphold the law. Others don't think twice about stopping a car on a deserted stretch of highway and soliciting a bribe to overlook some invented infraction."

He glanced down. "And you. What do you believe? Were you a random victim?"

Callie searched her heart, thought over the course of events. The suicide vest. The surprised look in the man's eye when he discovered she was pregnant. His death. Cole's rescue. The downing of the chopper that had been meant to whisk them to safety. Most of all, the chilling demand by a faceless voice that Cole hand her over.

Was it a coincidence?

Her hand swept through her hair. "I don't know. You tell me."

Cole's jaw tightened. "Someone is out to kill you, and we'd better figure out why…and soon. Because if they have a good enough reason to, they'll find you. And kill you. No matter who they have to take out to do it."

NINE

Moss traced Cole's probable route on the map. "I'm betting he'll stick to the roads, rather than following the rail line."

General Richard Markesan stood next to him. "Train line is a straighter shot. It'd take less time."

Moss wasn't exactly sure why Markesan had requested this meeting, or why he'd excluded the rest of the team. But he knew better than to ask. If his superior wanted to brief him, he would. If not, it was better for Moss to go with the flow until Markesan worked through whatever was bothering him.

Tapping the area where the road belled to the south, Moss said, "With eight days to play with, I'm betting he'll go with the safer route."

"Since when has Scalini ever gone with safe?" The general ran a hand over his thinning crew cut. "If he'd waited for orders in the first place he wouldn't be in this mess. And we wouldn't be chasing his ass halfway across the African continent."

The general's attitude might seem cold, but Moss knew better. His superior officer would lay down his life for any member of his team. Including his buddy.

"Cole wasn't going to let that woman die. If he hadn't gone in, I would have."

"That's not what I heard come over the wire. You told him to hold up and wait."

"He acted faster than I might have, but all of us…you, included, sir, wanted that civilian out of there unharmed." He tapped Calandula Falls on the map. "Besides, I don't know of anyone more equipped to get that woman safely to the extraction point than Cole."

"I hope you're right. I'm getting pressure from above to make sure that woman is retrieved unharmed."

Moss frowned. Now he was getting somewhere. "What kind of pressure?"

Markesan shook his head. "Seems the woman Scalini rescued is kin to Senator Parker."

"Fuck me. The Senate Majority Leader? You sure about that, sir?"

"Yep. He and I have had some interesting chats over the last day or so. Dr. Nascimento is his sister-in-law." The general paused. "Parker's wife was killed in Angola several weeks back. He got word through unofficial channels that Dr. Nascimento might have traveled to Angola to pay her respects to her dead sister and that she was somehow caught up in the embassy evacuations. Let's just say he's a very unhappy man at the moment."

"No wonder there was such a rush to evacuate. If Parker suspected she was there, he'd have demanded action. Who clued him in that she was at the embassy?"

Markesan clasped his hands behind his back and stared at the map. "That's where it gets sticky."

Moss straightened, waiting to be filled in.

"It seems there's some cause to believe Senator Parker's wife was targeted in Angola, that the plane crash carrying his wife and a Doctors Without Borders team wasn't an accident."

"What?"

"The official version is that the fuel system malfunctioned and a spark set it off. No survivors, all bodies incinerated beyond recognition."

"You said the official version. So what's the unofficial one?"

"It's farfetched."

"How farfetched?"

"Senator Parker is convinced his wife's plane was tampered with. Says he's got people quietly looking into it."

This just kept getting better and better. "Does he have any proof? A grief-stricken man sometimes looks for a devil where there is none."

"He's convinced he's right, but he doesn't have anything definitive. If he did, he wouldn't be sitting on his hands asking us—quietly—to make sure the sister-in-law gets out without incident."

"Shit. Cole said the bastards knew Dr. Nascimento's name. That they wanted her dead. Said those very words, that she'd been 'meant to die.'"

"Dammit, why didn't you say something sooner?"

"I didn't know she was related to the senator." Moss stared at the map as if he could visualize Cole's position at this very instant. He was getting a bad feeling about this whole setup.

"So Parker may be right about the accident being no accident," Markesan said.

Moss let the idea move through the slow-turning cogs in his brain. His best friend was out there somewhere, and there could be a price tag on his head. "Who is Parker looking to pin the incident on?"

"The Angolan government among others. It seems Parker and a few like-minded senators have been putting pressure on the U.N. to impose sanctions if the country doesn't change its policy on dislocating people from the capital's shantytowns." Markesan braced his arms on the steel table. "Maybe killing Parker's family is meant to make him change his mind." He stared at the map. "Getting them out is a priority. And not just because of Parker."

"I know. We'll get them. Six more days and they'll be on a Black Hawk headed home."

"I don't think it's going to be that easy. Parker's convinced that someone in the government isn't happy with his party's interference." Markesan circled Calandula on the map.

"That's probably true. No country likes to be told by another one how to conduct its internal—"

"Not someone from the Angolan government. Someone inside *our* government."

Moss stared at him. "You can't seriously believe someone in our government is behind Parker's wife's death? You saw those rebels as well as I did. If anyone's behind it, they are."

"Maybe. But it doesn't matter what I think. It's what the good senator believes is true."

"Since when do we take orders from Senator Parker?"

"We don't. We take orders from the president."

"So, what's the problem?"

Markesan turned to him, his thick grey brows pulled to the center. "That is the problem. Senator Parker is convinced that the person responsible for the attack on the embassy—for his wife's death…is the President of the United States."

COLE WATCHED AS A WOMAN filled their water bottles from a well. He wouldn't drop in the chlorine tablets in front of her; he'd wait until they were out of sight. Thank God they were still close enough to Luanda that everyone spoke Portuguese, rather than one of the myriad tribal tongues. The farther they moved into the countryside, though, the more difficult communication might become.

He glanced to the right and encountered Callie's stare. Seated in a hammock, she had one leg curled beneath her, while she used the other to push off the ground. As the hammock swung gently back and forth, he could swear there was a gleam of triumph in her dark eyes.

Okay, so she'd been right about the hammocks being halfway comfortable, even for someone of his size. But he'd have been a hell of a lot more comfortable if he'd been able to keep her close. As it was, he hadn't gotten a lick of sleep. He'd been too busy making sure Callie slept unmolested.

But would having her sleep next to him be a wise idea? Hell no. Two nights down, six more to go. And he was already in serious trouble.

The villager handed him the last of the bottles with a shy smile.

"Obrigado," he managed.

He stuffed the water into the backpack and hefted it onto his back. His rifle went over the other shoulder, but he was careful to keep the movement unobtrusive. Like Pedro, these people didn't seem to trust soldiers. It had taken some smooth talking on Callie's part to convince the folks that he wasn't a government spy.

Not being able to take the lead in negotiating irritated him. He'd found himself wanting her to trip over her words, even though he knew they desperately needed these people to give them shelter for the night.

What was wrong with him? So she was good at using her mouth.

Crap. And he was terrible at keeping his mind out of the gutter.

Crossing to where she sat, he glared down at her, as if she'd been the one to instill the image stuck in his brain.

"What's wrong?" she asked. "Mad that you had to sleep in a hammock after all?"

"No."

She cocked her head. "What then?" Giving the item in question another little push with her foot, she sighed. "I think that was the best night's sleep I've gotten since arriving in

Angola. Of course, being exhausted helped. And being able to bathe this morning was icing on the cake."

Seeing as he hadn't gotten any sleep at all, and the bath had only succeeded in raising images of her beside the river, washing every inch of her body, he turned up the heat on the glare.

She smiled, evidently not intimidated. "And the tapioca crepes reminded me of *bejú* from Brazil. Delicious." She drew her tongue along her lips as if she could still taste them.

The action sent his body haywire. He'd thought the rubbery pancakes were kind of bland and gummy, but anything that could get that kind of reaction out of her couldn't be all bad. He might even have to try another one someday.

The strap of his rifle slipped and he readjusted it, cursing softly.

"Didn't you like it?"

Had she read his thoughts?

A frown puckered her brow. "The crepes. You didn't like them?"

"They were fine."

She slid from the hammock and stretched, ending with a shrug. "I'd like to check your head wound before we go. Did you take your antibiotics?"

"Yes." The word snapped from his tongue.

"What's wrong with you today?" Her voice was a little sharper this time, her good mood seeming to slip away.

He was a regular black hole of good cheer, sucking it away from everyone he came in contact with.

"Nothing's wrong. Just in a hurry to leave, that's all."

"Well," she said, reaching up to push her fingers into his hair, angling his head toward her. "We'll go as soon as I check your head."

Her eyes narrowed in concentration and he noticed she had flecks of green surrounding her pupils. They weren't entirely brown like he'd originally thought. Her fingertips explored his brow with a gentle touch.

Cole suddenly realized how close they were. Way too close.

"I don't want to take these bandages off for a couple more days, so I can make sure the skin has had time to seal together. You're going to have a scar. Sorry."

"Doesn't matter." He had plenty more where that came from. Outside and in.

"Scars don't matter to you?"

Was that a trick question? His gut told him to pull away... but his feet weren't paying any attention. "Not really."

She blinked and the fingers at the back of his head moved slightly.

Cole swallowed. If she would just look away...

She didn't. He dropped his gaze to her mouth, remembering the way her tongue moistened her lips. Almost against his will, he found himself leaning forward, watching as Callie's lids closed.

Alarmed shouts caught his attention, forcing him upright and dragging him away from her tempting mouth. He turned to see men running toward the nearby road.

"O que foi?" he asked someone hurrying by.

"A man. They've found a man a few miles down the road. They are carrying him to the village."

Callie jerked from his grasp and turned to follow. "Is he injured? I have to see if I can help."

"No." Cole wrapped his arms around her waist and held her back. There was no way he was letting her rush into the middle of something. "Let the villagers deal with it."

"What?" She twisted in his arms until she stood toe to toe with him, her belly pressed tight against his. "I'm a doctor!"

His mind hardened. "No, you're a shrink. Stick to mind-melding and leave the real medicine to someone else."

The words had the desired effect. She stiffened and stared up into his face. "What did you just say?"

He couldn't bring himself to repeat the words, no matter how much he believed them. "I don't want you rushing out there half-cocked. For all you know it could be one of the rebels. Or a trap."

"Let. Me. Go." The words were quiet, contemptuous and oh-so-very effective. He released her and took a step back, his hands going behind him in a military stance.

When she swung away from him and headed in the direction of the villagers, he had no choice but to follow. He fully expected to have to shoot someone before this was all over with. Maybe even himself.

Cole pulled up beside her just as he spotted a litter in the distance heading toward them. He didn't see anyone other than villagers behind the stricken figure. But that didn't necessarily mean there wasn't someone there. His jaw tightened. Something didn't sit right about this whole scenario. How often did these small outposts come across an injured pedestrian?

Gripping Callie's arm, he pulled her to a stop and edged her to the side of the road, into some thick growth. "Stay in the bushes until we know what's happening." When she acted as if she were going to struggle, he leaned down. "If it's on the up and up, I'll let you help in whatever way you can. Just give me a minute to make sure there's nothing else going on."

She did as he asked, but her cold stare said she hadn't forgotten his earlier remark.

Well, that was just fine. He didn't need her to like him, he didn't even care whether she did or not. He just needed her to cooperate until they were out of this mess.

At least, that's what he told himself. His action a few minutes earlier didn't bear out that particular theory. He'd been on the verge of kissing her.

Would she have let him?

His mind snapped shut. Stress. Adrenaline. And Callie was a beautiful woman. For someone who didn't have a stellar reputation when it came to controlling his impulses, what had he expected to happen?

She didn't know what he'd almost done. And he wasn't about to tell her. Nor was he going to let it happen again. Six more days. Surely he could last that long.

Callie's horrified, "Oh no!" jerked his wandering attention back into place. The crude stretcher was passing by their position, and he saw immediately why she'd reacted.

"Dammit. I knew it," Cole whispered, shoving Callie farther into the brush and urging her to move.

They had to get out of here, now…before anyone realized they were missing. She didn't argue, just set out at a quick clip. Despite their need for speed, Cole was damned glad that she knew how to be quiet as they raced away from the area.

He tried to blot out what he'd seen, but failed. He couldn't erase the sight of the ruined, bloated face staring sightlessly out from the stretcher. Nor could he shed the crush of guilt at knowing he'd probably been the cause. Cole prayed the same fate hadn't befallen the rest of the man's family.

The body on that stretcher belonged to Pedro, their host from the first night. And contrary to what he and Callie had both assumed, the man wasn't injured. He'd been beaten, and then his throat slit from ear to ear.

TEN

CALLIE TRIED NOT TO THINK, just ran, being careful not to trip over roots. Despite her best efforts, though, Pedro's broken body kept appearing before her mind's eye.

"Oh God, that poor man. Who could have done something so horrible?"

Cole either didn't hear her question or chose to ignore it. He pulled in front of her to take the lead, his hand gripping hers with a fierceness that struck terror in her heart.

Her carefree attitude this morning poured over her, drenching her in guilt. Had Pedro been suffering at the hands of some monster even while she'd been joking about hammocks and *bejú?* While she'd been anticipating Cole's lips closing over hers?

She'd been so hopeful that the man on Cole's earpiece had discovered her name by chance, a freak accident, despite what Cole said. She'd also allowed herself to believe the rebel would give up once she was out of town and out of reach.

But Pedro's death, just one day after they'd left his house, couldn't be another terrible coincidence.

The rebels might even be following them at this very moment.

A branch smacked her cheek and she shoved it away, allowing Cole to continue dragging her along at break-neck speed.

Was Pedro dead because of her? But how? How could anyone have known she and Cole had stayed at his house?

Cole's hand tightened on hers. She imagined him saying, *Don't think. Just run.*

She pushed her thoughts away and focused on putting one foot in front of the other. Pedro was dead. Letting her guilt get her or Cole killed wouldn't help him. Putting a hand on her belly, she hoped the baby couldn't feel her panic, that the adrenaline pumping through her veins wasn't whipping his tiny heart into a frenzy. She'd wanted Micah to grow strong and healthy, protected by a calm, happy environment.

Her jaw tensed. The only environment she was providing at the moment was one of chaos, confusion and fear. "I'm so sorry, baby," she panted.

At her words, Cole pulled up and turned, pushing her behind his body. His gun came off his shoulder, ready to inflict serious damage on anyone who came bursting through the brush.

"You okay?" He threw the question at her.

She caught sight of a water bottle peeking from a small tear in the bottom of poor Pedro's backpack. It was her undoing. She covered her face with her hands, wrenching sobs fighting with her body's desperate need for air. She gulped oxygen in fits and gasps, but there was no way she could do it quietly. She wrapped her arms around her middle and rocked back and forth, trying to comfort herself as much as the baby.

Cole took a step back, his eyes and weapon still trained on the area in front of him. His free arm came around her shoulders and hauled her against him. "It's going to be all right, Callie."

All right?

It was going to be all right?

She knew he was trying to calm her down, but it wasn't working. Nothing would.

Except one thing.

Her brain latched onto the solution. Straightening, she pulled away and took a long shaky breath.

"I want to go back and face them."

His head swung toward her. "What?"

"If they're really after us...after *me,* specifically, then I need to go back. Pedro's life was no more important than my own. Why should he have had to die in my place?" The thought brought a fresh round of moisture to her eyes, which spilled over. "I—I can't let others die just to save myself. Maybe I can reason with them. Talk to them—"

"Talk to them? Lady, I don't know what kind of ego trip you're on, but you can't save the whole fucking world with a few well-intentioned words." He shook his head. "You really want to make that man's death a joke? Then go ahead. March out there spouting a bunch of philosophical bullshit. Show us how *you* can make the world a better goddamned place."

She reared back. He could think whatever he wanted, but she sure as hell didn't need his permission to do what she felt was right.

The second she went to take a step forward, though, he pivoted, making a quick hundred-and-eighty degree turn, until he stood in her path, the barrel of the rifle pointing in her direction. She stepped back in shock.

"You don't seriously think I'm going to let you skip out there just to be mowed down in a hail of bullets, do you?" He gave her a sinister sneer. "Or maybe, if you're lucky, they'll keep you around for a while. Maybe they'll let a few groups of men have at you...take turns using you. *Before* they kill you."

His ugly words and threatening posture brought up a sickeningly clear vision of her stepfather. He'd used intimidation tactics, just like these, to get her and Sara to toe the line and obey. And when that hadn't worked, a few well-placed slaps had done the trick.

Bile rose in a wave and she took another step back, her hand lifting to cover her mouth. Why had she thought Cole was any different?

Before she had time to react, he closed the gap and wrapped his hand around her arm, the grip tight enough to hurt. His gun lowered to his side as he yanked her flush against him. "Let's get this straight once and for all. You are *not* going out there. I'll do whatever it takes to stop you." His lips, white around the edges, barely moved. "Whatever it takes."

Her heart nearly stopped beating. His pupils were so huge she thought they might swallow her whole. Where she'd expected to see blind rage at her rebellion, there was none. What she saw instead was fear. Boiling, gut-wrenching fear.

Fear that she'd impulsively dash out of the woods and get herself killed. Fear that he wouldn't be able to stop it.

He was afraid for her.

She stared up at him, unable to tear her eyes away. She'd never experienced anything like what she was seeing. Differing shades of emotion ran through her system like quicksilver, each splashing onto the one before it, until the colors blurred and thickened. Her hands lifted, wrapping around his neck to pull him tight against her. She desperately wanted him to feel her own fear. To know he wasn't alone.

And he was right. She wouldn't—couldn't—take for granted the sacrifices that he, and Pedro, had made for her. For Micah.

"I won't go. I promise." She whispered the words, making them her own private vow. "I'll stay here with you."

Lifting as high on her tiptoes as she could, she put her lips to his.

RELIEF SWAMPED THROUGH Cole's system so fast he almost didn't realize she was kissing him.

Almost.

On some level, he'd been aware of the exact second her soft, trembling lips meshed with his.

Warning bells went off. He was neglecting his duty. Abandoning his post. Whatever he wanted to call it, he was going to get her killed by not stopping this now.

Oh man. He'd jeered at her, ridiculed her, even threatened her…all in an effort to stop her from putting her life on the line. But not only because of that. He'd had to do something to stop the fear that was threatening to grind his gut into hamburger.

And she'd reacted not by slapping his face. Not by screaming at him, or running in the other direction. She'd breathed the words he desperately needed to hear and put her lips to his.

It had taken his unprepared defenses by storm.

Defenses? Who was he kidding? He had none. Not anymore.

She'd destroyed them.

His free arm went around her back, pressing her closer. It was only dumb luck that kept him from dropping his rifle to the ground in the process.

Hell, she was right about the talking bit. A few well-placed words, a whisper against his ear, and she'd brought him to his knees like a quaking fifteen-year-old at his first make-out session.

He angled his head, and her lips opened to him. He hesitated for a fraction of a second.

Put a stop to it here, Scalini.

He couldn't.

His tongue slid along the sharp edge of her upper teeth, and his body no longer asked. It demanded. Cajoled. Begged. Before taking over completely. His tongue invaded the warm moistness of her mouth. Callie made a low sound deep in her throat. A sly, feminine sound that knew exactly what it did to a man.

Cole was no exception. And the sexy little moan did more than switch his body over to high-test and rev him up.

In the last two days, he'd fantasized repeatedly about what it would be like to kiss her. And the reality was light years from the mind games he'd played with himself.

Shit, in his mental merry-go-round he'd done a whole lot more than kiss her.

That thought pulled him up short and refunded a small portion of his sanity. A very small portion.

He was doing the very thing he'd accused Callie of just moments earlier. Crazy, impulsive behavior not based on logic.

Only he wasn't impulsively jumping off a bridge with only do-gooder intentions for his safety net.

His transgression was much worse.

He wasn't thinking at all. His dick was. And that was one part of his body that had an even worse track record than his dysfunctional brain.

Bracing his rifle against the ground, he pushed off, forcing himself back until her hands detached from his neck and fell away. He kept moving until she was out of reach, and then he turned his back, his rifle going up as if he were looking for sudden intruders.

In reality, he was trying to gather his scattered wits and catch his breath.

Never had he behaved in such an unprofessional manner. He was a career soldier. A member of the Corps and now a part of the elite Echo Charlie Group, and as such, he'd imagined himself above the fray.

Evidently not.

His eyes closed for a second while he dragged his self-control back around him and focused on the mission:

Get the girl out.

Pass her on to someone else.

And get the hell away.

His short-term goal summed up in three simple steps. Hell, he couldn't even make it through the first maneuver without screwing up royally.

"Cole?"

He sucked down another deep breath before turning around.

"Hey." He kept his bearing stiff and formal. "Sorry for manhandling you like that. I needed to find a way to get through to you."

Her eyes flashed fire and visions of a repeat performance slipped through his mind—and his groin. He needed to defuse the situation without dragging her back and finishing what he'd started.

He cleared his throat. "Sorry. That didn't come out right."

To his surprise, she smiled. "I know. I'm sorry too. I should have thought before I acted."

He smiled back. Well that made two of them. Maybe she was all right after all.

Twisting her hair, she pulled it over one shoulder where it cascaded over the slope of her left breast. He swallowed.

"So, what do we do now?" she asked.

What we do now is look at her face, Scalini.

He motioned past her. "First we make sure no one's following us, then we move. If I remember right, there's a rail line about five miles to our north. I think we need to travel along them for a while. The tracks were supposed to be repaired and operational by now, but I'm not sure if that's happened."

"Then why do you want to head for them?"

He hesitated, not wanting to bring up what sent them fleeing through the woods, but he had no choice. "Pedro was beaten. I doubt they killed him until they got the information they were looking for."

"That poor man." Callie shuddered. "Maybe he lied to them."

"And maybe he didn't. He knew our destination and even helped map out our route and stops along the way. If the rebels know what he knows…"

She nodded. "What about Pedro's family?" Her voice wavered for a second, but she lifted her chin and looked him in the eye.

He hoped the family had somehow been spared, but Cole couldn't rule out any possibilities. If it weren't for Callie, he'd have headed back and taken out at least a couple of the bastards himself. But he couldn't risk it.

"I don't know. Since the villagers didn't find his wife or kids, maybe Pedro hid them, or maybe the rebels weren't interested in anyone else."

"I hope you're right."

"Me too." He stepped past her. "You up to traveling?"

"Yes." She reached up to touch his arm.

"What?"

Her lips curved. "Sorry for manhandling you too."

Cole actually laughed. "No problem. We all get desperate sometimes."

Some of us more than others.

"Thank you—" she nodded at his rifle, "—for stopping me earlier."

He knew the weapon made her nervous, so he slung it over his shoulder, somewhat out of sight, and then changed the subject. "We'll follow the train tracks and pray the towns along it haven't shriveled up and died. It's a straighter shot than the road anyway, so there's a good chance we'll make Calandula sooner."

"And the rebels?"

The one thing he didn't want to think about at the moment. "We'll try to outrun them."

"And if we can't?"

He started walking.

She grabbed his hand and tugged, forcing him to stop and look at her. "Cole...what if we can't outrun them?"

"Then we do the only thing we can." Threading his fingers through hers, he pulled her into motion. "We turn and fight. And pray the cavalry shows up in the nick of time."

ELEVEN

CALLIE STUMBLED OVER a discarded railroad tie and would have fallen if Cole hadn't caught her around the waist. She leaned on his steady strength for a long moment before pulling away with a resigned sigh.

If only this numbness would go away. But she couldn't seem to shake it.

She turned to thank him, but his attention had already shifted to something else. Something evidently a whole lot more interesting than she was.

Kicking the block of wood in disgust, she muttered, "Thanks for nothing," and plopped down on top of it to rest—facing away from Cole, out of spite.

Not that he'd notice.

That was another thing. He'd been almost as quiet—no quieter—than she'd been since that desperate kiss. She knew he was busy doing his job, but the lack of conversation was starting to get on her nerves.

Pretty soon they'd be reduced to apelike communication. A couple of grunts, a few good hand slaps against the ground and you'd have evolution…in reverse. Maybe she could even get Cole to beat his fists against his chest to complete the picture. Unbidden, her mind drew up a picture of him shirtless, his—

"Hey, can I get a little input, here?" The image dissolved at the sound of his voice. Not the sexy rumble from her daydream, but an irritated growl.

"What?" She pivoted on her makeshift perch and faced him.

Yep. Definitely irritated. His dark-eyed gaze was narrow, focused on her face, which was warm…and probably blushing up a storm.

"How does this sound for lunch?"

"Lunch?"

He waved a hand in front of her face. "Where have you been for the last few minutes?"

"Uh, right here. The same as you."

"Oh yeah? Then how did you miss—" he reached down with a long thick stick and lifted something off the ground, "—this?"

Callie frowned, trying to figure out what that limp piece of…

She gave a small shriek and slid off the back of the railroad tie—butt planted on ground, legs sprawled over the thick wooden beam. She didn't attempt to get up. The farther away she was from…*that thing,* the better. "It's a snake!"

"A dead snake." He lifted it higher. The thing was long and seemed to get longer the more she stared at it.

She shuddered, then narrowed her eyes when she saw his grin.

Pig. He was enjoying making her squirm.

"I can see that it's dead. I take it you're responsible for its demise."

He shrugged. "It was either him or me."

In a split second, Callie realized why he'd been ignoring her a few moments earlier. "It's poisonous?"

"Slightly."

She gulped. "Oh my God, if the terrorists don't get us, the wildlife will."

He lowered the snake to the ground. "I thought you liked camping…swinging in hammocks and all that."

She laughed, glad beyond all reason that he hadn't simply

been blowing her off, but slaying dragons instead. "What can I say? The camping was in an RV—a comfy, air-conditioned one—and the hammock was in one of my aunt's bedrooms."

Dropping the stick, he propped his hands low on his hips. "And here I was worried that I wouldn't be outdoorsy enough to impress you."

Man oh man, in that sexy pose, he could "outdoors" her anytime he wanted. She shook away the image. They were running from a band of killers. It wasn't like he—or she—should even be thinking about things like that.

She changed topics before something in her expression gave her away. "You aren't really thinking of eating that, are you?" She jerked her head toward the unmoving reptile. "If it's venomous, won't we be poisoned?"

"Nope. We'll cut the head off. Cooking neutralizes the venom anyway."

Callie hoped her face wasn't as green as her churning insides at the thought. To cover it, she struggled to pull herself back onto the railroad tie.

Maybe he noticed her look of disgust, because he came over to her. "Here, give me your hand."

She hesitated and he smiled. "Don't worry, a little hand sanitizer and you'll be good as new."

Was he making fun of her little bottle?

"You can even use some on me, if it'll make you feel better."

He was definitely making fun. But it sure as hell beat the awkward silence she'd gotten from him for the last couple of hours.

"Deal," she said, letting him help her back onto the railroad tie. She patted her tummy, making sure everything inside still felt well attached.

Cole glanced at the hand smoothing across her abdomen then looked over at the snake. "I'm serious, though. Do you think you can stomach eating it? It's high in protein which will probably do you good." He nodded at her midsection. "Both of you. And I can't promise we'll get another opportunity to eat meat."

Her stomach roiled at the thought, but he was right about the protein. "Are you sure it's safe?"

"I've cooked and eaten snake before. We'll make sure it's well-done to kill any possible parasites." He smiled. "I would say it tastes like chicken, but then so does everything when you're hungry enough."

Callie couldn't imagine what he'd had to eat during his career. Maybe even roadkill, when the need arose.

The closest she'd come to exotic fare was the ostrich meat she'd eaten in Brazil. Oh, and the gator tail in Florida. But neither of those came from a slimy, poisonous creature.

"I'm not sure I can eat it, but maybe once it's cooked and no longer looks like…like…snake." Another shudder ran over her.

"I won't cook it, if it'll make you sick to watch."

She shook her head. "It's not the actual skinning and cleaning that bothers me. I'm a doctor, remember?"

When he remained silent, she stopped. That's right. He didn't think she was a "real" doctor at all. He'd said as much.

She wouldn't admit how much his attitude hurt, but she knew there were lots of people who thought psychiatrists were nothing more than a bunch of tea-leaf readers who went around performing lobotomies for kicks.

That wasn't who she was at all. Couldn't he see that?

Somehow the need to show him there was more to her than he thought made her glance at the snake. Surely she could eat it. Just a little.

Do you really think eating a squiggly creature will make him respect you?

Maybe. It was worth a try.

She stood and looked up at him.

"Fine, let's have lunch. You cook and I'll wash up afterward."

A flare of surprise went through his eyes, but he held out his hand. "Deal."

She shook it, noting that he released hers immediately. Not even a hint of the passion he'd shown in the woods.

Pulling her hair to the side, she twisted it into a rope to keep the wind from blowing it and let it hang over her shoulder.

Time to lighten up, Callie.

"I think you may have missed something obvious when you shook on our little agreement." She held her arms out and turned a slow circle. "Look around you. It looks like we're using disposable utensils tonight, honey. No dishes for me to wash. So it's up to you. Take that thing somewhere far, far away, and work your magic on it. But don't bring it back until you've transformed it into something that looks like… what did you say? Oh yeah. *Chicken*."

GARY PARKER'S THUMB stroked the embossed name on his leather agenda as the roll call continued and, senator by senator, his colleagues cast their votes on some trivial issue. His mind was not on the proceedings. It was on his sister-in-law. Where was she? His repeated calls to Markesan had yielded nothing more than curt, to-the-point updates. The man refused to speculate, which Gary found maddening. He supposed he couldn't blame the good general. No one wanted to put his ass on the line and come out on the losing end.

Nor had his meeting with the president gone any better. President Bryson maintained his do-no-harm smile that had won the hearts and votes of the American people, but his popularity was quickly fading, and Gary was under no illusions. Beneath that cool, unflappable surface lay a hatred of everything Gary's party stood for. The gulf between them was wide and deep. He'd get no cooperation from that front.

No, it was up to him. He had to stay on top of the military, until Callie...

"Senator Parker, may we have your vote please?"

He blinked, realizing the heads of his fellow legislators had swiveled to look at him. He'd missed hearing his name.

Sitting up straighter, he tried to remember exactly which issue was up for grabs. Coming up empty, he cast his vote for whether or not he would locate his sister-in-law before it was too late. In a loud voice, he said, "Aye."

CALLIE GNAWED AT ONE corner of the chunk of meat skewered on a stick. He'd actually cut the thing into small segments reminiscent of McNuggets—if you discounted the backbone and ribs in each piece.

Well, she'd told him to make it look like chicken. Given what he'd had to work with, he'd come up with a reasonable facsimile. He'd even charred it a bit, giving it a nice smoky tang, which almost made up for the lack of salt or other seasoning.

In fact, Cole appeared to be Mr. Boy Scout incarnate from the way he'd started the small fire. Unlike her own laughable attempts in years past with matches and piles of dried leaves, Cole's fire was hot with very little smoke. And all done without matches. Not even a magnifying glass.

She was impressed.

"Not bad," she admitted, holding up her half-eaten portion, "if you can just get past the memory of what it started out as."

He shrugged. "Do you think of a cow when you eat beef?"

"Well...no, but that's different."

His brows went up.

"Okay, so it's not different. But you won't see me chowing down on every grasshopper that flies by, either, no matter how well you reason away the facts."

"Actually, grasshoppers taste kind of like—"

Callie held up her hand. "I know. Chicken. Spare me the grisly details."

He laughed. "No, I was going to say sardines."

"Ugh!" She couldn't even believe he would know something like that. "Good thing I hate sardines."

"Too bad. I was already planning a tasty dinner."

She picked up her stick and showed it to him. "If you want to see this meal a second time, keep talking, buster."

Cole went over and knelt by the fire, turning the three remaining meat-laden branches.

"Ready for another one?"

"I think I'm good. I've had two already."

He stood. "I'm going to put the fire out, then, and cover the remains, so no one knows we were here. I want to keep close to the tree line in case there're signs of trouble."

She glanced down the long length of railroad tracks. So far, not a single train had come by. Nothing but weeds and brush as far as the eye could see. Was he expecting them to sleep out in the open?

"Will we run into more towns along the way?"

"Probably. But I don't want to wait too late to start out."

"I'm ready when you are."

He touched her cheek, his roughened fingertips sending a shiver across her skin as he looked into her face. "Sorry if it seems like I've been pushing you too hard."

"It doesn't. I'm sure you're going slower than you would if you were on your own."

"But I'm not on my own." He dropped his hand and turned to kick dirt on the small fire. It sizzled for a second before snuffing out completely.

"Bet you wish you were."

"Were what?"

"On your own."

His gaze shifted to hers, then away again. "I chose this course of action."

Not exactly the kind of reassurance she was looking for. But then, what had she expected him to say? Something to placate her? No. She'd have been angry if he tried. But he was right. He had chosen this course of action, when he hadn't had to.

"Cole?"

"Yeah?" He squatted, digging a small trench with a stick.

"I'm sorry for what I said earlier."

"About the snake? No problem, I understand why—"

"Not the snake. About what I said after you shot the man at the embassy."

He stopped what he was doing and his mouth opened to say something.

She cut him off. "Let me finish, please." Twisting her hair, she continued, "I implied I was better than you, that I would have taken the high road and talked him out of what he'd planned."

"Maybe you were right. Maybe you could have."

She shook her head. "I've been thinking about it. A lot. After I saw what happened to Pedro…and when I think about what might have happened to his family…"

Her voice wavered for a second and she cleared it, determined to get through her little speech without breaking down. "I realized if you hadn't done what you did, I probably wouldn't be here—" she motioned to the remains of the meal now lining the trench, "—eating snake and relishing being alive."

Moving toward him, she laid her hand on his shoulder. "So, thank you. I want you to know I'm grateful for what you did."

Cole glanced at her, his face hardening. "I was following orders."

"I know you said you were ordered to, but—"

"Don't make me into something I'm not. People before you have tried. It didn't work then and it won't work now. I'm no hero." His look chilled her. "I was told to shoot. *Ordered* to. I fired that shot knowing there was a good chance you might be killed in the process."

Callie gasped, dropping her hand from his shoulder. For some reason she'd wanted to believe he'd done what he did for a nobler purpose than just "following orders." "Surely not."

"Believe it. One wrong move when the target went down and he'd have triggered the switch, blowing up his explosive vest. And you along with it."

Her stomach twisted, the meat she'd eaten sitting in it like a rock. There had to be more to it than that. "I don't believe you."

"You can ask Moss when we get back to the States. He received the same order I did. I fired. He didn't."

So he was saying Moss hesitated and he stepped in to fire the shot instead? "But why?"

"There were embassy personnel inside. We needed to get to them. You were blocking my team's way."

The wave of hurt that crashed over her was enormous, suffocating.

She'd been blocking his path. Nothing more. "How can you talk about people that way? Like they're obstacles to be removed when they don't fit in with your plans."

And why had Callie allowed herself to believe he wasn't like her stepfather, when it was so obvious, in every way that counted, he was. Don't like someone? Shove them aside or mow them down, depending on where you were and what consequences you might have to face afterward.

Cole stood and stared down at her. "What do you want me

to say? Do you want me to lie and pretend I'm someone different just to fit in with your sanitized version of the world?"

"No. I don't want you to lie. I want far more from you than that." She blinked away a sudden rush of tears.

He gripped her by the shoulders, drawing her closer. "Then what is it? What exactly do you want?" He paused, a muscle working furiously in his jaw. "I can't make myself into something I'm not. Not for you. Not for anyone. I've tried. It doesn't work, dammit."

She wished she could see past the swirling currents in his eyes to whatever lay behind the tormented words. Callie had the desperate sensation he was trying to tell her something. But, like him, she couldn't lie and make up something. She owed him the truth.

"I don't want you to be someone you're not. I want one thing, Cole. Just one."

While flies buzzed in the background and heat rose in stifling waves around them, she gazed into his face and pleaded with him to help her believe in him. To tell her that whoever lay beneath his hardened façade was different than her stepfather. A man who, like Cole, moved obstacles when they stood in the way of what he wanted. No matter how dishonorable his methods. Obstacles like Callie, when she dared to stand between him and her sister.

Please, God, let him be different.

"What do you want?" he repeated, his hands tightening their grip.

The words spilled out, coming from a well of pain that she'd sealed shut for far too long.

"I want you to tell me you're an honorable man."

AN HONORABLE MAN? If she knew what his thoughts were at the moment, she'd know just how little honor he had.

He wanted to throw her down on the ground and make her want him.

Him. Cole Scalini.

Not her rose-colored version of who he should be. Of how he should act.

He stared at the tears spiking her lashes, his teeth grinding against each other as he fought his impulses. A tinge of fear colored her face and he stiffened. Released her. Took a step back, then another.

"Cole?"

"Don't." He slammed his lids closed, trying to shut her out. "I can't give you what you want."

Dragging a hand through his hair, he swore when it shook. "I'm not honorable. You've already seen the evidence of it. Don't slap on a slick coat of paint and call me ready for society." He held his arms out from his sides. "I am what you see."

Callie's hands went to her midsection as if protecting her baby. From him. It tore his gut up one side and down the other.

"I see," she said. Nodding, she gave a small sigh. "I guess we'd better go, then. The sooner I'm out of your way, the sooner you can get back to what you really want out of life."

What he really wanted out of life.

And what was that?

Hell if he knew. And he had no desire to stand around and talk it to death. She was right about one thing, though. The sooner she was out of his way, the sooner she'd be safe in her own little bed. He couldn't be what she wanted him to be, but he could do his duty and make sure the bastards that had gotten Pedro didn't lay a hand on her.

"Let's get moving, then."

Callie took out her bottle of hand sanitizer and squirted a small portion on her hands.

Probably sterilizing herself after touching me.

He couldn't blame her. Sometimes he felt the same way. Only he couldn't get rid of who he was. He could only work with what he'd been given and hope to hell it was enough. And when it wasn't, he just gave whoever complained the finger and moved onto the next task. And the next. And hoped that someday, it *would* be enough.

TWELVE

THE STENCH OF DEATH finally washed from his body, José sank into the clean tub of water, shutting his eyes as the steam enveloped him. The heat never failed to relax his muscles, especially after a particularly difficult kill. He still had a lot to accomplish today, but it could wait.

The embassy was back under the current government's control, but that was okay. The hotel where he'd taken up residence was more comfortable anyway, and the owners were friends of his cause. He'd have a lot of favors to repay once he was back in power. *All in good time.*

His eyes took in the pastel colors of the bathroom, while the clean floral scent of soap tickled his nostrils. He had other things to think about at the current moment. Like how to accomplish his task and get his money. He wasn't overly worried, because he now knew which rabbit-hole his quarry was scurrying to. Malanje Province, where Calandula Falls was located.

According to his generals, the woman and the marine had been at the village in Vitória just this morning. They'd fled, but even now his men were quietly searching. Once the pair was located, it would be easy enough to reach out and snatch them back into his grip. One whispered command was all it would take.

José smiled. Had they liked the little gift he'd sent them? Imagining the woman's horror as she realized who the dead man was, he leaned his head against the smooth porcelain surface of the tub. She knew he was coming for her now. His

penis stiffened, growing hard beneath the sudsy surface of
the water. He savored the decadent sensation and expanded
on it, enjoying the ability to control his body at will.

Maybe he should have kept Pedro's wife around for a
while instead of letting her go. Or Rosa.

His mouth twisted. No. Neither of them would satisfy this
particular craving. And he didn't want their faces flashing
before his eyes at the most crucial moment. He wanted all
his senses to be on high alert when it happened. Wanted to
smell the sweetness of the American woman's skin, feel her
move beneath him as he whispered her fate into her ear. All
while taking his pleasure in her body.

It would be his little secret. The American who paid his
salary wouldn't know he'd defiled her before killing her. But
José would and it would only increase his power.

He was still superstitious enough to believe that strength
could be acquired by devouring something belonging to your
enemy. Preferably his heart. He couldn't do that in the lit-
eral sense. Not even his arm was long enough to reach into
the United States government and strike down the object of
his contempt, absorbing his power along with his money.

But he could do the next best thing. He could place a sym-
bol or amulet representing his quarry onto a different person
and use it as a substitute. It would be almost as effective.

The American woman. The talisman of a traitorous nation that had betrayed him during his country's civil war.
The same nation that had tried to betray him yet again, even
while he'd been doing its bidding.

The woman. The center of all this turmoil. A source of
matchless power, especially in her current condition.

Yes. His prick stiffened even farther.

He would devour her in an entirely different sense. Not
only would he accomplish what he'd been paid to do—which

he would—but in doing so, he'd demonstrate to anyone who dared defy him exactly what he was capable of.

Including his American sponsor.

He drew up the woman's face in his mind, his closed eyes skimming her ripening form. He inhaled the subtle floral scent of the water and imagined it belonged to her. Shuddering with need, his hand slid beneath the water to fulfill his body's demand. With a promise that he'd partake of the real thing in the very near future.

COLE HANDED HER ONE measly bottle filled with river water. She accepted it with a sigh. He'd refused her request to bathe in the slow-moving body of water, first using the excuse that they needed to be ready to run if the rebels came upon them unexpectedly.

When she promised to keep her clothes on, in case they needed to make a quick getaway, he'd changed his reasoning to include the possibility of crocodiles lurking beneath the dark surface.

Well, that worked, because there was no way she was getting into the water after that statement. And he was right. But she resented the universe for ruining a perfectly good river.

She curled her arm around the bottle and held it close to her body. "And *where* am I supposed to go to use this? I can't exactly stand right here in front of you."

Not that it would matter if she did. He'd pretty much ignored her since their argument. Callie wasn't even sure what had started it. She'd tried to thank him…to give him a compliment, and he'd thrown it back in her face with some horrible statements about following orders whether it killed her or not.

Four more days of this. Although, Cole was pushing them harder than before, so maybe they'd make their destination that much sooner. He was obviously as ready to be rid of her as she was to be rid of him.

He was doing his best, though, orders or no orders. He'd even gone out and scrounged up some wild mint leaves when she mentioned missing toothpaste. She needed to focus on the bright side and try making his job as easy as possible.

"Cole, thank you." She jiggled the water bottle to let him know what she was talking about. "I'll go up by the trees to wash, okay?"

"Don't go far." There was a short pause before he added, "I won't look, so don't go into the woods."

Yeah, right. She wasn't going *way* into them. Just far enough so she had a tree or two between her and Cole while she undressed.

If he was worried about snakes, he didn't need to be. After their lunch yesterday, she'd kept a wary eye out for anything slithering.

"I'll be back in fifteen minutes."

"After ten, I'm turning around whether you're done or not. We need to get moving."

Callie glared at the back of his head and debated pouring the bottle of water over it instead of using it on herself. She was trying her best to be cheerful, but he seemed determined to thwart her at every turn. Besides, after his statements yesterday, Callie saw him in a different light. She'd thought she'd deduced a lot about his character, based on his heroic actions…not to mention that kiss they'd shared.

But what if all his actions had simply been the dictates of a superior officer? What would he have done if left to his own devices?

Was the fear she'd witnessed in his eyes on the trail real? Or just desperate imaginings projected from her own reckless cravings?

And if she made him angry…really angry, what was he capable of?

Ten minutes. He might not be bothered by her naked-ness, but she would be. No way was she going to bathe in the open. The thought of him looking at her…that she'd search for desire in his eyes and see indifference, would do her in.

No. Her self-confidence couldn't handle another batter-ing at the moment.

She didn't plan on being close enough to witness his re-action. And if he blasted her for it later, well then so be it.

Going to the edge of the trees, she tried to peer into the growth. Her eyes adjusted to the murky shadows quickly, and she noted several trees on the outer borders of the area that could afford a fair amount of privacy. She wouldn't really have to go past this spot. She sniffed. Clean, earthy scents met her nostrils. The woods smelled inviting. And, more importantly, cool.

There were a few aged concrete posts scattered around. Maybe there'd been some kind of village along the ruined tracks at one point in time. She shrugged, using the nearest post as a place to set her water bottle.

Keeping behind the largest of the trees, she stripped off her clothes and picked up the bottle, uncapping it. But Cole's presence made her nervous. What if he didn't stick to his end of the bargain?

Her lack of a watch didn't help. She gave a quick peek from behind the trees to make sure he was still there.

Empty. The log where he'd been sitting was deserted. Her breath caught in her throat. She scoured the area with her eyes, a quick sense of panic welling up.

He'd promised not to look.

Promised.

Her insecurities poured out. He'd never claimed he was

honorable. In fact, he'd scorned her when she'd asked. But surely he wouldn't stoop to spying on her like a peeping Tom.

The bottle was still in her hand. What should she do? She didn't have much of a choice, unless she wanted to re-dress and go out hunting for him. If she did that, she might lose this one chance to wash away some of the grime from their trip.

Nothing to do but get on with it. She used her teeth to start a small tear in the bottom of her threadbare skirt. Ripping the fabric, she was grateful the tear followed the material's horizontal grain, rather than heading up toward the waistline.

Voilà, instant washcloth.

She folded the strip, then wet it, washing her face and neck first. With that done, she bathed the rest of her body as best she could. She used a little more water to rinse off her newly scrubbed skin, shivering as the cold liquid connected with her overheated body. Goose bumps lifted along her arms. But at least she was cleaner than she'd been before.

How long had she spent? Her ten minutes couldn't be up quite yet. She peeked out from behind her tree again and promptly dropped the water bottle. A small squeak burst from her throat.

Cole hadn't disappeared at all. He was trudging up from the direction of the river. His pants were slung low on his hips, but his T-shirt was draped over one arm. His bronzed, muscled chest was bare, streaming with...

Water!

Fury erupted. He'd taken a bath in the river after expressly forbidding her the same pleasure.

He was going to get it as soon as she...

Her anger turned to renewed panic as his gaze went to the line of trees where she was hiding and moved along the row.

Even from this distance, she could see his brow furrow. He was not happy.

And she was still naked. What if he came up here?

As if reading her mind, he dragged his shirt over his head in one quick motion, still surveying the tree line. Then he started moving.

Fast.

She grabbed at her skirt, dropping it on the ground…right into the spilled water.

Crap.

Turning her back on him, she snatched it up, cursing at the muddy sludge dripping down the front of it. But she didn't have time to worry about that right now. She found the elastic waistline and stretched it wide.

Before she had a chance to step into it, his voice, low and commanding, came from several yards behind her. "Don't move. Stay right where you are."

Callie froze at the sound. For all of one second. Then she hauled the length of fabric to her breasts and turned to face him.

"Shit!" His reaction was immediate. "I said don't move, dammit."

Naked and barely covered, she didn't have much choice.

Worse than her state of dress, Cole's expression struck fear in her heart. The skin over his cheekbones was stretched taut and pale. He was deadly serious.

Her eyes widened. "What is it?"

"Just don't move." Sweat beaded along his brow. "Didn't you see the markers?"

"Markers?"

"Look to your left—but don't move your feet."

Her head swiveled in a slow arc until she spied the post where her shirt was draped. It snagged her attention. The same concrete pole where she'd balanced the water bottle. "You mean the posts?" She had no idea what he was talking about.

"They're not posts."

Tilting her head, she studied it. No. He was right. It wasn't really a post after all. It was curved on the top, kind of like the headstone on a grave and banded with a red stripe around the middle. But she still wasn't sure what he was getting at.

"Callie." He caught her attention and she glanced back at him. "I need you to stay very still while I find a stick. Don't move your feet."

Suddenly the world spun in slow motion as she remembered exactly where they were. Angola. A country ravaged by over twenty-five years of rebel fighting and civil war. A country just emerging from an era of horrible human rights abuses. A country in the middle of its reconstruction process.

And its *demining* process.

It was another of the reasons her sister had come to Angola.

Callie was in the middle of a flagged danger zone. And the markers stretched along the tree line...

As far as the eye could see.

THIRTEEN

COLE'S HEART THUNDERED in his chest as he searched for the right kind of branch.

He should have stayed with her. Shit, it would've been safer to let her dive headfirst into that river than make her take that damned water bottle up to the trees.

Selfish, selfish!

Part of the reason he'd given her was valid. Crocodiles were rife in parts of Angola and he hadn't wanted to risk it without checking the area. But the bigger reason had to do with his own unholy urges. He hadn't wanted to watch her undress and plunge into the river. A pregnant woman of all things.

And turning his back would have been out of the question. He'd have had nightmares of turning to find her gone. Pulled under the surface by a hungry creature.

So he'd taken the safe route. Let her go to the trees. Given her some privacy. Drowned his own hellish desires in the icy water of the river.

But he'd told her *not* to go into the woods, dammit. He'd trusted her.

Had tried to keep her safe.

Instead, he'd ended up forcing her into the middle of a landmine zone.

He located a long, thick stick and turned back to where Callie stood like a statue. The image of her moving and blowing off a limb…or worse, tore at him.

Hurry it up, you bastard.

He tried smiling at her, but the action felt more like a death mask stretching of lips over teeth.

Just stay there. Don't move. God, please don't move.

When he was about fifteen feet from her position, he crouched, surveying the ground around her. "Callie, I'm going to make my way toward you, but it's going to take me a few minutes." He glanced up at her. "Did you feel anything when you stepped down?"

She clutched the skirt tighter. "No, I wasn't paying attention." She licked her lips. "I'm sorry. I didn't know. I should have been more careful—"

"It's okay, you had no way of knowing."

"But I should have realized they weren't just posts. They're painted white and red."

Cole carefully pushed the end of the stick into the dirt, feeling for anything harder than packed earth. Nothing. He continued using the stick as a feeler, making a horizontal line about a yard wide. "The posts should have all been labeled. There's probably one along the line with a warning sign. We just haven't found it."

"I—I feel so stupid."

He was the stupid one, not her, but this wasn't the time to dwell on that.

Clearing the first section, he moved forward and stood on the line he'd made. He then checked the area two feet in front of the first one, using his poke marks to draw a second line. "Let's not worry about anything other than getting you out of there, okay?"

He cleared a third section, moving as quickly as he dared. Just three more and he'd be at her side. "Do you see the lines I'm drawing?"

Callie nodded.

"Those are the areas I've checked. When we move away from your location, I need you to be absolutely careful about stepping only on those lines. Not in between, not to the side. Only on those lines."

"I understand."

Her body shivered, although Cole's was dripping with sweat. "Don't worry, we'll get you out."

"I know you will."

Something about the way she said it made him look up. His jaw tightened. She had the same trusting look in her eyes she'd had earlier, before he'd crushed it with his words.

He didn't want her hero worship.

What he'd told her was true. He was no hero. And there was something in him that needed to keep reminding her of it, to be proactive.

He'd rather smash her ideals up front than wait to see the disappointment in her eyes once she realized what he was. The problems he had.

But first he needed to get her away from the minefield. "You're not out yet. Just stay still."

Another area cleared. Two more to go. He stepped onto his second drawn line. He didn't have time to check the places between his grid. If she moved…

Just keep going.

His stick came within two feet of her bare toes.

Pink polish. Delicate boned feet. Ankles that…

Dammit. Keep going!

He felt along the ground, pushing his stick into the soil inch by torturous inch. Each line seemed to take an hour to clear, although it was surely only five minutes.

When he finished that line, he stood to his feet and stepped on top of it.

She shifted as if to move toward him.

"No. Stay put. Let me check the area around your feet, all right?"

She shivered again.

"You okay?" he asked.

"Fine, just hurry, my stomach is starting to cramp."

He noticed her free hand had gone to her abdomen and was holding it there. "The baby?"

"No, I think it's just nerves."

Checking the area between her feet first, he made sure she hadn't inadvertently stepped on a pressure switch. It was clear. He then tested the area outside of each foot.

Nothing. He threw the stick into the bushes and held out his hand. "See the line I'm standing on? I want you to hold my hand and step on it. Center your foot right on top of it."

He watched her secure the fabric to her breasts by laying her forearm across it. With her other hand, she reached out and gripped his. Her palm was damp with sweat and icy cold. He longed to chafe some warmth back into her skin, but he could do nothing until they reached the safety of the clearing.

"It's going to be all right." He forced his voice to stay calm, hoping it would relay a confidence he was far from feeling.

She pulled in a deep breath. "I know. Tell me what you want me to do."

"On the count of three, step onto my line, just like I explained," he said. "Can you do that?"

"Yes."

"Okay, then. Here we go." He captured her eyes with his, held them. "One…two…three…"

She stepped across the space and hit the line in the perfect spot.

Nothing happened.

Cole breathed a huge sigh of relief. "Good girl."

He pivoted so they were standing side by side, both facing the same direction.

Five steps to safety.

Keeping hold of her hand, he put his arm around her waist

to support her. It wasn't until his flesh connected with her bare skin that it dawned on him she was naked.

He'd been too worried about getting her out to think about it.

You'd better still be worried, Scalini.

"We did it," she murmured, as if afraid talking too loudly might trigger something terrible.

"Not yet. We still have to hit all those lines. You ready?"

"Yes." She gave a soft laugh. "More than ready."

He slid close to her, making sure they were connected. He wanted them doing everything perfectly in sync. "On three, we're going to step onto the next mark."

She paused. "I'm scared."

"I know. Me too." Why bother hiding it? Anything that made her more cautious was a good thing.

"On three," he repeated. "One…two…three…"

They stepped as one onto the next line.

She stiffened suddenly. "Cole, the water bottle. M-my shirt. My shoes. They're still back there. You told me not to move."

She twisted as if to look behind them. His fingers dug into her waist to hold her in place.

"You're not going back."

"I'll just stay on the lines you drew. You said it was safe."

"It's never safe. You're not going back." He eased his grip. "I'll get them after I make sure you're on the other side of the markers."

She shook her head. "No, it's not fair for you to—"

"Stop arguing, dammit. I know what I'm doing." He sucked in a deep breath. "On three."

Cole repeated the process until they had stepped beyond his grid onto safe ground. Even then, he didn't trust the area to be totally clear. It was possible a mine had been missed in the marking process.

Before he realized what she was going to do, Callie wiggled out of his hold and turned, still holding the skirt to her body. She wound her free arm around his neck and pressed close, her face buried in the soaked fabric of his shirt.

"How many times does that make?" Her voice was muffled, but he heard the quaver.

He swallowed his own emotion. "How many times, what?"

She lifted her head and looked up at him. "How many times have you saved my life so far?"

"I'm just doing my duty."

"Bull. Not that time. You could have left me there."

No way in hell. "My duty is to protect American citizens."

Keep telling yourself that, dickhead. Maybe someday you'll believe it.

She blinked. "So, I'm just any old citizen?"

What the hell did she want him to say? Those damn eyes kept staring at him, digging into his soul like miniature pick-axes.

Raw emotion rose up in a wave.

"No, you're not just any other goddamn citizen." He reached out and gripped her arms, putting some distance between them. "I wish to hell you were." He clenched his teeth, trying to staunch the flow of words struggling to exit. It did no good.

"Why didn't you just do what I asked? I told you to stay in front of the tree line." Blood pulsed through his temples as anger replaced relief. "Don't you realize what could have happened back there? I've seen more people with limbs blown off from stray mines, not to mention—"

"Cole." Her soft word broke through his tirade, halting it.

He dropped his hands but didn't move away.

She closed her eyes and sucked in a deep breath. When her lids parted, something in her expression made his body come to life.

"Yeah?" Even his words were different. The inflection behind them seemed to come from another portion of his mind. The irrational side.

"I'm alive." Her breath slid out on a long sigh. "*We're* alive." She touched his arm. "I don't want to fight with you. Don't you understand? We're still here. Still alive. You and me."

His stomach did a back flip.

She took a step closer and it was all Cole could do not to stumble away from her.

"I'm going to ask you to do something." The fingers of her free hand slid up his arm, until one palm rested on his shoulder. "Please don't say no."

More than just his stomach was jumping now. He held his breath and waited.

"I want you to kiss me."

Cole stared at her. Surely he'd not heard her correctly. "What did you say?"

Her fingers slid into his hair as her eyes met his with a steady intensity. He was very aware that she was naked beneath that skirt; he'd felt the smooth bare skin of her back when he'd put his arm around her waist earlier. The knowledge had about killed him when they were dodging landmines.

If he kissed her, now that the danger was over…

Crap, he didn't even want to think about it. But telling himself not to think didn't do a lick of good, because his body was already demanding his surrender. Anticipating it.

"Kiss me."

Could he stop where this was heading? Just one more time. "Callie, I can't. You've just been through a traumatic situation. You're not yourself. You're a psychiatrist. You know the implications. You don't really want me to—"

Before he could finish his sentence, she'd stretched up to place her lips against his, silencing his protest in an instant.

Hell, he'd been through a traumatic moment or two himself when he'd first realized she was standing between landmine markers. Didn't he deserve a little time to recoup? To kiss away his own fears?

He kept his hands at his side, but he couldn't bring himself to pull away. Or to save himself.

It was way too late for that anyway.

Her soft lips nibbled from one corner of his mouth to the other, the light friction almost tickling, driving him insane with need.

She stepped closer, her body pressing against his. Her breath hissed in on a gasp. His jaw tightened. She'd evidently felt the truth of the matter. He wasn't nearly as indifferent to her as he was trying to appear.

"Cole, kiss me back." Her eyes were closed, her words soft and dangerous.

He shut his own eyes to block out the sight, willing his body to fall into line. That too, failed.

In a split second, his choice was made. His arms went around her waist, the skin of her back cool against his own superheated flesh. He splayed his hands across the firm surface. The small bump in her midsection didn't interfere. If anything, it snuggled her even closer.

She muttered something. He didn't even try to pick the sound apart to make sense of the syllables. The murmur itself had been arousing enough. He didn't need words making it any hotter than it already was.

Her mouth opened to his and he didn't hesitate. His tongue dipped inside, tasting the clean mint she'd chewed earlier. And her skin exuded a feminine scent that hovered in his senses and implanted itself on his brain. It was a scent he'd never get out of his system.

And that tiny spot behind her ear…

His tongue deepened its exploration, twining with hers. He shuddered, imagining what it would be like to have it sliding along his…

His mind pulled back. This was going way too fast, and if he didn't stop now, he'd lose the ability to call off his hounds before it was too late.

She had to know exactly where this train wreck was heading. She was a damned psychiatrist.

A mind melder.

He hoped to hell she couldn't read his mind right now, because the direction of his thoughts was blowing a few fuses in his own skull. He hated to think what would happen if that desperate energy was transferred to her own mind.

His hands moved up her back, despite the fact that he'd called them back to his sides. Insubordinates.

But then, so was he. He always had been.

His fingers slid into her hair and tangled the long lengths around his hands, forcing her head back. Wresting control away from her was a heady sensation. Too heady. And the low moan that emerged from her throat only augmented the feeling.

He deepened the kiss to almost savage proportions. He recognized the need to control her for what it was: the desperate attempt of someone who too often felt completely *out* of control. Someone controlled by outside forces, whether it be his mother, or the doctors, or now his superior officers.

The realization made him pull back. This was wrong. This shouldn't be about one person trying to exert control over the other. Sex had always been a shared event, both people putting something into it in order to get something out of it.

It was different this time. There was almost an urgent need to dominate Callie, to possess her. He'd never acted like this with a woman in his life.

He needed it to end right now before someone got hurt. And it was as likely to be him as anyone.

Forcing himself to gentle his kiss, he tried to think. She muttered a protest and bit his lower lip, the sharp sting almost propelling him back into action.

No. Do something. Anything.

Call her bluff. Scare her into stopping.

He pulled away from her mouth, his breath coming in heavy gusts that blew long strands of her hair away from her face. Her dark eyes, luminous with need, called out to him.

His heart in his throat, he knew it was now or never. He dropped his hands and took a step back, allowing his eyes to rake over her. He hoped to hell the act didn't look as shaky as it felt.

"Cole?" Her kiss-swollen lips curved around his name, reigniting his senses.

Time to hurry this little act up.

He propped his hands on his hips, trying to come up with a brilliant line that would do the job he wanted it to.

The hand clutching the fabric of her skirt tightened into a fist and pulled it closer.

The answer came to him in a blinding flash. "Drop your skirt."

Standing back, he waited for the fireworks to start, for his insolent demand to be met with a slap across his face. Or worse, a swift kick to his balls.

So sure was he of her reaction that it took a second or two for her slow smile to register.

He frowned, uncertainty beginning to crowd his mind with "what ifs."

And in slow motion, her fisted hand opened. The skirt— and all his vain attempts at self-preservation—fluttered to the ground, leaving Cole more naked and infinitely more vulnerable than the woman standing before him would ever know.

THE RELEASING OF HER SKIRT was met with a muttered "God help me" before he closed the gap between them.

Fast.

So fast Callie didn't have time to experience any insecurities about her pregnant body.

She half expected him to swoop down and snatch up her skirt, demanding she cover up, or throw it over her and do it himself.

He did neither. Her discarded skirt lay ignored while his eyes scorched a path across her body.

Callie shivered. He didn't touch her for a long moment. A muscle leaped in his jaw, the only sign of his struggle for control.

"I don't have any protection with me." His finger drew a line down her jaw in a move so gentle, it made her chest ache. She'd expected him to roughly grab at her, to consume her in a fiery burst. But instead of being disappointed, she was moved by his concern.

She touched her mounded belly. "You can't make me any more pregnant than I already am."

Some dark emotion flashed through his eyes and then was gone.

Trying to figure out what it was, she hesitated. "I haven't been with anyone in a while and I was tested before they implanted the zygote. I'm healthy."

He chuckled, his fingers moving from her jawline to her chin. "Zygote, huh? Only a doctor…"

Was he making fun of her? She had a hard time telling sometimes what made this man tick. He hid something deep inside of him. So deep she couldn't see it, couldn't get at it.

But it didn't matter, not now.

"And you?" She turned her head and kissed his palm, allowing her tongue to slide across it.

His eyes closed for a second. "Yeah. I'm healthy." He swallowed. "I've had a few partners, but I've always used protection."

The "until now" hung unsaid in the air between them. She forced herself to face reality. His statement was the result of circumstances. She shouldn't attach any kind of special significance to it. Although her mind was leaping to all kinds of crazy fantasies.

Fantasies. That's all they were.

And then her insecurities hit. Hard. Any man would react physically in the presence of a naked woman, right? Even one who was pregnant.

She wasn't anything special.

She had to force herself not to reach down and snatch up her skirt and cover herself. "If you'd rather not…" Her gaze skittered away from the sudden narrowing of his eyes. "I—I'll understand."

Using gentle pressure on her chin, he forced her to look at him. "You started all this. Just say the word and it stops here."

She crossed her arms over her chest. "I don't want you to think I'm some sad, desperate pregnant woman who's ready to jump anything that moves."

Cole shook his head. "That thought never even crossed my mind. If anything, I've been trying to find a way to keep my hands off you since the moment we met. I wondered if you'd think I was a pervert or something."

"A pervert?"

He shrugged. "For wanting a pregnant woman."

"I know about two million pregnant women who would kill to hear a man say that to them."

"Say what? That they feel like a pervert?" He smiled at her.

Callie tilted her head back, her toes digging into the soft earth. "No, silly, that they found her attractive."

His smile faded. "You are. Attractive."

"Really?"

His hands went from her face to the bump on her abdomen, curving over it. "You're perfect." He bent and kissed her lips. "Too perfect."

Callie swallowed the lump in her throat and kissed him back, hoping to show him how much those two simple words meant.

When his hands moved to her hips and pulled her close, she knew he was serious. His erection grazed the middle of her bare stomach.

From landmines to making love. It was crazy, but it felt right.

Tunneling her hands under his T-shirt, she brushed her palms over his powerful pecs, and then around to the firm flesh of his back.

Dear lord, the man was a solid wall of muscle, not an ounce of flab anywhere. Still kissing him, she couldn't resist trying to pinch-an-inch where his love handles should be. Nothing.

He pulled back. "What are you doing?"

"Nothing."

Before he could say anything else she pulled his head back down and kissed him.

She was ready for him. Already. Maybe it was pregnancy hormones that made her so needy. Or maybe it was the result of being with a dangerous man in the middle of a wild and dangerous country. And she had no doubt that Cole was dangerous. Oh so very dangerous. Every inch of his delicious body oozed it.

And he wanted her.

A sound crept up from the bottom of her throat, low and hoarse.

Was that her?

She tugged at his shirt, wanting it off so she could feel him skin to skin. He helped by ripping it over his head and casting it aside.

His drawstring pants were thin. Elastic waist. She could just slide her hands beneath it…like so. His skin was so hot. And his narrow hips made it easy to move her hands toward the front. Cole groaned and grabbed her wrists before they reached their destination, easing her hands back up and out.

She murmured her displeasure.

Against her ear, he whispered, "Not so fast."

Fast? He was going painfully slow, when all Callie wanted to do was rush, to shove him to the ground and mount him right there.

He was a man, wasn't that what they were programmed for? Rough, fast sex that was over almost before it began? At least that's what Callie had always experienced.

And yet this man was complaining that she was rushing things.

Maybe she should start worrying about what kind of equipment he was hiding under those pants.

No, he was definitely all man. She'd felt the evidence. More than once.

It could be he was worried about hurting her, or nervous about the baby. She bit his chin. "I won't break. Or even chip."

"No?" He gave a soft laugh. "Let's make sure, shall we?"

He kissed his way down her collarbone, over the upper curve of her breast until he reached her nipple. Drawing it between his teeth, he captured the sensitive peak between his tongue and upper teeth. An immediate shaft of pleasure arced from her breast to her belly and settled between her legs. The ache grew as he continued stroking. He wasn't touching her anywhere else, but she could feel him everywhere. Pulling, kneading, drowning her in sensation.

Just when it became too much, he pulled away, soothing her with soft kisses before he knelt, kissing over her belly, his tongue dipping inside her navel.

His mouth reached the lower edge of her stomach, and she held her breath, her pulse pounding in her ears…wanting him to, not wanting him to. Needing to stop him, but powerless to open her mouth to do so.

Oh God, she wasn't going to make it. The second he touched her, she was going to…going to…

He reached her center and her world exploded in a tight cluster of colors and sounds. Her hands gripped his short hair in a desperate attempt to keep from falling. If she was hurting him, he didn't complain. Instead, his arms went around her buttocks, holding her against him as the siege continued, as he coaxed more from her than she ever dreamed possible.

Struggling to retrieve her scattered thoughts, she pushed him away, dragging in huge gusts of air. "You, you…"

He looked up at her, a crooked smile on his face, completely unrepentant.

Using his shoulders to brace herself, she lowered herself to his level. She gave a shaky laugh. "You are in so much trouble, mister."

His smile grew. "You think?"

"Yes." She shoved him backward and then climbed up his partially clothed body. "Because now—" she leaned down and licked her way up his neck, "—now it's my turn."

FOURTEEN

"YES, MR. PRESIDENT. I understand."

Moss lifted his attention from the map in front of him in time to catch General Markesan's jaw tighten.

"I respectfully disagree with that assessment, sir." The hand gripping the telephone pulled the handset an inch or two away from his ear.

The president was evidently not happy with the report Markesan had given him. But why? Unless he really was involved in the rebel takeover in the first place, like Senator Parker had implied.

Moss wasn't sure he bought it. Was it possible this particular president was dirty? It had happened before, and it would happen again.

If so, what then? What did you do when your commander-in-chief was more corrupt than the forces he claimed to be fighting?

"I understand, sir. I'll keep you apprised of any further developments."

As the general listened to whatever the president was saying, he picked up a dart from his desk and hurled it toward the dartboard on his office wall. The dart jabbed squarely in the center of the target and quivered from the force of the hit.

"No, sir. I'll inform you of any intended action on my part."

General Markesan put down the phone with a growl and picked up another dart. "Prick."

Moss watched as he squinted at the target and started to take the throw. At the last minute, he turned the tip toward the map spread on the stainless steel surface of the desk. He tapped the tip on a spot that Moss recognized as Malanje. Cole's pickup point.

The name-calling, combined with pointing at the map didn't bode well for Moss's mounting headache. For the last three days, he'd been antsy to go in and drag Cole's ass out of that godforsaken place. And for three days he'd had to sit on his hands and wait. Cole wasn't due at the falls for another four days, but Moss wanted to go in now. In case his friend made an earlier-than-projected arrival. Knowing Cole's impatience, anything was possible.

He waited for Markesan to let him in on the reason for the president's call. Since his stomach was already spewing acid up his gullet, he figured the news wasn't going to be good.

Glancing up from the map, the general's answer came soon enough. "President Bryson has informed me that any planned rescue mission involving Lieutenant Scalini and Dr. Nascimento is to be aborted. As of immediately."

"What the hell? On what basis?"

"On the basis that it'll further inflame the Angolan government. They've already got a bug up their ass about the embassy evacuations. The Angolan president intends to take on any future search and rescue efforts himself. He'll notify us of the outcome."

"Bullshit, sir. They just want carte blanche to go in and mow down anyone they can put a rebel label to. If there are rumors of hostages involved, they figure they've got all the justification they need. And if those hostages die in the process, it'll only strengthen their position that the rebels must be wiped out. Whatever the cost." His hands fisted on the map. "Besides, without outside witnesses, no one can challenge their methods."

"I realize that, but it's out of my hands now. I have my orders."

Moss couldn't believe what he was hearing. "You can't tell me you're going to let Scalini and an innocent woman be captured—and in all probability killed—for the sake of diplomacy."

"We've done it before."

Moss straightened his spine. "Request permission for leave time, sir."

General Markesan's eyes narrowed. "Excuse me, Lieutenant?"

You heard me, you cowardly fuck. If you're not going to rescue your own man, then screw you.

Moss carefully squashed his fury before it surfaced in his voice. "Respectfully request personal leave time, sir."

"Personal leave, eh? And exactly how much leave time do you need?"

"Not entirely certain at this point, sir."

"Anything you'd care to share with me, Lieutenant?"

All of a sudden Moss got it. This is exactly what General Markesan had hoped to goad him into. His anger deflated. His superior officer had no intention of leaving Cole in there to die. He just couldn't openly disobey orders.

"Not at the current time, sir. Maybe once I see the situation first hand."

"Go through channels and file all the necessary paperwork." He checked his watch. "You've got exactly four days' leave, and then I expect you to report back, whether your personal situation is resolved or not."

Four days.

"Yes, sir." Moss retrieved his cover and flipped it onto his head. He turned to leave.

"Lieutenant Moss?"

He turned to face General Markesan. "Sir?"

"This is off the record."

Moss nodded. "Understood."

"Tell Scalini, when you hear from him, that his ass had better be in one piece next time I see his ugly mug."

"I will, sir."

General Markesan reached out to shake his hand. "Bring him back. Make sure the woman's with him."

"Yes, sir."

JOSÉ'S HANDS TIGHTENED on the wheel as he stared at the collapsed asphalt a hundred yards in front of him. He braked to a stop, the two vehicles ahead of him pulling over as well. The damned government. They'd promised to fix these roads. And look at them. In ruins, every one of them.

Governments bred corruption. Even the American system wasn't the pristine, benevolent face it presented to the world.

He resisted the urge to lay his head on the wheel and sleep away his frustration…his exhaustion. As long as his quarry eluded him, he would push his men hard. He'd push himself just as hard. To show weakness at this point would be fatal.

So he'd had two groups of men in four-wheel-drive vehicles travel the decrepit main road that led to Malanje. The first group had driven straight across the pothole-ridden paths without stopping, looking for the missing woman and her companion. He'd received a radio report an hour ago. There was no sign of them.

No U.S. military helicopters, no ground troops, no signs of any foreigners at all.

If they'd been rescued, José would know about it by now.

The second group of men had been ordered to stop at each town and village along the way and bribe or threaten the inhabitants for information. No strangers had passed through according to the reports. Nothing since that first village, where the Americans had been given water and shelter.

José couldn't order his men to torture everyone they spoke to. Besides, oftentimes the clink of a few coins spoke louder than a closed fist.

But he was running out of time. The Angolan government had ordered its military to crack down on all the UNITA groups. President Foresteiro assumed the rebel faction was behind the chaos in Luanda, as well as the fall of the U.S. embassy building.

Foolish on the president's part, but for José it was a blessing in disguise, because he wasn't part of UNITA. Not anymore. Not since the group had allowed itself to be tamed and domesticated like a herd of cattle who were too stupid to evade the slaughter. These days, José fought for his own causes: his empty coffers and to regain his lost power.

Angola's sitting president was every bit as corrupt as he claimed José's compatriots were. More, he told himself. But if José had his way, he himself would soon be either in charge of the country, or rich enough to buy a big chunk of the action. He would get his power, one way or another.

One of his men hurried from the other vehicle and thrust his head into the jeep. "We received word that a woman filled a water bottle for a foreigner a little over a day ago."

"Chinese?" He held his breath, hoping it wouldn't simply be someone from one of the Chinese demining crews.

"No. Western. White. Probably American."

His stomach tightened in anticipation. "Where did this occur?"

"Vale Cortida."

He wracked his brain for the town's location. "One of the outlying villages?"

His man nodded. "Halfway between here and the old rail line. We got lucky. One of the villagers from Vale Cortida came in to get supplies and overheard our men asking questions." He rubbed his fingers together. "For a few *moedas,* he was willing to tell us what he knew."

"Perhaps that's why the first group found no sign of the Americans," José muttered, half to himself. "Could they be traveling through the bush?" He tapped the wheel, his mind grappling with the new information. "Why would they travel through the *mata* when the road is safer? The minefields alone would kill them if they attempted it."

"Perhaps the soldier knows of the dangers. No one has heard an explosion."

José put a wealth of contempt into his glare. "I am aware of that. I was speculating that they could not have traveled directly through the bush. It would be suicide."

"Why have we not seen them, then?"

Why, indeed. It was a question he would have to contemplate without the irritating whine of his underling in his ear.

"Take me to Vale Cortida. I wish to speak with the woman who filled the water bottles myself."

"Vale Cortida is hours from here by foot, but the other villager is still in town. We could talk to him. He might be able to tell us everything we need to know."

José committed the man's face to memory. "If you question my orders one more time, it will take more than just 'hours' for anyone to find you."

The man slunk away, leaving José alone with his thoughts.

He glanced at the black box that housed the satellite phone. He had not heard from his sponsor in over a day, but he had no doubt that he would. Soon.

He needed to have the woman in his possession by then. Or he would have no bargaining chip, and all his efforts would have been for nothing.

The stakes were higher this time than simply taking care of those meddling foreign doctors who'd flown through with all their pompous ideologies. Not clear out the shantytowns? Absurd. Those slums were a blight on Angola. It was the one point he and the current government agreed upon. The shacks needed to be bulldozed. Every single one of them. The sooner the better.

The two vehicles ahead of him pulled out, swinging wide to traverse the narrow isthmus of pavement that connected one ruined portion of highway with another.

Several hours' worth of travel. He glanced again at the black box and willed it not to ring. If the American just gave him one more day, he could resolve all of this and secure the woman.

More than ever, he felt his additional efforts should be rewarded with a larger quantity of American dollars. Was it José's fault his American sponsor had tried to cover his own ass by launching that sham of a rescue mission?

No.

His sacrificial lamb had been taken out before he could detonate the explosive vest and kill the woman. Thanks to the soldier. And José Rodrigo dos Santos Coelho had no intention of letting that insult go un-punished.

He hit a pothole while deep in thought, and his teeth cracked together. Pain slashed through his head and something landed on his tongue. Furious, he spat the object onto his hand. White enamel. One of his front teeth had broken.

Raw hatred swirled through him at the faceless sniper who'd snatched away his prize. José would make that man die a long painful death.

And the woman would watch. Every last second of it. Knowing she was next.

He smiled. After she spent a few quality hours learning exactly what it meant to fall into enemy hands. *His* hands.

FIFTEEN

COLE CAME TO WITH A SENSE of unease. Something was wrong with his body. A thousand needles prickled through his leg from thigh to ankle. Had he been hit by gunfire? Was there a tourniquet cinched tight at his groin to cut off a spray of arterial blood?

A cold sheen of sweat broke out on his upper body as his eyes flew open, his hands going to his leg.

Instead of his thigh, he encountered an expanse of soft, obviously female...

Callie.

Thank God, it was just Callie. Relief washed over him. He remembered whispering to her to stay right where she was after they finished. He'd wanted to hold her. Keep her close.

He smiled. His leg was asleep. No artillery fire, no sniper attacks, no...

Landmines.

The past hours rushed through his brain. Exactly how long had he been asleep?

Oh fuck! What the hell had he been doing sleeping? Out in the open, where anyone could have snuck up on them... killed them.

Killed Callie.

And he'd been too busy screwing her to care.

Well, he'd better damn well *start* caring, if he had any hope of getting her out of here alive. If this was how he be- haved when he thought with his dick rather than his brain, then he'd better stuff it back in his pants and keep it there.

His hand trailed down the silky skin of her thigh.

And he'd better get up and retrieve her shirt from the mine marker, so she could get dressed.

His palm glided back up her smooth flesh, absorbing the sensations with his fingertips.

Do the smart thing for once in your life.

He reached beside him for her skirt and spread it out on the ground the best he could, then he eased her on top of it. She sighed and her hand came out as if reaching for him.

He forced himself to roll out of the way, pushing to his feet, just before she connected. If she touched him, he was lost. He tried to avoid looking directly at her, but his mind filled in the blanks, remembering every curve, every straining second he was inside of her, and his cock sprang to attention, wanting more.

Turning his back, he debated going to the river and jumping into the frigid depths to ice down his body and his thoughts. But he didn't dare leave her alone. That thought solidified when he heard a faint rumble in the distance and caught sight of the darkening sky.

He glanced down at his watch, afraid to see how long they'd slept.

Shit. Six hours, lost.

No chance of reaching the next town by nightfall now. The sun would be down in less than an hour, and those rain clouds appeared to be moving in fast. They'd be out in the open—in a landmine strewn wasteland, with nothing to do but…

His gaze slid back to Callie's nude body.

Ah hell. He was doomed.

The best he could hope was to get her clothes and make it as far as they could in a half hour. He needed to either find shelter or batten down the hatches and pray the storm bypassed them.

COLE'S LUCK JUST KEPT getting better. Before they'd made it a half mile down the road, the heavens had opened up, seemingly intent on dumping everything they had inside right on top of them.

Callie huddled against him in the dark as he tried to shield her from the worst of the blowing rain. If they had to be in the open, this was probably the best scenario despite the discomfort. No mosquitoes, few animals out hunting…and hopefully no rebels searching for them in this weather.

A flash of lightning split the night sky, the intense crack of thunder following less than a second later. Cole could swear the electrical charge was close enough to stand his hair on end.

There was always the chance they could get struck by a stray bolt, which would solve all their problems.

As if sensing his thoughts, Callie pressed a little closer.

They hadn't spoken much since he'd tossed her shirt onto her body, waking her up.

If she felt the same awful pull of regret, she didn't show it. In fact, she didn't mention what had passed between them at all. She'd just picked up her clothing in silence, turned her back to him and pulled them on.

He frowned, trying to figure out where they were according to the map he'd read. The main road had probably looped south by now, while the rail line they were following kept to a straight westerly course. But from what he remembered, the road was due to swing back toward the north and then run parallel to the tracks. You wouldn't be able to see one from the other, but the two would be a stone's throw apart. Cole just hoped the rebels had stuck to the roads and hadn't thought of the tracks yet.

Yeah, he could hope. Frustration swept through him. First the landmines and now this. No matter which way they turned, something seemed to go wrong.

He reached for the sodden backpack and removed a partially empty bottle of water. "You need to stay hydrated."

"I think Mother Nature's taking care of that for me." She pushed wet hanks of hair off her forehead, making no effort to take the bottle.

"You can dehydrate, even in the rain."

Still she sat there. Cole uncapped the bottle, his irritation growing hotter by the second. "Take a drink."

"Yes, sir." The two words snapped together with a sharpness that rivaled the cracks of thunder. She took a couple of swallows, then handed the bottle back. "There you go. Are you happy now?"

He wasn't the only one cracking under the strain, evidently. Or was she fuming about what had happened between them? He could at least reassure her on that account. He had no intention of losing it like that again.

"Listen, ah…about yesterday. It should've never happened. I acted unprofessionally, and…" He forced the words from between tight lips. "I apologize."

If he'd expected an instant sigh of relief and a smile, he was sorely mistaken.

Callie's face turned stormier than the night sky. "Since you weren't the one initiating things, it seems kind of odd for *you* to be apologizing. In fact, if anyone acted unprofessionally, it was me." Tossing her head, she stared up at him, her eyes glittering. "I've never thrown myself at a man in my life."

A woman like Callie wouldn't need to. She probably had men swarming around her in droves. That thought pissed him off more than their current situation.

"I'm sure you've never had to. You've probably got those metrosexual boys falling all over themselves to take you out."

"Metrosexual? Is that supposed to be an insult? Enlightened, well-groomed, educated men happen to be very sexy to most women."

"As opposed to what? Testosterone loaded apes?"

"You said it. Not me."

If he was pissed off before, he was steaming now. So a "normal" man basically had to primp and coddle himself nowadays to be considered sexy in her book. Yeah, great. One more box he'd never fit into. Not that he'd try.

Not even for her.

He glanced into her face, her red cheeks showing how passionate she was about this particular subject. Even angry, she was beautiful.

Gorgeous.

And she'd never want a man like him. Not on a permanent basis. She said so herself. His type was not what she found sexy. He'd never be cultured and well-spoken.

Cole was who he was, like it or not.

Since he'd *never* liked who he was, why would he expect her to?

"You're right. I said it." He shoved the water bottle back into the backpack and fastened it, shutting the door on this particular conversation.

"Wait, Cole, I didn't mean that *you* were a—"

"It doesn't matter. I just wanted to clear the air and get yesterday behind us. You won't have to worry about anything else happening. I'm not what you're looking for, and the feeling is mutual."

"What's that supposed to mean?"

Years' worth of anger frothed inside of him, looking for any available exit. "Meaning if I were listing traits I wanted in a woman, the title *shrink* wouldn't even make it to my top ten thousand."

He knew he should stop, he even tried to jam his mouth shut, but some devil inside prodded him to continue. "You asked me once if I was honorable. I couldn't give you a straight answer. But before you cast any more stones, take a good look in the mirror, doc, and ask yourself this: how honorable is a profession that earns its living manipulating a person's mind until he thinks and acts in a way you deem acceptable?"

He pushed to his feet and stared down at her, too far gone to temper his words. "Dr. Nascimento, answer me this...how honorable are you?"

HOURS AFTER COLE had lobbed his cryptic question and stalked away, Callie still didn't have an answer. They'd stopped at a village for water and were back on their way, but the question burned in her mind.

Was she honorable?

She liked to think so, but was she sure?

Her father would have known. She closed her eyes for a second and conjured up his features. His always smiling face. That ready smile was deceiving, though. Beneath his Brazilian laissez-faire attitude beat the heart of a lion. A wise and discerning lion. He could look at people and sum them up in five seconds flat, almost before they opened their mouths. He was rarely wrong.

But he wasn't here to ask. And Callie missed him terribly. Her mother had too. She'd married again within a year of his death.

What a disaster that had been. Cole's lashing out at her was certainly something her stepfather would have done. Only he would have used far more than just his voice.

That's where the two men were different.

Cole had never once lifted a hand toward her in anger. He'd been overbearing at times...had thrown around orders right and left, but she'd never felt in any physical danger from him. In fact, he'd yanked her from one dangerous situation after another, with no thought as to what could happen to him.

Yes, he'd said it was his job—that he was under orders to protect American citizens. But yesterday, after he'd gotten her away from the landmine area, he'd intimated she was more than just that.

She quickened her steps as Cole pulled farther ahead. He never once glanced back to make sure she was still following him. It was as if he wanted nothing more than to leave her far behind. To forget she even existed.

That hurt, almost more than his words had.

To be honest, they'd both tossed some pretty ugly comments around, but while she already regretted hers, she wasn't so sure about Cole. Why was he so very angry?

Because she'd questioned his integrity earlier?

Maybe. He'd taken some jabs at her profession before, but something about the way he attacked it this last time gave her pause. It was as if her being a psychiatrist was a personal affront to him.

Was he lashing out at her or against something that had happened in his past? She'd done the same thing when she'd first met him. Had practically proclaimed him a murderer.

Because she had something against soldiers.

No, that wasn't exactly true. She had something against *one* soldier. Her stepfather.

Callie could admit it. She tended to judge all military personnel based on the sonofabitch who'd exercised icy control over her mother, demanding the impossible from her. And when she couldn't keep up with the demands, he'd ridiculed her until she became a beaten down shell of the woman Callie remembered from childhood. After she died of cancer, the control had snapped and he'd started drinking. Heavily.

The haze of alcohol had finished the job the military had started. It turned the man into an automaton programmed to lash out at anyone or anything that threatened him. While drunk, that included Callie's sixteen-year-old sister, Sara, who was the spitting image of their mother.

Callie had gotten herself and her sister out of there as soon as she turned eighteen.

A week after they left, Colonel Milburn Louis Tucker—decorated Vietnam veteran—had taken a round to the head in the office of his shipshape family home. The home he'd once ruled over with an iron fist. A half-empty bottle of whisky sat on the desk beside him. With the lack of any other perceived threat, he'd become his own worst enemy. And he'd dealt with that enemy in standard Colonel Tucker fashion. By reaching out and destroying it.

Callie sighed and stared at Cole's back. This was another tough soldier, as much a part of some vast military machine as her stepfather had been.

But he'd made love to her with a thoroughness and gentleness that belied his hard outer shell. He'd made sure she was taken care of first, and even then, Callie had had to take over, fearing he might stop before his own needs were met.

A lump rose in her throat. Why wouldn't he tell her what was really bothering him?

She rolled her eyes. Because she was a stranger, that's why. Why should he tell her anything? He didn't even know her.

Oh yeah he did. He knew more about her than most people did. He'd seen deep into her soul when he made love to her. She'd held back nothing and revealed everything. Even the growing sentiments she'd fought for the last five days.

And after witnessing her most intimate thoughts, her deepest feelings, he could still question her motivations? He'd twisted her profession, making it sound like she was some depraved mental voyeur who gained her highest pleasure from controlling the minds of others—bending them to her will. A person who liked to watch people squirm in their seats as she grilled them about their darkest fears.

Had someone done that to him?

Maybe a military psychiatrist?

She swallowed. Oh God. Was he unhinged? Trigger happy? He'd shot that terrorist fast enough.

Under orders. He'd only shot when he'd been ordered to.

Cole might not have let her inside his mind when they'd been together, but she saw enough to know he wasn't mentally unbalanced. Insecure?

Maybe.

Exerting a self-control that went beyond super human? She gave a quiet laugh.

Definitely.

He turned unexpectedly, and she gulped back the rest of the laugh, changing it to a cough. He wasn't as oblivious to her as she'd thought.

"Something wrong?"

She bit her lip, unsure what she should say.

"No," she lied.

He studied her with narrowed eyes for a second before swinging back to the front and walking again.

Maybe she should just ask him what he had against psychiatrists. That would be the most direct route and it beat the hell out of guessing.

Hurrying, she pulled up next to him. "Can I ask you something?"

He didn't even bother to look at her. "Is it about the trip?"

"No."

"Your pregnancy?"

"No."

Cole stopped in his tracks and faced her, his arms folding over the broad expanse of his chest.

Already defensive as hell. It didn't bode well for an open discussion.

"Okay. What is it?"

Crossed arms. Forbidding expression.

Since when had that ever stopped her?

"What have you got against psychiatrists?"

He blinked. "What?"

"You heard me. You've been jabbing little barbs at me ever since we met. Something's behind it. I want to know what, so we can come to some kind of understanding."

"Some kind of understanding." One brow went up and he swatted at something on his neck. "Why would we need to do that?"

"To make this trip a little more bearable."

"Bearable."

Why did he keep repeating her words? That was her job. Was it as irritating to her patients when she did it?

"Stop it."

"Stop what?"

She threw up her hands and let them drop to her sides. "Oh for heaven's sake. Never mind. Just keep walking."

"You're the one who wanted to talk, not me." He rolled his shoulders.

Her brows went up. "Well, you were happy enough to do all kinds of other things weren't you? Things that didn't involve talking."

His movement stopped and a flush crept from his neck all the way to his hairline. "I've already apologized for that."

He had. And it had been wholly unnecessary. Why then was she bringing it up?

Getting a little of her own back. Teaching him to keep his pointed spears to himself.

"I think our little episode calls for some kind of…er, détente, don't you?"

"Détente?"

She laughed. "Would you please stop repeating my words? You're making me nervous."

Cole's arms uncrossed and he propped his hands on his hips, his fingers unconsciously drumming against them. He did that a lot.

But at least they were getting somewhere. He was still on the defensive side, but his posture had opened up a bit.

His head tilted. "I'm making you nervous?"

"See?" She made a little flourish in the air with her hand. "You just repeated back what I said."

A smile crept across his face. "And how does that make you feel?"

Okay, so he *was* making fun of her. Callie could laugh at herself as easily as the next person.

She put her finger on her lip as if considering his question. "It makes me feel a little…scared and vulnerable."

His face changed, darkened, and he rocked back onto his heels. "As if you'd know what that was like."

She took a step toward him and touched his arm, realizing they were getting closer to the target. The bunched muscles jumped under her fingers. "I *do* know what it's like. I promise you."

He stood motionless as a stone, not answering.

It was do or die. Try or give up.

Callie wanted to try. One more time.

"Tell me," she said.

"Tell you what?" One hand scraped through his hair.

"Tell me what happened. You've been to see a psychiatrist haven't you?"

His hand went back to his hip. "Yeah."

"Through the military?"

He shook his head. "No."

Had he been suicidal at some point? Addicted to something? Her mind struggled to find the answer.

"Was there a tragedy in your family?"

He smiled but it didn't reach his eyes. "Yeah. You just hit the nail on the head. There was a big tragedy in my family."

Callie leaned forward. Here it came. "What was it?"

His arms went out from his sides, his palms opening. "You're looking at it. The tragedy was me."

SIXTEEN

A WIDE RANGE OF EMOTIONS flashed through Callie's eyes: shock, outrage…and doubt. Cole waited for the inevitable question or for her to repeat back his words.

Mirroring.

Wasn't that what they called that charming little technique?

"No. Whoever told you that was wrong," she finally said.

His mouth had already opened to cut off all questions about how being a "tragedy" made him feel. He snapped his jaw shut. It was his turn to be shocked.

"I never said anyone told me that. I just knew."

She shook her head. "They may not have said it in words, but you perceived it."

Dammit, why did she always have to be right?

That was a shrink for you. They stood over you and told you what you were thinking and feeling. All through a very clever system of tricks. All geared to trip you up.

This was not what he wanted to be doing in the middle of Angola. They had to get through three more days in each other's company. And he fully intended that to be a hands-off, almost silent affair, until he could get to Moss, dump Callie into the chopper and get on with his life. A life that didn't include relationships with mind melders.

"You're wrong. I didn't *perceive* anything. I had some serious problems as a kid."

"What kind of problems?"

Cole looked past her to the dilapidated railroad tracks.

In the same way those tracks spelled disaster to a train that tried to navigate them, this woman could spell disaster to all he'd accomplished in his adult life, if he wasn't careful. She was shaking the iron rails and bringing back memories he'd pushed out of sight.

He lifted a shoulder in irritation. "Typical kid stuff. Behavioral problems."

"Your parents took you to a psychiatrist because of it?"

"Yeah. You could call her that. She had a shingle and she wasn't afraid to hang it." Another shrug. "Only it wasn't my parents. By that time there was only my mom and me. My dad skipped out."

"By that time..." Callie frowned. "You think your dad left because of you?"

"The shrink did. I heard her and my mom talking before I was allowed into the room with them. My mother was crying. Talking about how much of a problem I was in school, how my dad hadn't been able to take it anymore."

"You heard all that from another room?"

"The receptionist went to get me some juice. I put my ear to the door."

"Haven't you ever heard the proverb about eavesdroppers?"

"Tell that to a six-year-old boy who doesn't understand why his father no longer comes home."

She reached out and touched his arm. "Oh God, Cole. I'm so sorry. But it wasn't your fault."

"No? The shrink thought otherwise. Assured my mother she'd find out what was wrong with me. That there were always treatment options."

He gave an exaggerated stretch to remove her hand from his arm and to cover his restless need for movement, the need to get away from the source of his discomfort. "My mother just wanted me to stop bouncing off the walls."

"Did the psychiatrist diagnose you?"

"Oh yeah. I didn't understand what the letters meant at the time, but whenever one of my teachers read the note from the school nurse explaining about the meds, their faces changed. You could practically hear the 'oh no!' bomb going off in their heads."

"ADHD," she said.

He checked off an imaginary box with his index finger. "Ten points to the lady with the highbrow degree."

"Cole, stop it. There's nothing to be ashamed of. Lots of kids struggle with—"

"*I* wasn't struggling. My mother was. Evidently my teachers were. My father couldn't take living with me anymore." He drew in a ragged breath, irritated that it sounded shaky. "A whole passel of people didn't know how to deal with a kid like me. And they didn't want to have to try."

"They were just trying to help."

"By pumping me full of speed?"

"Didn't it work?"

"Yep." Anger marine-crawled up his spine. "It worked just fine and dandy." He wasn't about to stand here and hash this out one more minute. "Now that you've dug up my deepest, darkest secret, can we get moving again?"

"You didn't like being on the meds."

Great, she evidently wasn't done yet.

"No, I didn't."

"Why?"

"Because they put me on them for their own sakes, not for mine. They wanted to control me, to make me more manageable."

She paused for a long second, and Cole wondered what was going on inside that beautiful head of hers.

"If they did it for those reasons, then they were wrong,

Cole. I'm sorry that you felt alone and couldn't tell anyone how you were feeling."

"Oh, I had my sessions with my shrink every month. I sat in a room with her for about twenty minutes. My mom got the last ten minutes. She always came out of that office with a crisp new scrip."

"Are you still taking medication?"

"Nope." He smiled. "As if you couldn't tell. I've been drug free since I was twelve. Rehabilitated."

"You're functioning well."

"Surprised?"

"No, not at all." Another pause. "Don't you think your treatment could be part of the reason you're so successful today?"

Successful. Hell, half the time he was in trouble for some shit or other. Including going off half-cocked when he pulled Callie away from that suicide bomber. He was going to have some angry jaws wagging at him when he got back.

"No. Actually, I don't."

"Maybe it helped you deal with the situation a little better, helped you to fit in with the other kids."

"And maybe that was the problem. Everyone expected me to be a cookie cutter replica of all the perfect kids. The ones who made straight As and didn't give the teachers cause to complain. Maybe that's not who I am."

"Who are you, then?"

Who was he? That was another problem. Cole had never been quite sure. But he wasn't going to make any more big confessions. Not today.

"I'm the man you see standing before you."

"Can I tell you who *I* see when I look at you?"

Before he had a chance to say "hell no!" she took another step forward and continued, "I see a man who's been hurt and who's stronger for it."

Cole was taken aback. Is that what she really saw? Not the impulsive, attention-seeking clown that had driven everyone crazy with irritation?

They were almost toe-to-toe at this point, and while he hated to be forced to take a step back, she was making him nervous as hell. And causing certain parts of his anatomy to take notice of certain parts of hers.

"Great," he said. "Now that we've gotten that earth-shattering revelation out of the way, can we get going? I think we can make Malanje by tomorrow afternoon if we're lucky."

She blinked as if surprised at the change of subject. "I thought you said it would take eight days. That's a day-and-a-half earlier."

"We've made better time than I expected." Cole had been pushing himself hard since that fiasco yesterday at the mine-field. He couldn't risk a repeat performance. And if he didn't move away—soon—that was a definite possibility.

"Oh." She seemed disappointed by the prospect of arriving early, although she should be glad. She was within a stone's throw of safety. Of getting back to her own people.

"The sooner you get back to the States where your…your sister's baby can get the care it needs, the better."

Callie's hand curved over her belly. "Yes, you're right, of course."

He couldn't take it anymore and edged back a step out of self-preservation. Now wasn't the time for weakness. Not when his goal was so close.

"I think I told you his name is Micah, right?"

He nodded, not sure what she was getting at.

"It was the name my sister chose. Gary, her husband, said he was fine with whatever name she went with. She never even got a chance to tell him what her final choice was going to be. She was hoping to surprise him when she got home from her trip.

"I think my sister would have wanted Micah's middle name to be Cole." She stopped for a second when her voice trembled. She took a deep breath, held it and then let it out. "Cole...after the man who saved his life."

"HELL NO!"

Callie's eyes widened in shock. She'd imagined all kinds of responses to her declaration, but "hell no" wasn't anywhere on that list.

"What?" What kind of person said something like that when honored with having a baby named after them?

"You heard me." Cole turned his back to her and scraped his hands through his hair. "You're not making me out to be some fucking hero."

"Watch your language!" Her voice was sharper than she'd meant it to be. Not because she was offended by the word itself, but because she hated him using it during a conversation about Micah.

He spun back around. "Why the hell should I? You wanted the real me. Well, lady, this is it. This is all I've got."

Callie was crushed. She'd meant the gesture as something that came up from the depths of her heart. "Forget it."

When she started walking, a hand on her upper arm stopped her. She turned and glared first at his face and then stared pointedly at his restraining hand.

He let her arm go. "Hey, I'm sorry if I hurt your feelings—"

"I said forget it."

"Look, it's not that I'm not flattered, but you don't even know me."

"You're right. So don't worry about it. Your name won't go down in the hallowed halls of bravery on my account." She tossed her head. "Micah will never have to know your sordid little secret. That you actually deigned to come down from your self-righteous perch to help a mere mortal. A *psychiatrist*, of all things. I guess it's a good thing you didn't know that up front, or the baby and I would have been splattered from here to—"

"Stop it, damn you!" His lips, pinched and white, barely moved as he said the words.

"Or what?" she taunted, knowing she was pushing him to the limit, but unable to stop herself.

"Don't go there."

"Oh, so first your name is off limits, and now talking about the rescue itself is off limits. What next? The time we spent writhing around on the ground together? You certainly didn't mind my using your name as you were—"

Before she could finish her sentence, she was in his arms and his lips were covering hers. Seeking, probing…a kind of angry desperation in his touch that she more than willingly returned.

He finally lifted his head and anguished eyes stared down at her. "Don't give him my name, Callie. I don't want him going through life saddled with what it represents."

Hot tears spilled over before she could stop them. "Oh God, Cole. Your name doesn't represent anything, other than the brave, kind man you are today."

He shook his head, his jaw working in spasms, but said nothing.

Reaching up, she touched his face. "There's so much I've come to admire about you. Those are the things I want to impart to my sister's child. Not the past, not what you went through. What you *are* as a result of the difficulties you passed through."

Cole brushed her tears away with the pads of his thumbs, before tucking her hair behind her ears. "I hate it when you cry, you know that?"

She smiled, but it was shaky. "Why?"

"Because it means I've hurt you," he whispered. "And I don't want to."

"What do you want, Cole?" She bit her lip and waited for his answer.

"You don't want to know."

"Try me."

He cupped her face. "You. Right now, I want you." Looping her arms around his neck, she stepped on tiptoes and rubbed her cheek against his, reveling in the press of her belly against his firm abs. "You have me. Right now, you have me."

"Do you know what you're saying?"

"I have a pretty good idea, but you can set me straight if I'm wrong."

His head lowered and his lips brushed hers, repeating the gesture until she was straining against him with need. Against her mouth, he growled, "This is what I had in mind."

She smiled. "I like the way your mind works, soldier. Now, carry on."

"With pleasure, doc."

COLE KISSED HER ONE more time, and then got to his feet, pulling on his pants. He didn't want to join the real world again, but there was no choice.

She looked up at him with a knowing smile and stretched her arms over her head, her breasts lifting as she arched her back.

Groaning, he turned away. "We need to go. The more you do that the less I want to move."

A laugh sounded from behind him. "We didn't have to move an hour ago."

Yeah, they did, he'd just been too infatuated with her to force himself to do the smart thing. Her request to give the baby his name had touched him to the core. He'd fought his reaction, knowing they were heading for this very moment if he couldn't derail his emotional roller coaster.

He'd done his job a little too well, because she'd cried and he'd been lost.

Again.

But as hard as he tried, he couldn't make himself sorry for the time they'd just spent together. He swung around, deciding they could wait another thirty minutes, but was surprised to find her on her feet adjusting her blouse over her skirt. She brushed the bits of grass from the garments and a wave of disappointment swept over him.

"No frowning." She smoothed her index finger between his brows. "It's not allowed."

"No? Then how about this?" Grabbing her around the waist, he nuzzled her cheek.

"Yes. That's definitely on the okay list." She sighed. "Mmm…I like you so much better like this."

"Like what?" He kissed her neck, unable to resist nipping up the delicate cords.

She pressed closer. "Relaxed. Lighthearted." Her head tilted so he could reach the area behind her ear. "Human."

"And I was inhuman before?" he whispered the words in her ear.

Her fingers slid into his hair, holding him in place. "Not inhuman, no. Just hard and cold. A typical military man."

He stopped and leaned back to look at her. "You think the typical military man is hard and cold?"

"The ones that I've known have been."

"And you've known enough of us to get an accurate picture of what we're like."

Callie frowned this time. "I think so. My stepfather was in the Marines."

"And he was a badass."

"You could say that. He and his friends used to laugh about how many 'kill shots' each had taken while in Vietnam."

Cole's jaw tightened. He was a sniper. It was his job to kill people from a distance. He didn't take pleasure in it, only shot when lives were at stake. He knew men who bragged about it, but for the most part, it was just talk. A way to downplay fear and come to grips with what they had to do on a daily basis. He personally stayed as far away from that kind of stuff as possible. "It's not an easy job."

"Whatever you say."

Well, hell, looked like the honeymoon was over already. He let go of her and took a step back.

Holding her hands up, palms out, Callie said, "Okay, I'm sorry. You're right. It's wrong to stereotype a whole group based on the acts of a few people."

Like he'd done with psychiatrists.

The words were unsaid, but they hung between them like a wall, effectively separating them.

He looked at her, and she returned his stare. Neither of them said anything to end the awkward silence.

What did she want him to say? That he was sorry too? He was, but saying the words probably wouldn't bridge the growing gulf between them. It was already too wide.

He could try rappelling down one side and scrambling up the other, but would it really solve anything? His life was on one side of the ravine and hers was on the other. And he saw no way to bridge the gap. Better to just keep moving.

"Right, then. Like I said earlier, time to go."

She nodded. "I think you're right."

SEVENTEEN

Moss STEPPED OFF THE SMALL charter plane and sucked in a breath of heat-soaked humidity. He scanned the area for signs of anyone who looked out of place. A handful of tourists of varying nationalities loitered by an out-building, evidently trying to get a lift to the falls, but no Cole or Dr. Nascimento. He looked at his watch. It was still a couple of days early, unless Cole had succeeded in hitching a ride.

Moss frowned when a jeep in the distance made a swift U-turn and headed his way. That was the kind of vehicle the rebels had used during their rampage.

Reaching into his overnight bag, he thanked his stars for thinking ahead of the game. He pulled out a *Les Canadiens de Montréal* ball cap and perched it on his head. Wrapping his tongue around a mouthful of French words—particularly the strongest curse word he could remember—he ambled across the narrow dirt runway. If he could make it to the small cluster of tourists, maybe the jeep men would assume he was with them. Hopefully they were of European descent and not a group of Asians or he was doomed.

The jeep angled between him and the group, cutting him off before he could reach them.

Shit.

He tried to appear slightly confused when a couple of armed gunmen leaned out of the windows.

"Where is your paperwork?" the one in the passenger seat asked.

Moss cocked his head and tried to ignore the pounding

of his heart. *"Je suis désolé, mais je ne parle pas anglais, monsieur. Parlez-vous français?"*

He hoped they bought the lie and believed he didn't speak English.

The man gave a slow smile that revealed he was missing a piece of his right front tooth. *"Mais, vous êtes avec la bonne chance, monsieur, parce que je parle français."*

Not only was his luck *not* good. The prick spoke French.

The rebel in the jeep aimed his gun at Moss's chest for emphasis and repeated his question. In French this time. "Where is your paperwork, *monsieur?*"

Grimly, Moss faced the man, aware that his service pistol was no match for three thugs with machine guns. He was glad he'd at least picked a language he had a fairly good grasp of.

"I'm going to reach inside my pocket for my passport."

"Slowly, *monsieur.*"

Moss nodded and pulled out his passport. The Canadian one. His real passport was safely tucked in his dresser drawer at home. Handing it over, he asked, "What's this all about?"

The man who appeared to be in charge didn't answer, just studied the passport and then glanced back at Moss.

He motioned to one of his men in the back of the jeep and said something in Portuguese. The man jumped out of the vehicle and snatched away Moss's overnight bag. Ripping open the zipper, he began rummaging through the clothing and assorted items. Moss was doubly glad he hadn't hauled a bunch of military paraphernalia with him. And his pistol was hidden in a spot he was fairly sure they wouldn't check.

"Why are you in Angola, *monsieur?*" A jab of the gun against Moss's chest brought his attention back to the first rebel.

He held his anger in check. "I'm here to view the beautiful waterfalls, like the rest of the tourists." He motioned toward the clustered group across the tarmac, whose attention was now avidly focused on the exchange.

Evidently not expecting an audience, the man lowered the tip of his rifle.

The rebel nodded at the small band of people. "You are with them?"

"I came separately, but planned to join them here." That was about as far as Moss dared to stretch the truth, because if the man decided to question the huddled group, he was in big trouble.

Moss glanced at the tourists again, praying they didn't go off and leave him hanging with the lie. He noted one of the tourists had lifted a camera and was either filming or snapping shots of them. He waved at them, diverting the rebel's attention back toward the group, hoping he would see the camera as well.

It worked. The man's eyes narrowed. He turned to Moss and closed the passport with an angry snap. "Very well, *Monsieur* Trentón. Please join your party." He called to the man who was ransacking his bag, who then tossed it aside to hop back into the jeep.

Half of Moss's belongings were now scattered on the asphalt. He reached down to stuff the objects back inside the overnight bag.

Then, trying to look suitably beaten down, he shuffled away in the direction of the tourists.

"Oh, *monsieur*," called the voice.

Moss's jaw clenched, but he turned to face the rebel. "*Oui?*"

The man switched to English and watched Moss's face carefully. "We will check the information on your passport against your country's registry."

Moss frowned as if he didn't understand what had been said. "*Je suis désolé. Je ne comprends pas.*"

"Oh, I think you understand me perfectly, my friend. But if we find you have been lying…"

"*Ce qui?*"

Slow color suffused the rebel's face, but he didn't reaim the gun in Moss's direction. He belted out an order in Portuguese and the jeep turned in the other direction and sped away. Stones, kicked up by the tires, pelted Moss in the head and chest as they left. He shielded his eyes and watched them leave.

He was under no illusions. If the rebels decided they wanted him, nothing—including fear of reprisals from a foreign government—would stop them from taking him down.

"GARY?"

"Callie?" Her brother-in-law's incredulous voice came across the line. "Thank God! Do you know how worried we've been about you?"

"We?"

Gary laughed, his relief evident. "Yes, everyone. My fellow senators, the House, all the way up to the president. Countless prayers have been lifted up. Where are you? Are you safe?"

She glanced at the corner of the concrete block building. Cole had disappeared inside the store after leaving her to use the restroom. She'd decided to call Gary first and then use the facilities afterward. Thank heavens she'd committed her credit card numbers to memory. And even more incredible was that the phone at this particular store was in working order. She'd tried one in another town, only to find the handset had been cut free and used to beat at the ancient mechanism in hopes of finding coins inside.

"Callie?"

"Oh…yes, sorry. I'm safe. I'm in Angola, in a town called Malanje. It's where the big waterfalls are."

"I'm not sure where that is. How did you get there?"

"One of the soldiers in charge of evacuating the embassy staff…oh it's too long of a story to go into right now." And she didn't want to think of the trip she and Cole had just made. She shook off the memories. "He says the military is supposed to send help in the next day or so."

"Damn," her brother-in-law said.

"What?"

"The mission was called off." There was a long pause. "We all thought the worst. And the president…"

Fear crawled up her spine at the trepidation in his voice. "The president, what, Gary?"

"He ordered the military to stand down. To abort the mission. Said the Angolan government was breathing down his neck for interfering in the first place. That the Angolan military was prepared to deal with the situation."

The rest of his words were like so much background buzz. All she heard was that the rescue mission had been aborted.

"Callie, stay where you are, okay? I'll get you out somehow. But I want you to be careful." He asked her to spell the name of the city so he could jot it down.

"We are being careful. One of the rebels in Luanda said they were after me. He used my name. I have no idea why."

"Oh God, Callie. It's true, then."

"What's true?" She glanced to make sure Cole wasn't coming.

"Are you sure they said they were after you?"

"They threatened the soldier with death if he didn't hand me over."

"Thank God he didn't. And the baby? Is everything okay?"

Callie's hands went to the precious bump, mourning the thought of giving him up. "The baby's fine."

"I'm so glad. Your sister, she wanted that baby so much

that…" His voice trailed away, and Callie heard a low anguished sound. Sara was right. The baby had helped heal whatever rift had been between them. And now her sister was gone. Her heart ached for his grief and her own.

He cleared his throat. "Okay…let me think for a minute."

"Can you get the military to remount the rescue mission?" she asked.

A beat passed.

"Gary?"

"One of the military commanders who helped evacuate the embassy said he thought someone on the American side had set you up as a target."

What was that supposed to mean? "Set me up? Why?"

"He's not sure. Maybe it has something to do with the upcoming elections."

"The presidential election?"

"Yes. There's a lot riding on the vote."

"What does that have to do with me?"

"I was planning on running against the president next year. Surely Sara told you."

"No, she didn't." Callie's mind raced with the information. Had that been the cause of the problems between them? Sara's comments made more sense now.

She drew a deep breath and focused on his words, the earthy scent of Angola filling her nostrils. "I'm not sure I follow you."

"The president's party is desperate to maintain its hold on the country."

"And?"

"I'm the frontrunner for my party's nomination."

Her mind slowly grasped the implications. "You think someone killed Sara to force you from the race?"

"I didn't want to think so, I hoped it was truly an accident…but if they used your name…"

"They did."

"Callie, I wouldn't go forward with the campaign if something happened to the baby in addition to Sara. I—I just couldn't."

Callie was horrified. Surely politics couldn't have played a role in her sister's death, or with the attempt on her own life. But it all made a horrible kind of sense.

"If it's true, who's behind it?" she asked.

"I don't know. The general I told you about is working on it outside of the normal channels. He's doing it as a personal favor."

"Surely you don't think the president is somehow involved."

"I hope not, Callie. I don't want to believe he'd be capable of it. But it could be one of his cabinet members."

"But the order to abort came directly from him, right?"

"It did, but again, no one can be—"

"Is there a way we can find out…"

Cole rounded the corner, and his face drew into harsh lines as he strode toward her.

She suddenly wondered if making the call had been a mistake. "Gary, I have to go. See if you can get the military back on the ball, will you?"

"I will. Stay put and we'll figure something out. Just don't trust—"

Cole reached her and took the phone from her hands, slamming it back onto its cradle with a sharp crack.

Wincing, she bit her lip. "I told you I wanted to call my brother-in-law."

His cold gaze swept over her from head to toe. "No, you told me you needed to use the bathroom."

"I did. I—I do."

"But you chose to make the call instead."

"I told you when we were in Luanda that I needed to call him. You never said I shouldn't."

"What did you use for money?" The calm, impersonal tone of his voice was more frightening than open fury would have been.

"I used my credit card."

"You said you'd left your purse behind."

"I did. I lost it during the scuffle at the embassy. I have my credit card numbers memorized."

"You could have just jeopardized your safety—our safety—even more."

She shook her head, realizing she had to tell him what she'd just found out. "You're wrong. But, that's not the important thing. Gary said the rescue mission's been called off. No one's coming for us."

His eyebrows dove into a dangerous position. "Called off? On whose orders?"

More afraid than she'd been in the last six days, she gripped his arm and looked up at him.

"The order came from the president."

COLE STARED AT CALLIE.

Aborting the mission had come on the president's order? He had a hard time believing that. They had the word of one lone senator. True, the man was Callie's brother-in-law, but still…

He knew better than to think General Markesan would abandon him or Callie, unless there was absolutely no other option available to him.

And even if by some twist of fate he did, Moss would be on his way, orders or no. His friend wasn't as impulsive as Cole, but he was tirelessly loyal and nearly unstoppable.

Cole wasn't worried about himself, but he wanted Callie out of here as soon as possible. Not only because of his lack of control around her, but because of the baby. There was something about seeing that curve of her bare stomach that made parts of him flip inside. He didn't want her losing it.

And not just because it would carry a piece of his name.

"They'll be here," he said.

Callie shook her head. "No, they won't. You don't understand. Gary said the order was to abort the mission altogether. He even implied someone in the president's office might be behind my kidnapping in the first place."

"What?"

"Gary also thinks Sara's death might be tied into the election. That the president's party is getting desperate because of the low approval ratings."

"But how would killing your sister affect anything?"

"By forcing Gary to drop out of the race before it even begins."

"Your brother-in-law was thinking of running for the presidency himself?"

"Yes."

"And Senator Parker thinks that by killing his wife and now you, the president will force him out of the race before it even begins?"

She nodded. "Gary's a popular senator. If he wins his party's nomination, he'll probably win the election. But if he was forced out before that happens…"

Cole tried to keep an open mind, but the idea was so far-fetched it stretched the cords of believability to their limits.

But it had happened before, hadn't it? In many countries, including the country they were currently in. Election rigging took many different forms. But forcing someone out of the race by killing off his family members was the act of a madman.

Was the president capable of such an act?
And if he was, where did that leave him and Callie?
Worse, where did it leave the United States?

EIGHTEEN

"THE PRESIDENT WILL see you now, sir."

Gary nodded at the aide and walked toward the open door of the president's office. Just before crossing the threshold, he adjusted his lapel, tapping the tiny button of a tape recorder as he did. He wanted a record of every word that came out of the bastard's mouth.

President Bryson stood as soon as he entered and came around the desk, smile firmly in place. "Gary, how nice to see you."

He could pretty much guarantee he was the last person this particular president wanted in his office right now. "Let's dispense with the pleasantries. I think you know why I'm here."

"Why don't you remind me?"

Gary didn't miss the fact that the president didn't offer him his hand. "My sister-in-law is trapped in Angola, and I'm told you've called off the rescue mission."

The other man's hands spread. "I had no choice. The Angolan government is breathing down our necks, blasting us for sending men in there in the first place. You were there for the briefing."

"My God, how can you just stand there like that? Callie is carrying my child. *Sara's* child, remember?"

The man's face reddened. "I'm well aware of the problems in your private life. So is the whole country. You've made sure of that. Maybe you're hoping it'll garner you a couple of sympathy votes in the next election."

"My wife is dead. So for you to talk about sympathy votes at a time like this—"

"You went behind my back and tried to send a black ops team in there after you were expressly told not to. Don't bother to deny it. I talked to the general in charge. He said you'd spoken with him about the possibility. That's unforgiveable."

Gary bristled at the pompous attitude. "You helped evacuate the embassy personnel after we got the intelligence information about the rebel attack, so why are you so unwilling to send anyone in for my sister-in-law? My wife died over there, dammit! How many more people were you willing to risk just to keep the peace?"

The president's smile finally disappeared, his voice rising. "Your wife died in a plane crash, not from rebel fire. And don't you dare lecture me on peace."

Gary knew he had to be careful. Getting into a shouting match would help no one. Better to try to steer the conversation in the right direction.

He took a deep breath and fought for control. "I did what I thought was right. I'm sorry if I overstepped my bounds."

The other man leaned back against his desk and folded his arms across his chest, but said nothing.

Gary tried again. "Callie called me from a payphone in one of the major cities."

"She did? When?" The president's face registered surprise.

"This morning. She's okay. She's with one of the military team."

"I just assumed…"

Gary leaned closer. "You assumed what, sir?"

The president waved his hand in dismissal. "Nothing. By 'one of the military team' do you mean one of the troops that helped with the evacuation?"

He squirmed. "Yes."

"I see."

"Look. Callie's alive. Just let me send one or two men in and see if we can get her—"

"Absolutely not."

"Why on earth not?"

"This presidency is built on trust and respect. I gave the Angolan president my word. I'll contact him and update him on the situation. He can have his own military pick them up."

Gary almost laughed out loud. "The *Angolan* military? You know as well as I do that most of them are as corrupt as the rebels."

"Your sister-in-law went there of her own free will. I'm not responsible for the consequences of her actions."

"I'm pleading with you." He paused when his voice cracked. "This is the only child Sara will ever have. The only piece of her I'll ever hold again."

The president's eyes softened. "I'm sorry for your loss, Gary, please believe that. I know how hard this must be on you, but I can't send anyone in. I can't go back on my word."

There was a fifteen second pause while Gary tried to call up a normal tone of voice. He remembered the tape and forced himself to say the words he needed to say. "Then you've just signed both of those people's death warrants."

JOSÉ HELD UP A FINGER to silence his men. Without his translator, he needed to focus.

"You're sure the phone call originated from Malanje?"

How could he have missed them? He and his men had driven to the city and seen no sign of them.

The American's call was fortuitous, though. It seemed the woman had just made his job a thousand times easier. No more requesting information from un-cooperative villagers.

With the Angolan government getting more involved by the minute, time was running short.

"Yes, Malanje." The voice on the other end grew agitated. "You promised you would take care of her within forty-eight hours. That was almost a week ago. And now she's got a Special Forces soldier to protect her. They were never supposed to have the opportunity to make phone calls."

"Not all things bow to the whims of man, my friend," José said.

He tilted his head. How poetic he sounded even in another language. Before he could forget the words, he scratched them into the dashboard of the jeep with the tip of his knife. He mouthed the phrase to himself, while the American blustered on. Things were coming together. If all went well, he would soon have an American president at his beck and call.

The man on the other end of the satellite phone was still ranting. "If she could contact a U.S. senator, who knows who else she was able to get in touch with. The press?"

José could imagine the man shuddering. He smiled. "If they had called the press, you would have heard something by now. They will not get the chance to make any additional calls. I am in Malanje even as we speak. We will pick them up."

"You'd better. You won't get another red cent until I have proof that you've taken care of the problem."

"Ah, proof." His smile widened. Americans liked to stay well removed from the ugliness of death. How sanitized everything had to be before it touched their plates... or their hands. "What kind of proof would you like? Pictures, maybe?"

"Of course not. Just a death certificate will do."

Just as he'd thought. They couldn't stomach doing the dirty work, yet they wanted to reap all the benefits. How was it they'd been able to maintain power for all these years?

"I will see what I can arrange."

"I want more than that."

"And what would that be?"

"I want her dead by the end of the day. Do you understand me?"

"Yes. I understand."

He understood, but that didn't mean this drama was going to play out the way the American demanded. No, the man would soon learn that José called the shots in this particular partnership. He already knew just how he was going to drive that point home. He'd planned this moment down to the last tiny detail. And he would exact a much tidier sum when the American realized how vulnerable a position he'd placed himself in. All it would take was for the gringo to hear the woman's voice pleading for her life.

When the transaction was completed, José would solidify his position as a strong contender in his own presidential race. With the backing of a powerful ally, he couldn't lose.

With a slicing motion, he underlined the words he'd carved moments earlier and pondered just how he could work them into his inaugural address.

MOSS RECLINED ON THE sagging mattress and stared at the ceiling. A spider the size of a coffee mug huddled in the far right-hand corner, its strong hairy legs clinging to its overhead perch. He should get up and kill it, but he was too busy formulating contingency plans to bother.

The rebels he'd encountered at the airport worried him. They'd been far too interested in seeing his papers to be merely corrupt military police trying to shakedown naive tourists. In fact, once ol' chipped-tooth bought his story, he'd spun away as if hurrying on to find someone even more important.

Like Cole and Dr. Nascimento, maybe?

If the rebels knew the pair was headed for Malanje, Moss's best moves were stymied. He'd hoped to spirit Cole and his companion to Zambia on the same private plane he'd flown in on. But if the airport was under rebel surveillance that was out of the question.

The rendezvous point had been Calandula. Maybe the pair would bypass Malanje altogether and head straight for the falls. Moss could simply head there and stake out the area.

But if they stopped in town first, they'd have no idea the trouble that awaited them.

Moss couldn't take that chance. He'd have to stick around. If they didn't show up in Malanje by rendezvous time, he'd head to the falls and wait there.

He eyed the spider one more time. It hadn't moved. Good. Settling into his pillow, he decided to grab a few hours of shuteye. He wouldn't be worth shit on a shingle to Cole or anyone if he was dead on his feet. Hopefully, his hairy roommate was as tired as Moss and would leave him the hell alone. He'd like both parties to leave this little tête-à-tête alive. But if that wasn't to be, Moss had every intention of emerging the victor. He'd leave it to the spider to decide the course of his own fate.

As COLE APPROACHED the glass doors of the Palácio Regina Hotel, the raucous sound of American laughter hit his ears. A burst of hope shot through him that he quickly extinguished.

These people could do nothing for him or Callie. In fact, across the street from the hotel was a UNITA headquarters building. The once-violent rebel arm had supposedly disarmed, becoming just another political party, but Cole didn't trust them. The rebels chasing them smacked of UNITA tactics, whether they officially belonged to the group or not.

The American tourists in the hotel made him just as nervous. The rebels would look for them among their own countrymen first. No, his hopes for Callie's survival were pinned on one person.

Moss.

Where the hell was he?

Edging Callie away from the building, Cole ignored her questioning frown. He would like to spend the night in a hotel, if they could get in quietly and without a fuss. It would give Callie a chance to rest and eat a nourishing meal. And hell, it wasn't as if he couldn't use a little downtime as well.

"They're speaking English." Callie's whispered words stopped him.

"I know. But we need to keep our distance."

"Okay."

He'd expected an argument, but got none. No time to wonder why. He needed to be grateful. "We're going to head for the other hotel I saw."

She sighed. "This one looks beautiful."

"When we get back home, I'll take you to a better one."

Where the hell had that come from?

Callie didn't acknowledge his words, but her hand slipped into his, and a painful knot gathered at the base of his throat. If he'd been going to disavow his statement, her action stopped him in his tracks.

And, he realized, he *wanted* to spirit her away to some quiet place and spend time getting to know her in a normal setting.

In spite of her profession?

Maybe not all psychiatrists were cut from the same cloth. She'd said as much, right?

He threaded his fingers through hers and gave her hand a soft squeeze before heading for the simpler hotel he'd seen a short distance away. If he could just hold off on his urges until they got out of here, he would give himself a medal of honor.

She'd asked if he was an honorable man. Right about now, he needed to dig deep and unearth that trait. For both their sakes.

NINETEEN

José MOVED INTO the lobby of the Planca Negra Hotel. His quarry was within the city. So close. The concierge eyed him from across the space with wary fear, but made no attempt to call security.

He leaned across the desk and held out his hand. "I would like to see your guest registry, please."

The man licked his lips and hesitated, but when José shifted his machine gun, he moved quickly to the computer and tapped on the keyboard. Within fifteen seconds José was in possession of a printed list. He'd already been to the Hotel Palácio Regina and had struck out. There was a block of American tourists staying there, but they'd all arrived together. None were traveling individually.

He figured he'd work his way from the top hotel to the bottom feeders.

The pair was here, somewhere. If he had to tear the place apart with his bare hands, he would find them.

He scrolled a finger down the printout. No Dr. Nascimento listed, but that didn't mean anything. He didn't know the name of the Special Forces soldier she was with, and none of the names rang a bell. There were several American sounding ones, however. Just like there'd been at the other hotels. They could be using an alias, he supposed. If he had no luck this time around, he'd start all over again, going room to room if need be.

Lifting his eyes to the still-cowering man behind the desk, he motioned him closer with a reassuring smile. "I'm looking for a man and a woman. Both white. Both Americans. The woman looks to be of South American descent." He nodded at the list. "Anyone here match that description?"

"I—I don't remember everyone who comes—"

"Think very hard, *senhor*. Your life may depend on it."

The man's face blanched, but he looked down at the sheet of paper in José's hands. "May I look?"

Handing the list over, he watched the concierge's face carefully. "How about now? Remember any of them?"

"A couple came in today, but they spoke Portuguese, not English."

"Brazilian accent? Or American?"

"The woman didn't speak, just the man. His accent was American. The woman appeared uncomfortable about being here."

José sighed. "How did they pay?"

"Cash. Large Kwanza notes."

"And they're here for how long?"

The man looked at the list again. "They're scheduled to leave tomorrow."

What luck.

"Room number?"

Swallowing hard, the man behind the desk hesitated again. "May I ask why you need it?"

If not for another couple entering the lobby, José would have killed the concierge and been done with it, but he didn't want his old UNITA buddies from around the corner finding out he was in town. "You could ask, *senhor,* but some things are better left unsaid."

"Ah…yes." The man blinked then turned his attention to the computer and typed in a command. "Room 208. Second floor."

José leaned across the desk and said in a slightly louder voice. "I seem to have left my room key in my vehicle, *senhor.* Would you mind loaning me a copy? I'll bring it back down momentarily."

Hands shaking, the man wordlessly took the list of names from José and went into a back room. If he called the police, he was a dead man, witnesses or no witnesses.

José would capture his quarry. His future depended on it.

The concierge came back, key in hand. "Here it is." He dropped his voice to a whisper. "If you could just keep things quiet, I would appreciate it."

José smiled. The man was smarter than he looked. He knew there was going to be bloodshed and he didn't really care…as long as it didn't affect his hotel's cash flow.

He lowered his voice as well. "Don't worry. You won't hear a peep." Winking, he tossed the key in the air and caught it one-handed.

One of his men stepped forward as soon as José moved away from the desk. "Are they here?"

"Yes. Our friends have arrived. We'll just go up and check on them."

Deciding on the stairs rather than the elevator, José and two of his most trusted men quickly mounted the steps and came out on the second floor. Signs directed guests to the right or left, depending on the room number. He veered to the left.

When he stopped in front of Room 208, he put his ear to the surface, but heard nothing. Maybe they were asleep. He signaled his men to enter as soon as he opened the door. Without a word, the two men nodded at him.

He unlocked the door as silently as possible and swung it open. The lights were out, but he could still see well enough. The foot of the bed was the only thing visible from this angle, but the lumpiness of the covers signaled it was occupied.

He pointed at the light fixture and one of his men found

the switch and flipped it on. Moving fast, he rounded the corner, his gun pointing forward.

"Hey! What's going on here?" The startled English phrase came from the gringo reclining against the headboard.

José ignored the question and focused on the empty space beside the man. "Where's Dr. Nascimento?" he asked in Portuguese.

"Quem?"

So the man did speak the language. So far so good. "Your companion. Where is she?"

The man's eyes widened and shifted to the door across the room. Ah, yes. The bathroom. José moved his attention back to the man and noticed a gun on the nightstand. Next to it lay an empty foil wrapper.

So that's how it was.

"Very unprofessional of you, my friend."

"What are you talking about?"

"Sleeping with someone you were charged with protecting."

The man's face flooded with ugly color but said nothing.

"Is she in there?" José pointed his own gun at the bathroom door, keeping his eyes focused on the bed's occupant. Drops of sweat formed along the man's forehead. The hatred gleaming from the American's dark eyes was unmistakable.

"No. I'm here alone."

Just as the lie cleared the man's lips, José heard the door to the bathroom swing open.

He and the man moved at the same time. Unfortunately for the American, José was faster at this particular game. He fired three rounds into the center of the man's muscular chest. When he fell back against the pillows, José landed one more shot to the middle of his forehead. A horrified scream sounded from the doorway.

Perfect. She'd witnessed the deed, just as he'd hoped.

Fear was his biggest friend in situations like these. After eluding him for so long, the woman would learn just what it meant to be afraid. And now, no one stood between him and his goal.

Without turning, he called out, "Dr. Nascimento, please come into the room so I can finally make your acquaintance."

MOSS BOLTED UPRIGHT in bed. Gunshots. Three of them in rapid succession, followed by an ominous fourth a few seconds later. Either on this floor or the one just below him.

Shit.

He jumped off the still made-up bed, shoving his pistol into the back of his jeans. The spider, still in the same spot, watched from its perch.

Had Cole arrived without him realizing it?

If so, had the rebels found him and Dr. Nascimento? Or worse?

The ball cap caught his eye, and he flipped it on his head as a safety measure, then pushed through the door. He took stock of his surroundings. An eerie silence permeated the hallway. One of the neighboring doors opened and Moss pivoted, gun drawn.

An elderly man's horrified face met his gaze. Moss held his finger to his lips and motioned him to shut the door, which he quickly did, probably with a sigh of relief.

So the shots hadn't been merely his imagination.

They'd been all too real.

But where had they come from? This floor? The one below?

He strained his ears but heard nothing. Another door opened farther down the hallway, but Moss didn't aim his firearm this time. He concealed it behind his back. It wouldn't do for him to be mistaken for the shooter and be detained. By the time he explained, it might be too late.

A beautiful blonde peered down the hallway at him.

He tilted his head and feigned ignorance. "Did you hear that?"

"Yeah," she answered in English. "I'm not sure what it was. I thought it was a gunshot, but surely not. Must have just been a car backfiring."

"You're probably right, but now that I'm up, I think I'll go to the bar for a drink. These foreign countries make me jumpy as hell."

He stopped just short of rolling his eyes at himself.

The young woman, evidently not put off by his sissy talk, opened her door a little farther and smiled. "Need some company?"

Great. Just what he needed. "Can I take a rain check? I just got in and I'm totally jetlagged."

Her full lips curved higher with sensuous promise. "Really? I know the perfect solution for jetlag. Are you traveling alone?"

"Actually I'm not." He nodded toward the door to his room and lowered his voice. "My *mom's* here and she hears everything."

The woman's pert nose crinkled as if she couldn't believe a man his age would be traveling with his mother. "Well, maybe some other time, then."

He sighed as if disappointed and shrugged. "Yep. Sorry."

"Yeah. Me too." Her door swung shut without so much as a goodbye.

"Fuck me," Moss muttered to himself. "You'd better still be alive, Scalini, because if you are, I'm going to kill you with my bare hands."

JOSÉ STARED AT THE shivering woman seated on the foot of the bed. She claimed she wasn't Dr. Nascimento. Was it a lie meant to save her ivory skin? He'd know soon enough.

His glance fell to the corpse staring sightlessly at the wall. The short cropped hair, the weapon, the powerful body all reeked of Special Forces.

"Who is he?"

The woman wrapped her arms around her still-naked breasts, bringing his attention to the heavy, glittering stones on her left ring finger. She shook her head and sent her long dark hair into motion around her shoulders. "M-my body-guard."

Disgust roiled through his gut. His mother had been a whore too, screwing men one after another as he lay listening to her coarse moans from his childhood bed. "*Puta!* And what of the man you're married to?"

Her eyes widened. "I—I… It wasn't like that. I told you, you have the wrong person. My name is Amanda Silva. I'm a fashion model. I just finished a shoot at the falls."

"You lie."

He didn't know what was behind his sudden fury. Perhaps the possibility that he really had cornered the wrong prey. Or maybe it stemmed from catching someone in an act of betrayal. He'd been betrayed far too many times by the very people he should have been able to trust. His mother, UNITA, his mouse of a wife, his translator, Rosa…and, he suspected, his American sponsor.

All had betrayed him in one form or another. All were unworthy of his mercy.

The woman's bloodless lips trembled and a single tear spilled over her lush lashes. Instead of being moved by her distress, he felt nothing but contempt. And a deep, seething rage. That didn't surprise him as much as the rising lust. Maybe he could work some of the anger out of his system and deal out a dose of retribution at the same time.

He glanced at his two men. "Out!"

They backed from the room without a word, closing the door behind them.

Yes. It was time for someone to pay.

Past time.

This woman's husband was not here to punish her for playing the whore, but José would take it upon himself to restore the man's honor. And he would discover the truth of her identity in the process. On the same bed where her dead lover lay covered in his own blood. Where she'd moaned to the tune of a thrusting cock and creaking springs. She'd brought death and destruction to the man she'd played the whore with. And now, he, José Rodrigo dos Santos Coelho, would bring destruction to her.

MOSS REACHED THE LOBBY via the stairs and concealed his weapon by shoving it in the waistband of his pants, making sure his shirt covered it. As soon as he pushed through the doors, he knew there was trouble. Two rebels lounged in overstuffed leather chairs. They were snickering to themselves. He pulled his ball cap lower on his head and tried to figure out his next move. These were some of the same men who'd questioned his arrival. But chipped-tooth was missing. The ring leader.

Time was running out.

Trying to appear nonchalant, he headed for the reception desk. The man behind it, his formal white shirt soaked with sweat, came forward, but his eyes shifted repeatedly to the men in the chairs. Not a good sign.

Moss kept his voice as low as possible and formed his phrases with care, hoping the man spoke at least a smattering of French. *"Que s'est produit?"*

The man started and glanced across the room, but responded in French as well. "There is no trouble. Please go back to your room, *monsieur*. You will be safer there."

"If you want to save lives, give me a room number."

The concierge's Adam's apple bobbed twice, but he didn't question the request. "*Chambre* 208."

The floor just below his. He'd been right. Shit, he had to get up there before it was too late. "Give me a bottle of water, so they don't suspect."

The man handed over a liter of chilled water.

"*Merci beaucoup.*"

He strolled to the elevator, conscious of eyes following his every move. Glancing at the readout on the wall above, he noted that the elevator ticked off the floors. Not good, but he had no choice but to board it when it came. Going back up the stairwell would only draw unwanted attention to himself.

The elevator arrived and he slid inside, pressing the button for the fifth floor. He could catch the stairs back down.

The machine crept upward.

"Hurry up, dammit!"

Valuable seconds ticked by before the elevator jerked to a stop. He exited and glanced down the hall. Empty.

He frowned when the elevator doors immediately closed and headed back down to the lobby. Had the rebels decided to follow him up after all? Giving the numbers one last glance as he prepared to take off, his stomach dropped to his feet. The elevator stopped on the second floor.

Plunging through the stairwell door, he took the stairs three at a time.

If he was too late…

He came to the second floor and stopped, knowing that to impulsively rush out could mean certain death. He cracked the door and saw an empty hallway. Where was room 208?

There, catty-corner to the elevator. The door stood barely ajar.

Retrieving his gun, he crept forward and waited behind

the door, listening. No sounds came from inside. His bowels twisted into a single hard knot as he pushed the door open.

"Holy shit," he whispered.

On the bed lay two figures, one male and one female. The woman was draped over the man in a way that hid both their faces.

Hot bile washed up his throat, but he forced himself to check the room for other occupants. The area was clear, save the blood soaked bed.

Someone had scrawled PUTA! in scarlet lettering on the wall above the headboard. Smeared blood coated the woman's buttocks and the backs of her thighs. A bloody towel, where the bastard had cleaned himself after the horrific act lay on the floor beside the bed.

Blind rage replaced the nausea.

He was too late. They were both dead.

Forcing himself to move forward, he thought he caught a tiny sliver of sound. He halted, watching. The woman's shoulders moved in a sudden violent shudder. Moss surged forward, until he reached her side.

He leaned down and pushed long strands of dark hair from her face. Her visible cheek was bruised and bleeding, her puffed eyelid barely opening to focus on his face.

"H-help me," she croaked.

His heart squeezed in his chest. "I will, Dr. Nascimento. Just hang in there."

She coughed and her lips moved. "N-no. I—I'm not—"

"Shh. Just lie still." He needed to check Cole, but wasn't sure how to safely move the woman to do it. He could only pray his friend was alive as well.

He eased her to the side just an inch or two. Horror flashed up his spine when the fatal mark on the forehead came into view. When his eyes skimmed the man's face, hot relief speared through him. It wasn't Cole.

Thank God.

Then who was he?

He glanced at the woman's glassy, pain-filled eyes and touched her hand. This, then, had to be someone other than Cole's traveling companion.

"Hang on, ma'am." Holding her hand as gently as possible, he picked up the phone to dial for help.

Moss could only pray the rebels didn't discover the truth, before he could locate Cole and Callie. Or before he had an opportunity to find the sick bastard responsible and show him what a real man did to those who preyed on innocents.

Chipped tooth?

Try no teeth at all.

TWENTY

COLE ROUSED HIMSELF from the dinette chair and tried to work the crick out of his aching back.

He'd done it. He'd spent the night sequestered in a hotel room with Callie and had actually kept his hands—and every other body part—to himself. Miracles were possible after all.

The sun was still well below the horizon, but since it was after midnight, he could still count it as morning.

In a few more hours, they'd be on their way. They were still a day ahead of schedule, but he wanted to scout out the most secure hiding place near the falls. Maybe they'd get lucky and Moss would be there a day early as well. Except for the landmine episode, the whole trip had gone smoother than he dreamed possible.

Of course, there was the problem of two incompatible people having the hots for each other, but that attraction would fade once they made it back to their own separate lives.

Callie would realize just how little she needed to be paired with a fuck-up like him. And he'd remember what little use he had for shrinks.

Yeah. Sanity would return soon enough. The faster they got out of this country, the better for both of them. His stomach churned at the thought, but that too would go away. Eventually.

He chanced a peek at her. Curled on her side with one hand tucked beneath her cheek and the other curved protectively over the swell of her belly, she was gorgeous. Hell, she looked like an angel.

And as much as he'd just lectured himself, he wanted nothing more than to stretch himself alongside her and wake her with soft, seductive kisses. To listen to her low sighs as she responded.

He took a quick step back when he realized he wanted more than just that. Wanted more than just one morning. He wanted to wake up beside her every single day.

He grabbed the back of the chair and tried to weather the sudden avalanche crashing down on top of him.

Holy Mother of God. He loved her.

Impossible.

You kill people for a living. She saves them. She's a mind melder. And you're defective merchandise. How long before she sees the truth?

As if she'd indeed read his mind, her eyelids parted and homed in on him, catching him mid-stare. His face heated, but he stood his ground and pretended everything was fine, when in reality the world as he'd known it was exploding… his heart pounding within his chest.

"What time is it?" she asked, her voice tumbled-from-bed sexy.

"Early. Go back to sleep for another couple of hours."

She yawned. "Why are you up, then?"

Good question. He should have stayed pretzled in the chair where he couldn't think past his physical discomfort. "Just stretching."

Callie's chest rose and fell in a deep sigh. "Are we going to the falls today?"

"Yeah. I want to see the lay of the land."

"But we're not leaving for another couple of hours, right?"

He hesitated, his mind still grappling with other issues. "No."

She patted the bed. "Then come lie down for a while." Nodding at his white-fisted knuckles, she went on, "I know that chair can't be comfortable. I told you the bed was more than big enough."

He gritted his teeth. "It's a *twin* bed." That fact had been his salvation. The perfect excuse. Fat lot of good it had done him. Maybe he should have jumped her bones after all. Now here he was getting all mushy and sentimental, when he needed to think rationally.

"I bet we can both fit." Her lips curved. "Or are you just chicken?"

Bingo!

She scooted closer to the edge and patted the area behind her. "See? Look at all this room. Even a big guy like you can fit."

When he didn't move, she frowned. "What's wrong?"

He shook his head. What the hell was he doing? How had this situation—and his life—gotten so completely screwed up?

"I promise not to try anything." She blinked at him. "Unless you want me to."

"Callie, don't." His voice came out strangled. He looked for an escape route and found nothing but gnawing need.

She held out her hand. "It's okay. Just come to bed."

"I can't."

"Why not?"

His laugh was the ugly grating of rusty hinges. "You want the truth?"

She nodded.

"Because I don't trust myself. Hell, Callie, you shouldn't trust me, either."

"But I do. I have from the very beginning, even when my brain told me not to." Her hand remained extended. "And I want you to lie beside me. It'll be all right. I promise."

Too late. It wasn't all right. And Cole wasn't exactly sure how to turn back the hands of time.

But as he stared at warm brown eyes that seemed to beckon him nearer, he took a step forward. And another. Until his hand was in hers and he was sitting on the edge of the bed.

And before he knew what hit him, his mouth was on hers, drowning in her scent, reveling in the soft skin of her shoulder, in the silky fall of her hair.

He couldn't get enough of her, and Callie welcomed him in, folding him close until all that existed was her…and the desperate rise and fall of the mattress beneath them. And then, finally…Cole—the man trapped inside an eternally restless soul—slept.

MOSS MADE IT TO THE FALLS just before dawn and crouched in the shadows, trying to shake off the horror of the events that transpired while he'd slept.

He'd known the rebels were in town. Why hadn't he kept an eye on them?

His stomach muscles, held tight with anger for so long, spasmed in protest, forcing him to ease up the pressure.

He didn't go as easy on his mind, however. And hell, if he hadn't lived up to his name tonight. A rolling stone gathers no moss? He'd gathered plenty while sleeping. By the time he reacted, it'd been too late to do anything. And an innocent man had died, and the woman…the woman…

After quietly calling down to the desk and telling the concierge to send a doctor, Moss had covered her with a bath towel and slid her as gently as he could to the far corner of the bed. There he'd waited—holding her hand and muttering whatever words of comfort came to mind. Time and time again, he'd brushed strands of hair off her bruised face while she cried, had sponged the worst of her abrasions with a damp cloth. All the while his gut burned with helpless rage.

When the doctor finally arrived, the man's face had held

the stoic patience that came from years of seeing the same types of atrocities during the country's civil war.

Moss's fury built as he listened to the powerful churning of the waterfalls in the background. It echoed everything he felt. He wanted to act…now, to pummel whoever had hurt the woman, but the desire would do him no good. Even if he succeeded in killing the bastard, someone else would rise up to take his place.

As long as there were crazed barbarians walking the earth, there would be rape and torture and murder. They were facts of life. But that didn't mean Moss should just roll over, smile and pretend they didn't bother him.

Hell no. That's why he'd gone into Special Forces in the first place. To try to right wrongs. To make a difference.

At the moment, that meant doing everything he could to thwart the rebel's ultimate goal of killing Dr. Nascimento. If he could do that and get her and Cole out of Angola, he'd consider this mission a success.

Continuing to stake out the waterfall was his best bet. If Cole was in Malanje, he'd eventually turn up here. His friend wouldn't bury his head in the sand and wait for help to come to him. He'd go out and grab it by the throat and wrestle it to the ground. It was both Cole's strength and his weakness. In this case, Moss figured it would land on the strength side of the equation. Thinking fast and changing directions like a jack-rabbit could only help.

In fact, if the good doctor had to be rescued by anyone, she couldn't have done any better than Cole.

He hunkered down and waited. Maybe, just maybe, this would be his lucky day. He thought of the woman in the hotel room and closed his eyes, drawing in a quick breath. No. A lucky day would be making sure the bastard behind her ordeal never harmed another living soul.

CALLIE SNUGGLED CLOSER to the warm body next to her, then opened her eyes. Cole was still asleep, while sunlight poured full-force through a crack in the draperies. She'd woken up before him. A first.

A moment's worth of panic hit her, before her system settled back down. He was exhausted. Ever since they'd taken off from Luanda, he'd gone to sleep after her and woken before her. The human body could only take so much abuse before it finally shut down.

Still, she listened to the sound of his breathing and sighed in relief. Slow and even. She knew she should wake him, knew he'd be anxious for them to be on their way, but couldn't bring herself to.

She needed a few more minutes to let reality sink in.

Her bladder twinged, reminding her that reality was what had woken her in the first place. The baby was pressed in just the wrong place.

She slid her hands over the small bulge, tears coming to her eyes. No. The baby wasn't pressed in the wrong place. He was in the perfect place. And her sister would never have a chance to know him. Would never get to hold him, to breathe in his baby scent. The last thing Callie wanted to do was give him up, especially now. But she would. Gary wanted this baby as much as Sara had. He'd treasure Micah.

But the next baby...

Her glance went to Cole, and she bit her lip. No, he wasn't in the running to be daddy to her babies. He'd slept with her, but she was the one who'd kept pushing for it, even when it was obvious he hadn't wanted to. Like this morning.

Her face heated in embarrassment. Once this trip was over, she was history. She'd just been a warm body to pass the nights.

Why had she insisted, even when he hesitated?

Working off stress. Proving that you're still alive after a traumatic experience.

She knew all the medical mumbo jumbo, but it didn't diminish the tiny leap her stomach took each time he whispered her name. The way her body tightened in anticipation when her gaze strayed to his firm lips.

Oh God, Callie. What have you gotten yourself into?

Nothing good. She was infatuated. With his strength, his quick thinking, his unfailing bravery. And ultimately, his sacrifice.

So very different from her stepfather, and yet they'd been trained by the same military. One man had become a monster, the other a hero. How could that be?

One of the mysteries of the human spirit that even psychology couldn't unravel.

Another mystery was how she was going to extricate herself from his arms without disturbing him. Better not to try. She should just wake him up and be done with it. They were both adults. They'd handled this particular situation before.

Okay…so their previous "handlings" had been pretty disastrous affairs. But the third time was a charm, right?

Right.

Threading her fingers through his, she kissed his cheek. "Cole?"

Lids parted and warm chocolaty eyes regarded her for a long moment, a tiny frown appearing.

Great, he didn't even remember who she was. Then he jerked upright in the bed, but their twined fingers reined him in before he could spring completely away.

She forced a smile. "Hey, sleepyhead."

He glanced at her, and then at their joined hands. "What time is it?"

"I don't know. I lost my watch, remember?" She tilted her head to read his. "It's just after nine."

He blinked a couple of times as if trying to come to his senses. "Dammit, I wanted to be out of here long before now." He shook her fingers loose and climbed out of bed.

She'd been right. He couldn't wait to get away from her.

"I need to use the restroom." She pulled the sheet up to cover herself. "Would you mind turning your back for a minute?"

His smile was unamused. "Isn't it a little late for that?"

No. Not when the man who'd made her feel so special hours earlier, now looked at her as if she were a recent escapee from a leper colony.

She wasn't in the mood for arguing. If he wanted to stand there and gawk at her, then let him.

Callie threw back the covers and stood in front of him, her chin tilted in defiance. When he swallowed and muttered a choice curse word before turning away, she should have felt at least a twinge of triumph. She didn't. All she felt was disgust for her childish behavior. She might as well have stuck her tongue out and said, "So there."

Gathering her clothes, she made her way to the bathroom, but couldn't resist glancing back one last time. He'd walked to the window, his back ramrod stiff. If he was ill at ease with his own nakedness, she couldn't tell. He was a soldier.

And she didn't care, she told herself. She might have given him her body, but that didn't mean she was going to throw her heart at him as well.

Too late, her mind whispered.

She slammed the bathroom door. "It's *not* too late. You'll see."

Another day or two and she'd be back in the States, back at her practice and back in her own familiar environment—where she belonged. She probably wouldn't maintain contact with Cole. There'd be no reason to. He'd just as soon put this episode behind him, like she would.

She used the restroom, took a quick shower then pulled her clothes on, telling herself she was looking forward to getting her life back on an even kilter. Each day brought her one step closer to that goal. She pulled a face. And each day would take her one step farther from Cole.

Why did she have to turn everything into a tragedy?

Think positive thoughts, Callie.

Sucking in a deep breath, she tried again. She'd carried out her sister's deepest wish to have a child. That was something to celebrate. She smiled. That was better.

Yes. In another five months she'd give birth to Micah Cole Parker and would place him in Gary's loving arms. That would be that. Everything would return to normal.

The pitted bathroom mirror reflected a pale, unhappy face. She forced a smile. Cheerful thoughts, she reminded herself.

Yes, everything would return to normal, and Callie would be absolutely, positively...

Alone.

COLE WAS AWARE OF CALLIE'S silence as they rode to the falls in one of the dilapidated local taxis. But he wasn't going to do anything about it.

This silence was no different than the oppressive stillness he'd endured over breakfast, where only the utensils spoke and mouths had clamped down on any sound other than chewing. The only time she'd said anything had been when he tried to pour her a cup of coffee. She'd held up a hand, her nose crinkling in something akin to disgust. "Don't."

When he'd looked at her quizzically, she murmured. "I don't like coffee."

The steady quiet was a good thing at this juncture, though. It was better than the rattling vibrations of gunfire and explosions they'd encountered in Luanda.

He was surprised. They'd made it this whole trip without any kind of real rebel intervention. At each village, he'd expected to be ambushed. With each bend of the railroad tracks, he'd expected to encounter a gun-wielding madman. Instead, they'd been met by silence.

Cole leaned back and stared out the window into the wooded surroundings.

So life was good. Just because Callie had stalked off to the bathroom like the injured party from one of those somebody-done-somebody-wrong songs wasn't his problem.

Keep telling yourself that, shithead. Maybe someday you'll believe it.

The falls had to be just ahead. Wisps of mist rose like smoke rings, and a low roar vibrated off his eardrums.

"How much farther?" he asked the driver, a private security guard the hotel had hired at his request. In order to avoid alarming Callie or drawing attention to the fact that they weren't normal tourists, Cole had asked the man to come dressed in street clothes. To complete the look, the guard had rented a taxi from a local cabby.

"Not far. Maybe a kilometer."

He nodded and had just turned his head to look at Callie, when a quick metallic glint caught his eye.

"Get down," he yelled. He dragged Callie flat against the seat and glanced up to make sure the driver had heard his warning. He had. The gun the man had tucked in his waistband was now on the front seat of the car.

The guard was still driving, but he'd ducked his head so low, he was peering at the road from between the spokes of the steering wheel. "What is it?"

"I saw something. Stop. Let me out."

"What?" the driver and Callie said in unison.

"You are crazy, *senhor*. There could be bandits. I will go with you."

Cole had ruminated too soon about the lack of trouble. He knew from Pedro's death that the rebels had probably discovered where they were headed. They were here. In the woods.

"Just stop the car and let me out," he repeated.

The guard pulled over to the side of the road, muttering in Portuguese, his gun now in hand.

"Cole, what is it?"

"I don't know."

"I'm going with you."

"No. I need to make sure no one's following us." He pulled out a large bill and handed it to the driver. "Take her the rest of the way to the falls and wait. If something looks suspicious when you get there, take her back to the hotel and accompany her to her room. Stay with her, no matter what."

"What about you, *senhor?*" the guard asked.

"I'll meet you at the falls. If you're not there, I'll catch a ride or hike back. But don't let the lady out of your sight."

The driver nodded, scanning the sides of the road. Cole hadn't seen any other vehicles up to this point, but that didn't mean anything. There could still be rebels in the woods. He wanted to make sure they were in the clear, before he let Callie out in the open.

"Cole, please don't do this. Let's stay together." Her brown eyes pleaded with him.

He had to force himself not to cave. The rebels would be expecting her to stick by his side. He needed to do the opposite. The hotel had assured him the security guard knew his stuff—he'd been in his country's military. "It'll be okay. I'll meet you up on the hill."

She sat up. "I'm sorry about this morning."

"This morning?"

"For forcing you to do something you didn't want."

He blinked for a second before he realized what she was talking about. When he did, remorse spurted through his veins, and he couldn't let her leave without setting the record straight.

Leaning down, he whispered in her ear. "I did want to, Calista. Hell, I still do." He paused, searching for the right words. Failing, he settled for something trite. "Wait for me, okay?"

Tears brimmed in her eyes, and she kissed him on the lips. "We'll both be waiting for you."

He shut his eyes for a quick second before meeting the driver's glance in the rearview mirror. "As soon as I get out of the car, start moving. And whatever you do, keep her safe."

"*Sim, senhor.* I'll guard her with my life."

Cole jumped from the vehicle and sprinted for the nearest tree, turning just as the taxi spit gravel as it sped on its way to the falls.

FROM THE OPPOSITE SIDE of the road, Moss—flat on his belly with his gun cocked and ready—had watched the taxi pull to a halt a couple hundred yards ahead of him. All he could see was the driver's head tucked low in front. Who the hell was that? Another rebel? He'd seen several jeeps go past about two hours earlier.

The appearance of the military-style vehicles made him decide to pull back about a kilometer from the falls and wait. He had to intercept Cole somehow before he walked into what could be a trap.

He'd strained his eyes at the taxi, but hadn't spotted any passengers. Strange. Maybe the driver was picking someone up?

The vehicle had stayed parked on the side of the road for about a minute-and-a-half then sped on its way, again heading straight for the falls.

Moss had a bad feeling. Why the lone taxi?

Could he be carrying a sightseer?

If so, where was the tourist? Stuffed in the trunk? With the price of gas the way it was, he couldn't see a hand-to-mouth taxi driver taking an afternoon off for a pleasure drive.

He stared ahead, watching the vehicle until it pulled out of sight. Should he go after it? Or hold his ground?

He'd wait until the driver came back. He could always flag it down and see what the hell was going on.

Cole was an early riser. If they were coming to the falls today, he would have expected them first thing. He checked his watch. Almost noon. Maybe he should just call it a day and come back tomorrow.

Except he didn't want to risk it. If Cole came while the rebels were still at the top and he couldn't warn him…

The grisly image of the couple in the hotel room came to mind. No. He'd wait, if he had to stay in this position until midnight tomorrow. Cole said he'd be here. And his friend hadn't reneged on a promise yet.

Sitting up, he retied one of his boots. Before he could finish, the sharp click of a gun came from behind him, along with the ominous press of metal to the back of his skull.

He put his hands up.

"*Vire, senhor. Devagar,*" said the voice.

Moss blinked. The Portuguese words had a definite twang to them. He smiled and scrubbed his hands over his face. "I told you not to stand me up, you bastard." He turned around, slowly…just like Cole had demanded. "Now, I'd appreciate it if you'd get your damn gun outta my face."

"Goddammit, Moss, what the hell are you doing here?"

"Meeting you. Like I said I would."

"That date was for tomorrow."

"You always did jump the gun, you S.O.B. Why should this time be any different?"

Cole lowered his weapon, and Moss stood, clapping him on the back. "I'm glad as hell to see you. Markesan's in the mood to kick someone's ass from here to Australia, and I didn't want it to be mine."

"So he didn't order you to abort the mission." Cole's face was a study in relief. Moss almost hated to spill the news.

"He did."

Cole's eyes closed for a second. "Let me guess. On the president's order."

"You know?"

He nodded. "Callie called her brother-in-law, Senator Parker"

"You're shitting me. When?"

"Yesterday. I have a feeling that's part of what this is all about."

"What the hell are you talking about?"

"It's too complicated to explain right now. Let's go get Callie and you can fill me in on what our next move is."

Moss's jaws froze and he had to force them apart. He'd assumed the doctor was waiting in the brush somewhere behind them awaiting Cole's signal. "You mean she's not with you?"

"No, she's on her way up to the falls in a taxi. Why?"

"The taxi that just left?"

Cole's eyes narrowed. "Yes. What's wrong?"

"Shit! She's heading right for the rebels."

"What?" His friend's voice rose to a shout.

"They're there, Cole. At the top of the falls."

COLE'S FEET WERE MOVING, but his brain for once was stuck in quicksand, frozen in one spot…on one person.

Callie.

He tore through the brush, ignoring the thorny vines grabbing at his shirt, tearing at his flesh. All he could think about were Callie's parting words. *We'll both be waiting.*

Following close behind him was Moss, who for once hadn't insisted on stopping to draw up a game plan. They'd both plunged into action at the same time. And for Cole, the strangled look on his friend's face had said it all.

"You're about two hundred yards out," Moss panted. "Don't crash into the open until we know what we're up against."

"Right." Except if Cole caught anyone putting a hand on Callie, he wasn't waiting around for permission to go in. He was going to kill someone.

The sound of the waterfall grew in steady increments. By the time Cole saw light coming from the tree line ahead, the sound was a relentless roar, drowning out everything in its path. He couldn't hear a thing, not even his own voice as he tried to shout something to Moss. When he got to the last portion of brush, he stopped.

Moss signaled for them to split into two different directions, Cole taking the flank. Before he had a chance to argue, Moss was gone. Fists clenched, he moved sideways until he could see through the trees.

He caught sight of the cab and relief almost brought him to his knees. He placed his hands on his thighs and struggled to catch his breath, staring at the vehicle. The windows were rolled up tight against intruders. He could see the guard sitting in the driver's seat, but there were no signs of any other vehicles…or rebels. Moss had been wrong. They'd either left or were in a different spot. Callie was safe.

Regardless of how serene the tableau appeared, he scoped the perimeter, checking the trees for snipers. Nothing. He frowned when he spotted Moss heading for the taxi without him.

Pushing through the last of the brush, he made it into the open and strode toward the vehicle. The roar of the falls was still deafening, making him uneasy. He wouldn't be able to hear the approach of other vehicles. The sooner they got Callie out, the better.

Moss ducked his head and looked inside the front seat. The driver didn't move.

Cole moved faster when his friend sidestepped, cupping his hands to peer into the backseat.

Something was wrong. His heart started pumping out danger signals.

Moss straightened up in a rush and came toward him, holding his hands out.

"What the hell's wrong?" His voice was immediately swallowed by the falls.

Moss's mouth moved, but Cole heard nothing his friend said. A hand came out to grip his arm, and Cole shoved him hard enough to send him staggering backward. He reached the taxi just before Moss.

The backseat was empty, save a dark spatter against the cream colored upholstery. His pounding heart stuttered then raced to life as he looked at the huge wet area on the back of the driver's head.

The man still didn't move.

No. It couldn't be.

But it was. When he moved to the front window, the neat round bullet hole in the center of the driver's forehead explained everything. And pinned to the man's chest with a pearl-handled hunting knife, was the Kwanza note Cole had paid for Callie's safety.

The money had been useless.

The guard was dead.

And Callie was gone.

TWENTY-ONE

CALLIE'S LIDS FLUTTERED open. Woozy and nauseous, she struggled to get her bearings, but she couldn't seem to focus on anything other than the enveloping darkness. She tried to put a hand to her head, but her limbs—like her eyes—wouldn't cooperate.

What was going on? Her lips were parched, so she licked them. At least her tongue still worked…but what was that strange taste? Almost like…

Chloroform. She'd been drugged.

She blinked and her memory came rushing back. The taxi driver was dead, and she was… Fear raced through her. She was in a chair, her arms and legs tied in place. She was blindfolded. But there was a familiar scent nearby. She tried to place it.

The baby! Had the drug harmed him? *Please, no.*

Shoving down the rising sense of panic, she shook her head and forced her mind to function.

A low voice purred through the silence. "Dr. Calista Nascimento. We meet at last."

The words came from behind her. No. From all around her. "Although it does sadden me that you've kept me waiting for so long. Surely you grew tired of your other escort after such an extended period of time. But you needn't worry, he won't stand between us any longer."

Was he talking about Cole? Had he done something to him as well as to the cab driver? The nausea grew in a wave, and she had to clench her teeth together to hold back the tide.

She drew a long shaky breath, hoping to clear her fuzzy thoughts. The speaker was Angolan, of that she was sure, even though he was speaking English. Despite his accent, his words were clear. And they chilled her to the bone.

"Who...are you?" Her words slurred together, probably from the drug.

"Surely you know who I am. I'm a long-time admirer, Doctor."

"I don't understand."

"No? I'm surprised you were not able to figure it out by now."

"How do you know me?" She moved her head in an attempt to locate the origin of the voice.

"We have a mutual acquaintance. Someone very close to both of us. Someone very close to your poor dead sister."

Callie's heart lurched. "My s-sister?"

"Yes, Sara Parker, right? A beautiful woman. Such a shame that she was cut down in the...how do you say it? In the prime of her life, yes?"

Anger swept over her, but she forced it back.

Don't let him control the conversation.

She took another deep breath and forced the gears in her brain to start turning. "I'm almost positive I've never met you, *senhor*. What's your name?"

His sudden laugh filled the room, booming much louder than a normal voice. Like it was amplified. The sound sent cold fingers tripping down her spine.

"You will not recognize my name. Not yet. But soon, very soon, the entire world will know of me."

Why? Was he planning some kind of 9/11 attack? Her pulse jumped, and she tensed, praying the sudden shot of adrenaline didn't send her into a mindless state of panic. No matter how she terrified she was on the inside, though, she needed to appear empathetic, make him believe she was on his side.

"Are you a freedom fighter?" she asked.

"Yes, in a sense." He seemed pleasantly surprised, but it could just be a trick.

As hard as it was for her to say the words, she needed to find out everything she could. "How can I help you meet your goals?"

"Very magnanimous of you to offer, Dr. Nascimento. I'm delighted. You can help my cause a great deal." A beat went by. "In a couple of hours we'll be receiving a phone call. Someone is very interested in your well-being. I think you'll be happy to hear from him."

"Him?"

"The interested party."

Was he talking about President Bryson? If he'd been involved in her sister's death, then…

How could someone be so evil?

Callie took another deep breath. The familiar scent hit her nostrils again, bringing with it a strong jolt of recognition, but she still couldn't put her finger on why.

Focus. "How will my hearing this 'interested party's' voice help your cause?"

"You misunderstand me. I don't want you to simply listen. I'll want you to speak. But you will say only what I tell you to say. Understood?"

She was afraid to ask, but she needed to know. "The man I was traveling with. Is he okay?"

"I wouldn't know. He abandoned you. Left you for me to find."

Cole was alive. Thank God.

Just then, tiny butterfly wings brushed her abdomen, the touch so light she almost missed it. A double dose of relief swept through her system. The baby was okay.

The rebel went on. "But don't expect your friend to come for you. We're in the last place he would think to look."

"And where is that?"

"Why your very own hotel room, of course."

The hotel room! That's why something had seemed familiar. Cole's unique scent still saturated the air. But the kidnapper was right. Cole would be searching for her frantically, but he would never think to look in the room they'd vacated just this morning.

How had the kidnapper even known where they'd stayed? Unless he'd been watching them all along. But how? Cole was positive no one had followed them.

"How did you find our room, *senhor?*"

Another low chuckle. "That was quite easy, Doctor. People are always willing to cooperate…with the right motivation."

Pedro's battered face flashed through her mind. Was that the kind of motivation he'd used? On how many people?

She purposely filled her lungs, willing Cole's essence to bolster her courage, which was flagging. "You're very adept at motivating people, then."

"Adept." He paused for a few seconds and Callie held her breath. Had she made him angry?

But then his voice came back. "Yes, I've been told I have the *pro-pen-sity* of motivation."

Callie frowned. He'd drawn out the word propensity in an odd kind of way and his usage was a bit off. Was he trying to impress her with his vocabulary? Maybe, but why?

"I'm sure you have a propensity for a lot of things, *senhor.*" Not the least of which was killing. Had this man played a personal role in her sister's death? Did she dare broach the subject?

She sent up a quick prayer. *Cole, please feel me. I'm in our room. The place we touched. Made love. The place where I realized I loved you.*

Loved him?

She searched her heart. It was there, chiming loudly in her ear. How could she have missed it?

And she'd never gotten a chance to tell him. Moisture pricked the back of her eyes. She had to get out of this. Had to find a way to let Cole know.

She made a decision. "I'll talk to your contact, *senhor,* if you'll let me get a message to my companion."

"You are not in a position to bargain, Doctor." His voice sharpened, telling her she did indeed have some kind of leverage or he would have dismissed her demand outright.

"You've already made sure he won't find me, so what's the harm?"

"*I* decide what's harmful and what's not."

He was becoming agitated. Not a good sign. Better to just back off and head in another direction. He seemed to revel in making sure she knew just how in control of the situation he was.

She blinked and realized something she should have thought of from the very beginning. He'd talked about the world soon knowing who he was. The classic sign of a narcissistic personality…a megalomaniac. Who did that kind of person love above all else?

Himself.

She opened her mouth and prayed she was making the right decision. "*Senhor,* you have a message for the world. A message you feel is of great importance. What is it you want people to know?"

GENERAL RICHARD MARKESAN strode through the rotunda of the Russell Building, his gaze taking in the statue of its namesake against one of the majestic columns. He wasn't looking forward to this particular meeting.

He had a feeling he knew why Senator Parker wanted to

speak with him in private, but hadn't decided what, if anything, to tell the man. It could go either way. Besides, Moss wasn't on a condoned mission. He was in Angola as a private citizen. As such, Markesan felt no compunction to share that fact with anyone. What his men did with their private time was no one's business as long as it didn't break any laws.

The senator's intern stood as soon as he entered the office. She lifted her hand to run her fingers through her blond hair, drawing his attention to the single button that was undone at her stomach. "He's waiting for you."

"Thank you." Without knocking, he turned the handle and pushed the door open.

Senator Parker stood in front of an ornate mirror, straightening his tie. Markesan had never liked the polished façade that most politicians seemed to display to the world. He guessed it was necessary to be attractive to get elected. Where Markesan came from, life was more than a pretty face. In fact, it was sometimes downright ugly. He personally preferred seeing the nitty-gritty truth to a bunch of superficial fluff.

"General Markesan, how nice of you to pay me a visit."

The man's genteel southern accent was as smooth and flawless as his appearance. It made Markesan squirm inside. He didn't like dealing with these pretty boys up on the Hill.

"You asked to see *me*, sir, remember?"

"Why of course I do, General."

He came forward with his hand outstretched and Markesan shook it. The man's firm grip made him feel a little more at ease.

The senator motioned to a chair. "Have a seat, General."

While Markesan lowered himself into one of the dark leather wing chairs flanking the desk, Senator Parker moved to his own spot behind the imposing surface.

"What can I do for you, Senator?"

Parker leaned forward and rested his elbows on his desk, regarding Markesan with an assessing stare. "Did the president tell you I've been to see him?"

"No, I haven't spoken with him in a couple of days." An overturned pencil cup on the corner of the large desktop caught his attention. A square wooden affair, it sported a decoupaged photo of the senator with his arm around a beautiful woman. His deceased wife, no doubt.

"I received a phone call from Callie."

"Who?"

"My sister-in-law. She's alive. I went to the president to ask for his help in getting her out of Angola. He refused." One of the man's hands fisted on the desk's surface. "He's not willing to do a damned thing to get her out of there, Dick."

Markesan's teeth went on edge. The senator's attempt to turn this into a cozy little chat by shortening his name was way off base. His men knew how much he hated that particular moniker. But it didn't pay to make men like Senator Parker angry by pointing out the lapse.

He decided to play it safe. "Exactly how can I help?"

"Did you know that Callie…my sister-in-law agreed to be a surrogate for Sara's and my child? She's almost four months pregnant."

He was taken aback. "No, I wasn't aware of that."

The senator looked at the pencil cup and frowned, reaching over to right the object and to slip several pre-sharpened pencils back inside. He glanced back at Markesan. "I still haven't fully come to grips with Sara's death—that she's not just going to walk through our front door. The thought of losing our child as well…" He shuddered. "I just can't face it, Dick."

The raw grief etched on the man's face earned forgiveness for the second lapse with Markesan's name. "I'm sorry, Senator."

"The president refuses to go in and get her out."

"I know. He ordered the mission aborted."

"But he was willing to help everyone else in the embassy get out safely." Senator Parker's voice held bitter anger. "It's just Callie he's willing to leave behind."

What did Parker want from him? It was on the tip of his tongue to tell him about Moss's trip—about Cole—but something held him back. "Again, I'm sorry, Senator. I'm not sure how I can help."

Parker leaned forward. "You've got a man in there too, don't you? Callie said there was a soldier with her. What are the chances of him getting her out alive?"

"I don't know," he answered truthfully. "I haven't heard from him since the embassy incident."

"But surely you're not just going to leave him there to be killed. I thought the military's motto was 'no man left behind.'"

"Scalini is special ops. He'll get her out if he can." Markesan paused, taking his time to assess the man in front of him. "Other than that, my hands are tied. I can't go against the president's orders."

Parker's face reddened and his lips thinned. "I want you to listen to something." He pulled out a tape recorder from a desk drawer and pressed a button.

President Bryson's voice came from the speaker.

Markesan was floored. The senator had taped a private conversation with—no, he thought as the voices increased in volume—a private *argument* between himself and the President of the United States. What had possessed him?

As he listened, he agreed with Moss's initial assessment. It certainly appeared the president was complicit in something, but the tape never actually made those suspicions concrete. Although the plane crash involving Senator Parker's wife *was* mentioned, the president did seem nervous as hell when he responded that it had been deemed an accident.

The senator was watching him as the tape rolled on. The longer it went, the worse it sounded for the president.

It also cemented his decision to say nothing about Moss's trip. If this man had taped a conversation with a U.S. president, what else was he capable of? Besides, there was no guarantee Moss would be successful. He didn't want to get Parker's hopes up just to have them come crashing back down.

The tape ended and the senator sat back, perusing his face. "So, what do you think?"

"What am I supposed to think?"

The man frowned. "Doesn't it sound like the president played a role in Sara's death? If it comes out that he did… I won't be responsible for my actions." He shook his head. "I think he's hoping Sara's loss will keep me out of the presidential race next year. And if I lose the baby… Well, he's right. I might not be able to run."

Did this man even realize how crazy the idea sounded? "Even if that…suggestion is possible, why single you out? Why not every other possible candidate?"

"He knows I'm the only one with a real shot at the nomination."

Parker leaned back in his chair and laced his fingers, putting them behind his head. Something about the senator's lazy, relaxed movements struck Markesan as odd. Where was the urgency? The outrage over the president's supposed betrayal? Instead, Parker appeared at ease with the world—drained of any hint of nervous tension. Almost like a soldier coming off a lengthy deployment.

The hair on the back of Markesan's neck came to sudden attention, and acid rolled like water from a broken dam into his stomach. His mind went from the pencil cup to the unfastened button on the intern's shirt. In that moment, his decision was made.

"I don't know what to tell you, Senator." He measured his words with care. "The tape sounds suspicious, I agree. Maybe even enough to warrant an independent investigation, if you pushed the issue. But again, unless he's impeached, I can't go against a direct order from my commander-in-chief."

Parker's head tilted to the right and his face cleared for a second. He came forward in his chair. "Impeached? You think there's enough here to warrant bringing it before congress? There's only a year left until the elections." He fingered his chin as if in deep thought. "It would take a massive breach of trust on the president's part to get Congress to go for it."

Markesan frowned. "I'm not suggesting you motion to have him impeached. I'm just giving you my position as a member of the U.S armed forces."

"I see." Parker's mouth twisted. "I'd hoped for a little more support from our country's military, but I can't just let this go. I have to do everything in my power to get Callie and the baby out alive."

He paused for a few beats, then sat higher in his chair. "Even if it means impeaching the President of the United States."

TWENTY-TWO

COLE DROVE THE TAXI as fast as humanly possible on the dilapidated roads, at times almost sliding off the worst sections. The dead guard lay in the back, a towel draped over his face. There'd been no choice. Neither he nor Moss would leave the man behind. Cole prayed that no one stopped them along the way to check the vehicle.

"I shouldn't have left her."

Moss, his forearm braced against the frame of the open window, shook his head. "You couldn't have known."

A low-hanging branch slapped the windshield, and Cole flinched with a curse. "What the hell does that matter now? For all we know she could already be dead."

"If she were, we'd have found her body or more blood. They wanted her alive." He hesitated. "I hope it's not because of…"

Cole glanced to the side. "Because of what?"

"Nothing."

"Don't bullshit me with half-finished thoughts, Moss."

"Your rebel friends found another couple they thought was you and Dr. Nascimento." He shook his head. "It was bad."

Cole swallowed. Did he really want to know? No. But the more information he had the better. "Tell me."

"The male—about your height and build—was shot three times in the chest, with one tap to the head. The woman was…" Again he stopped.

"Moss."

"The woman was beaten, sodomized and left for dead.

The bastard wrote on the wall with her blood. She said he'd called her Dr. Nascimento."

"Shit." Cole's fingers dug into the steering wheel at the thought of Callie suffering a similar fate. He had to shift away from the image before he broke down. "We've got to find her."

"They can't be more than a half hour ahead of us. An hour tops."

"Then we've got to narrow that head start."

"They're traveling in military-style jeeps. Let's see if anyone's spotted them."

He gave a harsh laugh. "Do you really expect someone to give you that kind of information? These rebels are known to kill anyone they regard as a traitor."

"I know just the person."

Within ten minutes, they'd pulled into the parking lot of a nicer hotel than he and Callie had stayed in. They parked the car in a concealed area, making sure to stay well away from any taxi stands.

Cole nodded at the building. "You know someone here?"

"No, but the woman I told you about was attacked here. The concierge couldn't stop it. I heard the shots and he gave me the room number, even when there were rebels sitting within feet of him."

"Let's hope he's still on duty." Cole's personality balked at stopping for anything, but it would do him no good to spin in circles. This was Moss's area of expertise. Slow, steady progress that brought results. Cole respected his friend enough to let him take the lead.

Walking through the doors, Moss immediately made for the desk. Cole followed, hoping this worked.

Leaning over the counter, his friend held out his hand to the man behind it. "Thank you for your help. Have you heard any word on the woman's condition?"

"She's still in the local hospital, but they expect her to recover. She asked about you, *senhor*."

Moss's eyes closed for a minute, then they reopened. "You're the reason she's alive, not me."

The man shook his head. "I saw her when the ambulance carried her away. She will never be the same."

Cole's heart thumped in his chest. If Callie were here, she'd know what to do. She'd be able to talk to the woman.

He blinked. Since when did he think shrinks could do anything beneficial?

Since he'd seen the caring way she'd dealt with him. She'd seen firsthand how messed up he was, and yet she'd wanted him.

He had to find her.

Stepping forward, he nudged his friend with his elbow to hurry him along. Moss tossed him a narrow-eyed glare that warned him to keep it to himself.

"Senhor," Moss said, "the men who attacked the woman may be in the process of hurting a friend of ours. Have they been back since the incident last night?"

"No, *senhor,* but another hotel manager called to warn me they were on the warpath, ransacking rooms."

Cole's hopes leaped. He jumped in. "A hotel here in Malanje?"

The man aimed a narrow-eyed glance at him and looked back at Moss. "He is a friend?"

"Yes, you can trust him."

"It is a hotel in the city, a few blocks from here. They came in jeeps. One of the party appeared sick, they carried him in with a remark about too much wine."

"Him?"

"That is the story the men gave."

"Are they still there?"

"The jeeps all left around a half hour ago. Tiago—the

other manager—and I are cousins. We look out for each other. I warned him not to cross the soldiers if they showed up."

"They've already left?"

"The jeeps left. Tiago is too afraid to go to the room and look. He said he heard a loud voice, like a god calling down thunder from heaven. The voice was talking to someone."

Moss frowned. "Did your cousin hear anyone else in the room besides this voice?"

The concierge glanced around the lobby. "He did not go close enough to hear. He was afraid someone would catch him."

"Which hotel?"

"The Galleria."

Cole's nerves shot to life. "Callie and I stayed there last night."

Moss turned to him. "Are you sure?"

The morning spent making love to her came rushing back, along with the pain of losing her. "I'm positive."

"What room did the voice come from, *senhor?* Do you know?" Moss asked.

The man shook his head. "I can call and find out if you'd like."

"Please."

By that time, Cole's hands were shaking so much that he could hardly think straight. If he had to fire his rifle, he'd have no chance in hell of making the shot.

The concierge dialed his phone and waited, looking nervously from one to the other. "*Eu preciso falar com Tiago... agora.*"

They all waited with bated breath.

The concierge put his hand over the receiver. "My cousin is not at the desk, they are looking for him."

Something didn't feel right. How much of a coincidence

was it that the rebels had chosen the very hotel he and Callie had stayed at?

A thought hit him. Unless the rebels knew where they'd been staying. But how was that possible? They'd killed one man and raped a woman, thinking they'd found them last night.

But their actions today said they realized their mistake and were setting out to correct it. That could only mean one thing.

At that moment, the concierge looked up and said what Cole had already deduced. "The voice came from room 328. The soldiers told my cousin they would check out of the room later today."

Cole nodded, his teeth clenched so hard he could barely speak. They didn't have time to waste. "I know right where the room is. It's the one Callie and I stayed in last night. I think he's going to kill her there."

"Oh shit," Moss said.

"What?"

"Dr. Nascimento's pregnant but not married, right?"

"She's a surrogate for her sister's baby. Why?"

Moss grabbed Cole's arm. "Remember I told you there was a word written in blood above the injured woman?"

Pressure began building in Cole's chest.

Before he could say anything else, Moss went on, "The word was *puta*. Portuguese for whore."

How much time had elapsed since she'd last heard the eerie voice? Thirty seconds? Thirty years?

Disoriented and deprived of sight, she couldn't keep track. She fisted and unfisted her hands in an effort to restore circulation. It didn't help. The restraints were too tight.

The rebel was deranged. He thought he was going to become the president of Angola with the help of the American government. It was absurd. President Bryson couldn't pull off something like that. Callie had asked for the identity of the person helping him, hoping her brother-in-law's suspicions were unfounded. But the madman just laughed, saying he wanted to surprise her.

She would be surprised, no matter who it was.

And her sister...

Her eyes watered. This same band of rebel thugs had tampered with her sister's plane, causing her death along with all the other passengers. Who ordered it? And why?

It didn't matter. Knowing her death was deliberate made losing her that much worse.

She sent up a silent prayer. Cole had to figure out where she was before it was too late. It wasn't just her life and the baby's which were at stake—although she desperately wanted to save Sara's child—she didn't want the Angolan people to suffer because of some egotistical maniac in her own country. But what motive could the president possibly have? To prevent Gary from running in the election? It was just too unbelievable to be true.

But these men would kill her. Of that she was certain.

She shifted on the hard wooden surface of the chair to ease the ache in her back. "Hey," she shouted. "I need to use the restroom."

Silence met her request.

In the distance, she heard a ringing sound. A phone?

She strained behind the blindfold, hoping to be able to discern at least whether it was day or night, but the thick cloth covered her eyes and nose completely, leaving no spaces for light to pass.

A creak came from her right...a door opening? Yes. It had to be, because someone was now speaking in accented English. The rebel from earlier?

The voice continued in low tones, but there was no response from the other party. So she was right. It had been a phone she'd heard a minute ago.

Rough hands yanked the blindfold from her head. Callie's pupils were flooded with so much light that they shrieked in agony, forcing her to shut them.

A voice close to her ear murmured, "Time for your big surprise, Dr. Nascimento. Are you ready?"

She blinked a couple of times before glancing around. The room was definitely the one she and Cole had shared. She spied the rumpled covers on the bed, and the memories threatened to drown her. Would she ever see him again?

She forced her attention to the man in front of her. His broad shoulders and rugged features were so different from the weasely figure she'd pictured in her mind. Thick black hair was slicked back from his forehead. A razor-thin scar ran along a high, defined cheekbone.

If she didn't know what the man was capable of, she might have found him attractive. Then she met his icy eyes and revised her opinion. Handsome…but lethal. His probing gaze dissected her the way a scientist's scalpel might explore a splayed lab rat. A tremor rippled through her, and she looked away.

His fingers gripped her chin, forcing her eyes back to his. "I have a script which I wish you to read, doctor. Recite it exactly as written, and you won't suffer. Veer from the words by so much as one syllable, and I will make sure we have a very special party. Just you and me."

He held up a photograph and smiled. "*This* kind of party."

Everything inside her warned her not to look, but her glance flashed to the photo before she could stop it. She gasped, bile rising in her throat in a huge searing wave.

Blood, death and…. Who was that poor woman?

Oh God, how could anyone do something so horrible?

"Do we have an agreement?" He untied her hands from

behind her back, showing her the gun in the waistband of his military-style fatigues.

Her desperate fingers itched to cover her abdomen and rub with gentle strokes, but she didn't dare draw his attention to the baby.

"What do you want me to read?" Her raw throat could barely croak out the words. She had to swallow several times before the nausea passed.

"I have the page here. You don't have time to rehearse. Afterward, I will permit you to use the facilities as you asked."

So he had heard her yelling earlier. Maybe she could still escape. Hope surged through her. *Yes. Cling to that thought.*

"Our guest is waiting. Are you ready?"

What choice did she have? She could only hope to delay the inevitable until Cole arrived. *If* he arrived. "Yes."

He held up a large notepad and the English words written on it made her eyes widen. Either this was a sick joke, or the man had some disgusting ulterior motive in mind. She tended to believe the latter.

"I'm ready," she said, her body beginning to quake as the hopelessness of her situation sank in.

The man picked up a handset from what looked like a black hard-shelled briefcase. "Are you still there, my friend? We've yet to make the final arrangements for payment, no?" He paused, and his eyes went to Callie with a smile. "Let me put my accountant on so she can walk you through the process, step by delicious step."

He pressed the phone to her ear and motioned for her to hold it. She tried, but her hand was still numb from the ropes, and the object slipped from her grasp, hitting the floor with a crack.

The man cursed in Portuguese, and then held it out to her once more. "Drop it again, and you will pay."

Curling her fingers around the handset, she willed them

to squeeze tight. When she was sure she wouldn't drop it, she shifted the phone to her ear and held it there, using her shoulder to help prop it.

The rebel knelt in front of her, the notebook in hand, and made a rolling motion. If her feet weren't tied to the legs of the chair, she could have kicked him in the throat.

Callie swallowed, before beginning to read, enunciating with care. "My name is Dr. Calista Nascimento, and I'm to instruct you on the final payment arrangements that will complete the transaction you agreed to."

"What is this, a joke? Callie? Callie, is that you?" The caller's voice came over the loudspeaker, filling the room just as her captor's had. Her stomach plummeted.

Gary.

Her free hand went to Sara's baby in a protective gesture. The madman in front of her noted her movement and gave a quick frown. He shook his head no, meaning she wasn't to deviate from the script. Her mind and her stomach were churning. This had to be a mistake.

A terrible, awful mistake.

She forced herself to continue. "The price has increased to twice the agreed upon amount, due to the mental anguish involved in apprehending me—"

"That bastard." Gary's harsh words spilled out, before he paused. When his voice came back, it was softer, the drawl firmly back in place. "You have to believe me, Callie. I had nothing to do with this."

But she didn't believe him, not this time.

Tears came to her eyes and sluiced down her cheeks. If she was right, Gary had killed her sister, his own wife. Despite his words to the contrary, she was sure he now planned to kill his own baby as well.

Why would he? Why?

She tuned out the horror and picked up where she left off.

"General Coelho needs the money deposited in his overseas account before the job can be brought to a successful conclusion."

"You believe me, right, Callie?" Her brother-in-law's voice cracked. "My baby. Is he all right? You didn't lose him, did you?"

Why was he bothering to pretend? She and Micah would both be dead soon enough. Just like he'd planned.

Maybe he never expected to be confronted with the evidence of his evil deeds. He thought she'd just disappear. Like Sara had.

Sara. Her sister had known something was wrong, but she never could've imagined her own husband would…

Callie's eyes burned. The fact that the bastard still referred to the baby in her womb as "his" struck her as obscene.

Her captor, in the meantime, had risen to his feet. He towered over her, staring at her midsection. Callie's fingers spread over the area. Why was he looking at her like that? Shaking the notebook, he motioned for her to continue, all the while staring at her with something between a sneer and disgust.

"If the m-money is not received by tomorrow morning, General Coelho will place me on a plane to Washington, where I will expose your plan to the world. Your aspirations for the p-presidency, as well as your career, will be finished, and you will be tried as the—" her voice dropped to almost a whisper, "—murderer you are. General Coelho has kept meticulous records of your conversations and each bank transfer. He knows you have a propensity for lying." She paused. The word *propensity* was underlined twice.

Gary's voice changed, thinned, until it was a pitiful wheedle, his charming southern drawl all but gone. "Callie, I'll get you out of there. We have several teams of troops on the ground right now. They're on their way. Just hang in there."

Liar. He'd told her the president had ordered the mission aborted—had emphasized that fact. He was the one who'd planted the idea that the president was involved.

That had been his plan all along.

To frame President Bryson. And she'd fallen for it. Just like everyone else would. They would believe a grief-stricken senator over an unpopular president. And no one would think sweet, gentle Gary Parker capable of killing his own wife and unborn child.

She longed again to demand he tell her why, but she didn't dare.

Her continued tears threatened to obliterate the letters in front of her. She blinked to clear her vision. "By eight o'clock tomorrow morning the money must be in the account. Don't be late."

Callie handed the phone back to the rebel. He took it, but held her stare for a long moment, then in a sudden gesture he spat, catching her on the left cheek. "*Puta!* You carry his child."

Horror washed over her as her forearm lifted to wipe away the spittle. He thought she was a prostitute. A whore, who'd given her body to her sister's husband.

Her voice hoarse, she whispered, "No, I'm a surrogate."

His hand cracked across her cheek with such force that her teeth rattled and her head hit the back of the chair. Her vision blacked out for a second.

She was going to die. Right now.

"Don't speak," he screamed.

Callie's foggy brain searched through the pain for a way to explain what surrogate meant in his language, but it was a word she'd never had to use while living in Brazil. She had no idea what the correct term was. All this man knew was that she was carrying Gary's baby.

And that made her a whore in his eyes.

He'd turned from her, his angry tones cracking through the phone's handset. Gary's voice no longer came over the loudspeaker, so he'd turned it off somehow. A low ugly laugh met her ears, but she tuned it out.

Gary's baby. She was carrying his child. A man capable of unspeakable evil.

The thought made her almost as ill as it seemed to make her captor. But the baby wasn't just Gary's. Half of Micah's genes came from his mother. His beautiful, big-hearted, loving mother. Surely that would override everything else. And he would carry Cole's name. A strong, honorable name.

If it was the last thing she did, Callie would make sure Gary never raised this child.

If she survived.

She didn't know whether her brother-in-law was willing to pay the extra money. But she evidently had until eight o'clock in the morning to find out. And to find some means of escape. Maybe if her captor let her go to the bathroom as he'd promised…

The rebel hung up the phone and stood with his back to her for several long seconds. When he turned around, his face was calmly resolute, his eyes empty black holes that lacked a soul.

Cole's words at their first meeting had been prophetic. She'd claimed you could appeal to anyone's humanity. She'd been so smugly sure of her position. Cole had disagreed. She could still hear his pronouncement in her head: *He had no humanity.*

Real fear swept over her, greater than anything she'd experienced in all her time in Angola. She didn't have until eight o'clock tomorrow morning. Her fate was going to be decided in the next several seconds.

The rebel's soft words confirmed her fears. "And now, my little *puta*…you and I have a party to attend."

TWENTY-THREE

MOSS AND COLE BURST INTO the lobby of the Galleria Hotel. Moss let his friend rush for the reception desk, while he paused to take in the surroundings.

The second his eyes landed on two seated individuals, an eerie sense of déjà vu gripped him. The rebels from the other hotel. Chipped-tooth wasn't with them.

As if the two goons shared a single brain cell, their eyes swiveled toward Moss, and a synchronized pause of two full beats went by before they both leaped to their feet.

He'd been made.

"Cole," he called, pulling his handgun just as the two men began a panicked grappling for their machine guns.

His friend was beside him in an instant, drawing a bead on one of the rebels, before either man had a chance to lift his gun. Moss took aim at the other one.

Moving a step closer, he kept his gun aimed and ready. "We can do this like civilized human beings, or we can shoot it out. I guarantee we'll win."

The rebel's eyes widened. The man evidently understood enough English to get the gist of the threat. He didn't dare look to see the other man's reaction. That was Cole's territory.

"Put your guns on the ground and we won't kill you," Moss continued. "My friend can put a bullet through the center of your friend's pupil. It's what he's trained for."

Out of the corner of his eye, he watched Cole shift his aim a millimeter to the right. "Which eye? Right or left?"

That rebel lowered his gun without a word and laid it on the ground, raising his hands and backing away.

"And you, my friend. What will your choice be? My aim's not nearly as good as my buddy's here, but I can still make a pretty big mess of your head. Either way, it's two guns against one, now."

The man shook his head. "The general will kill us if we let you pass."

Chipped-tooth. It had to be.

"Your choice, then. Die now. Or choose a safer profession, far from your boss's reach." Moss shook his head. "Although I don't think you'll have to worry about him much longer. If he hurts my friend's lady, he's a dead man."

The second rebel dropped his weapon as well. "We will leave then."

"Not until we get your general. Is the lady okay?"

"He ordered us from the room ten minutes ago. Like last time." The man's swallow was visible. "He doesn't like anyone to watch."

COLE HANDED HIS rifle to Moss. "Keep them here."

They traded guns, Cole taking Moss's pistol. Without another word, he sprinted past the desk. "They're in the room I reserved?"

"*Sim, senhor.* But you must hurry. The voice from the heavens has stopped talking."

"Stairs?"

"To your right."

Cole didn't need to be told twice. He wasn't waiting around for the elevator. Slamming through the doors two floors above him, he glanced down the hallway but saw nothing. Nor did he hear anything.

He swallowed and prayed for time.

The door was there, to the right. Shut tight. He hugged the wall and put his ear to the wooden surface. Nothing.

A scream and the sound of glass shattering forced him into motion. He backed up a step and rushed the door, planting his full weight against it. The barrier groaned but held. He backed up and tried again, but the damned thing wouldn't budge. He remembered the key.

"Shit!"

Cursing himself for his lapse, he found it in his pocket and slid it in the lock. Another scream met his ears.

Shoving through the door and pushing it wide, he held the gun in front of him as he entered, swinging the weapon in a wide arc.

Empty. The room was completely empty.

Where were they?

It was then Cole spotted the small speakers on the dresser. Some kind of panting came through them, like the sound of an animal…and then a pained squeal.

Taped? No, it was live.

Where the hell were the sounds coming from?

A chair in the center of the room. Ropes. *Oh hell.* A shirt lay crumpled on the ground. Callie's.

Nausea roiled through his gut. He had to find her.

Now he could hear her, talking in low tones to some unknown person. Pleading with him. The other party laughed, but said nothing.

Cole checked the bathroom, his pulse racing with dread. It was clear. The speakers were wireless. The range would be short…

It had to be a nearby room.

"Hang on, baby, I'm coming."

He rushed back into the hallway and worked his way down the row of rooms, listening at each door until he struck pay dirt on the third try.

Callie moaned and cried out.

Oh, fuck, fuck, fuck.

Cole backed up several steps and said a quick prayer before releasing every ounce of strength he possessed. Miraculously, the door gave way and he nearly fell into the room.

The general, his face dripping blood from a long ugly-looking gash, gripped Callie from the side. She was naked from the waist up. Her long hair was fisted in the man's hand, her head yanked back so far it looked like her slender neck would snap at any second.

Her eyes met his across the room. "Cole!"

The man's crazed gaze fastened on him as well. It was then that he noticed the shattered window behind the pair; the long lethal shard of glass gripped in Callie's hand, the bloody fingers, her swollen right eye…the man's unfastened pants.

Blind fury roared through his gut, and he aimed his gun at the man's forehead.

The rebel sneered. "Put it down, soldier boy, or I will kill your *puta* where she stands, along with the bastard child she carries inside."

Cole held his ground.

"Cole." Callie's voice came out as a sobbing plea. "Just let him do what he wants."

"No." The sound, low and feral burst, from his throat. She might say she was willing, but it was obvious from the slash on the rebel's face and the glass in her hand that she'd tried to stop him.

"Listen to your whore, soldier boy." The man drew a gun from behind Callie's back. Before Cole could move, he pressed the weapon to the bare skin of her pregnant abdomen, the barrel digging into her flesh.

She stared at him, her head still wrenched painfully back. A tear tumbled from her undamaged eye and tracked sideways, disappearing into her hairline.

As he watched, her trembling mouth formed three distinct words: I. Love. You.

Then, before anyone could react, she moved fast and Cole's world exploded in a roar of sound. Once from his gun and once from the rebel's. He stared in disbelief as, in slow motion, both Callie and her rebel captor went down.

CALLIE STRUGGLED TO sit up, pain shooting through her elbow.

Cole was beside her in an instant. "Are you hit?"

Her hands flew to her abdomen, her fingers running over it. A tiny reassuring flutter met her touch. She shut her eyes for a moment. "We're fine."

She glanced at the rebel beside her. "Is he…?"

"No. You moved so fast I was afraid of hitting you by mistake. I shifted my aim at the last second. He caught the shot in the shoulder."

Her heart was still thumping a million miles a minute and her whole body shook. But she was alive, when she'd expected to die. The rebel had planned on killing her no matter what.

She'd pulled free and smashed the window with a nearby lamp as he was wrestling with his zipper. She'd only gotten in one slash, before he'd screamed and overpowered her again. Just a few seconds later and…

Her eyes shut again, and Cole's arms went around her. "You're fine."

Callie leaned closer, his low voice soothing her trembling heart. "Thanks to you."

"You did most of it. You fought like a tiger." He glanced to the side and gave her a quick squeeze. "I'm going to leave you for just a minute to secure him, okay?"

She nodded, wrapping her arms around her middle to cover her breasts as Cole ripped the cord from the overturned lamp and shoved the rebel onto his side. The man groaned and shifted, but didn't open his eyes. Cole's movements were sure and quick as he looped the cord around the rebel's hands and fastened it tight.

He took hold of the bedsheet and started to pull it free, then stopped and stared at it. His eyes lifted to the wall. And he turned in a rush. "Did he…"

Shaking her head, she relieved his thoughts by opening her palm. "He cut my hand and made me write in blood on the wall."

She shuddered as the word *puta* stared down at her from above the bed. She'd tried to explain what a surrogate was, but her sister's killer had not wanted to listen, declaring her body polluted with adulterous seed.

Cole abandoned the sheet and brought the bedspread instead, wrapping it around her.

She glanced at the downed man. "The taxi driver tried to protect me. He killed him." Sorrow washed over her. Yet another victim of her brother-in-law's treachery. So much bloodshed.

"I know. We found him."

"We?"

"Moss is here. He's guarding the others in the lobby. I need to give him the all clear."

Making the call, he gave Moss an abbreviated version of events. He told him to tell the flunkies in the lobby that their leader was out of commission and unless they wanted the same thing to happen to them, they'd better get out of town.

He hung up, and then hunkered down in front of her, touching her cheek with a hand that wasn't quite steady. "You sure you're okay? The baby?"

"I think so. He's still moving. I just want to get out of here."

"Moss has probably already made the arrangements. We're going to get you home. And when we do, we'll go to my higher-up, General Markesan, and tell them what the president tried to—"

"No." Her head tipped back to look at him, still unable to fathom how close she'd come to death. Still not believing who'd given the order. "It wasn't the president."

"What?"

Her shoulders heaved and the acidy sting of bile washed up her throat in a rush. She swallowed hard. "It was Gary."

There was a long pause. "Your brother-in-law?"

She told him about having to read the script over the phone and the shock she'd felt when Gary's voice had come over the line. "He lied…said he was trying to get us out. The rebel said the money was on its way. That Gary agreed to pay it to avoid being discovered."

"Bastard. Why?"

She'd been asking herself that question ever since she heard his voice. "I don't know. But he was involved in Sara's death as well. The rebel said he tampered with her plane on Gary's orders."

"What motive could he possibly have? You're carrying his child, for God's sake."

"Maybe he thought by implicating the president he'd have an easy win in the election." She touched his arm, her throat still burning. "Imagine how the public would feel about a man who'd recently lost not only his wife, but his unborn child to terrorists. Wouldn't you elect him?"

Cole's laugh was strained. "Actually, I was planning to vote for the other guy, until he refused to send troops in to get you out. Now—" his hands went up, "—I have no idea who to vote for."

She pulled the bedspread tighter and offered a small smile. "Maybe you should consider running for office yourself."

"With my scatterbrain?" He sat next to her and looped

his arm around her shoulders, pulling her close. "I don't think so."

Callie smoothed the hair off his forehead, her fingers brushing the area just beneath his wound. "This scatterbrain has saved my life quite a few times already. And somehow even concocted a way to make snake look and taste like chicken."

At Cole's soft chuckle, she glanced at the rebel leader. "Will the police come for him?"

"I doubt it. There's still quite a bit of corruption in the various government agencies. I don't think the desk clerk is going to be calling them anytime soon."

"How did you find me?"

"The clerk of this hotel is the cousin of Moss's hotel clerk. Moss evidently made a good impression during his last hotel stay."

"Remind me to thank him."

He kissed her forehead. "You ready to go?"

The wheels in Callie's head had been turning for the last fifteen minutes or so. "I am, but first I want to make sure Gary is brought to justice for my sister's death."

"He will be. We'll go to the authorities—and General Markesan—and tell them what we know."

"I'm not sure that'll be enough."

He shrugged. "What else can we do?"

"I have an idea."

Cole tilted his head and studied her. "I'm all ears."

TWENTY-FOUR

José glared at the American pigs from across the room.
They were talking in subdued tones, daring to ignore him.
He'd tried in vain to free his arms and legs from the bindings,
but the slightest movement detonated pain in a fiery wave
and sent it shooting through his shoulder. He broke out in a
cold sweat just thinking about it. He was in the same chair
the *puta* had occupied earlier.

How much time had passed?

He lifted his chin. His men were probably planning to
liberate him even now. They would make these American
capitalists pay. And that whore…she would finally get what
was coming to her. His eyes crawled over her swollen stomach. He'd cut that demon seed out of her with his own hands.

The woman's gaze turned toward him in that moment.
She touched one of the soldier's arms and inched closer.
There was an intimacy between them that made raw fury
rise in his chest.

Was she spreading her legs for this one too?

José opened his mouth. "My men will come for me. They
will kill you." His voice came out as a croak, and he was
irritated at the slight quaver he sensed beneath the sound.
Raising his chin, he tried to outstare the man who had his
arm around the whore.

There was a cold hatred in the eyes that stared back at
him. A hatred that rivaled his own. He wondered why they
were holding him prisoner. Why hadn't they just killed him
or, as Americans were so prone to do, turned him over to the

police? He had contacts in most of the bigger departments. He'd be out by nightfall.

The woman separated herself from the soldier and moved toward him, stopping about two feet away. She spoke to him in cultured Portuguese. "Your men aren't coming. They ran as soon as they were given the chance."

"Liar. I do not speak to whores." He looked at the third person occupying the room, another soldier, and switched to English. "You! Come release me."

The woman didn't cringe like he'd expected her to do. Instead, she stepped in his line of sight, cutting off his view of the soldier he was speaking to. She continued in Portuguese, murmuring in low calm tones that made his own speech sound like that of a petulant child. "You will have to deal with me. I'm sorry if that makes you uncomfortable."

Uncomfortable? He laughed. He'd soon see who felt more uncomfortable: her when he wrapped his hands around her neck and choked the life out of her…or him as he rammed his cock into her lifeless corpse.

His lips curved. "I choose who I will deal with."

She continued as if he hadn't spoken, "I have a proposal for you. If you do as we ask, you'll live to see another day. Refuse and…" She snapped her fingers.

His smile widened. "You think the yammering of a foolish woman frightens me?"

"No. I don't imagine it does."

Why were the men behind her saying nothing? Were they so weak that they were willing to let a woman—*a whore*— take the lead? These Americans knew nothing about reality. Give a woman your ear and she would soon cut it off and feed it to you in your evening meal.

"So, will you do as I ask?"

"A whore's words mean nothing."

The woman crooked her finger, and the soldier he assessed

to be her lover came forward. José kept his gaze focused and steady, but the man was larger than he remembered. Angrier.

It is because you are sitting down, you fool.

Was it true that his men had fled? If they had, they would soon pay with their lives. Just as these Americans would.

Something about their calm manner made his insides quiver. He'd expected some kind of physical violence from the start, had braced himself for it. Yet their attitudes were subdued. Friendly, even.

The man draped his arm around the woman's shoulders and José's back teeth ground together. Could he not see the woman was playing him for a fool? Making him weak?

"Is he not cooperating, Callie?" the man asked.

She raised her brows. "I don't know. He hasn't actually given me an answer yet." She turned her gaze back to José. "Will you do as we ask?"

He glared. He would not give her the pleasure of a response.

She smiled. "My friend will snap your neck like a twig, if you don't do exactly what we say."

Her companion turned to look down at her, his eyes widening. "This from the person who believes it's possible to reason with anyone's humanity?"

She shrugged. "Like you once said, 'he has no humanity.'" They both turned to look at him. The soldier's face carried the slightest trace of a smirk.

José got that liquid feeling in his bowels. The one that came only when his life hung in the balance. Normally he had his men to walk in front of him and protect him from danger, to take a bullet in his stead. But he had no one to go before him this time. He struggled against his bonds, and then gasped, slumping in his seat when fire burned through his shoulder and spiraled to the far reaches of his body.

He panted, holding very still as he waited for the pain to

subside. With it, his will to resist seeped away little by little. Better to do what they wanted. Or appear to. He could always get his revenge later. These Americans were still in his country after all.

But he would not bargain with a whore. Just with the men. He focused on the soldier beside her. "What do you want me to do?"

The man shook his head and tilted it toward the woman. "Ask her, not me. She's the smart one. I just snap necks on her command."

José licked his lips. What choice did he have? He had no doubt the man could easily kill him where he sat. What good would that do his cause?

He could still salvage his reputation. It was even better that his men were gone. They would know nothing of the humiliation he'd suffered in this room.

He focused on the woman's face. "What is it you want me to do?"

CALLIE, WITH THOUGHTS OF her sister and justice winging through her head, held up the same notebook the rebel had used on her. "I want you to read this exactly as written. If you veer so much as one syllable from the script you will be sorry. Do you understand?"

The man gave her a black stare that told her what would happen if he got loose. She forced herself not to flinch, although images of those horrific photos he'd showed her flashed through her mind.

Despite the murderous look, he said, "I understand."

"I'm going to call Senator Parker, the man you received the money from and you will read this to him."

The rebel sneered. "I don't know his number. He never gave it to me."

"That's okay. I have it memorized."

His face twisted with rage. "Yes, so you could arrange a place to do your whoring."

Cole moved fast, icy intent in his eyes, but Callie grabbed his arm. "Don't," she murmured, "that's what he wants."

She turned back to the rebel. "I'll dial, and when it's time for you to speak, I'll signal you. Remember. Only read what's written, nothing more." Her fingers slid down Cole's arm. "Can you figure out how to use his equipment to record?"

"We've got it covered."

Fifteen minutes later, they had what they were looking for. The terrorist had stuck to the script and Gary seemed to buy the ruse, his voice swelling with arrogance toward the end of the conversation. Little did her brother-in-law realize that his own words would soon be used to hang him. At least she hoped they would.

"What are we going to do with him?" she asked, motioning to the rebel. Callie hadn't really thought past this point. She wasn't even sure the rebel would go along with her plan. But he'd caved faster than she ever dreamed.

Bullies. Push a pin in them and all the hot air rushed out, leaving nothing but a shriveled substance-less shell.

Cole glanced at Moss. "What do you think?"

"A lot of these rogue fighters were once members of UNITA. They formed splinter groups when the cease-fire accord was signed. They're just another political party now." He shrugged. "They might be interested in retrieving a former member."

"No! UNITA has betrayed the cause," the rebel shouted.

"UNITA didn't betray their cause," Moss said. "They just found a greater one—peace."

"There can be no peace until I am Angola's leader." The man's chest puffed out. "The Americans were helping me, trying to make sure that happened."

A megalomaniac who believed he was the savior of his

country. He had no idea that "the Americans" weren't helping him at all. Just one greedy man, who had his own hungry quest for power.

"You said there can be no peace. You're wrong," Callie said. "There already is. Peace came when the fighting stopped."

"The war is not over."

It would do no good to argue with him. He would hold onto his irrational beliefs until the day he died.

"Will UNITA kill him?" she asked.

"I don't know," Moss said. "But we can't let him loose to murder again. I've seen his work, firsthand."

Callie nodded. "You're right. But how do we find a UNITA representative here in Malanje?"

"They have an office building across the street from the Palácio Regina Hotel, the big hotel in the center of town."

Moss came forward. "We'll drop him off. But once we do, I have a favor to ask, Dr. Nascimento."

I LOVE YOU.

Those words circled through Cole's mind as he watched Callie murmur to the woman in the hospital bed. Pride swelled in him when the brutalized woman touched Callie's hand, reaching out to her.

He'd dismissed her psychobabble as nonsense, but Moss evidently believed in it, or he wouldn't have asked her to come. And Cole had to admit, she was quickly making a believer out of him as well. Look at how she'd handled that terrorist in the hotel room. She hadn't caved or shown weakness. She'd been as strong and tough as any soldier he knew. Her words were sure and confident, and they'd gotten results.

And now this woman. Cole wouldn't have known the first thing to say to her. He'd have dumped her on someone else as soon as he had the opportunity.

And what about the words she'd mouthed the split second before Cole shot the rebel? Had she meant them? Had he even read them correctly?

I love you.

Hard to mistake those three words. But had she meant them? Or had she merely said them thinking those minutes were her last on earth?

Cole warmed inside. He'd finally acknowledged his own feelings. What if she really did love him back? Could he give himself to a woman like her? And would she accept him, warts and all?

Who the hell knew? She was strong, and yet she still wanted him. Seemed able to look beyond his past and the fact that he was a soldier like her stepfather. He was no longer a child being forced to do something he feared. He was an adult who could choose freely what to do with his life. And he chose Callie.

He shook himself. There was nothing he could do about it right now. He'd hold off mentioning anything until they were back in the States, then he'd ask her out. If she didn't balk, he'd work up the nerve to tell her how he felt.

For once, he wasn't going to jump in with both feet and screw things up. He was going to plan his course of action and not stray from it.

A huge weight lifted from his shoulders. That was a plan.

Callie turned to him. "I need a piece of paper and pencil."

He nodded and pushed through the door to find the nearest nurse, his heart lighter than it had been in years. His plan could very well work.

If it did, he'd be the luckiest guy alive.

SENATOR PARKER WAITED behind the scenes as the podium for the press conference went up. He'd read over the notes for his speech, but his mind was on José, the weasel terrorist in Angola who'd tried to blackmail more money from him yesterday.

The bastard chickened out in the end—said he'd been forced to shoot Callie just minutes after he'd put her on the phone. Neither she nor the baby had survived. He'd even emailed close-ups of her face. Battered and bruised, her features had been so distorted, she was unrecognizable as the woman he'd known. He straightened his tie to hide a shudder. But those pictures would cement his position in the run for presidency.

Gary couldn't have asked for a better scenario, though, or a more incriminating one. His sister-in-law's soldier chaperone had burst into the room where she was being held, guns blazing and José's men had shot and killed them both. Their bodies would be flown home within days.

This president would take the blame for the fiasco. Would be impeached more than likely. But either way, his career was over, his reelection prospects practically nil.

And Gary's success was all but assured.

He had every confidence in his country's judicial system. The tape-recorded conversation between him and the president would be added to the testimony of a witness who was beyond reproach. General Richard Markesan. The general had admitted he'd argued with the president about the order to abort the rescue mission. Gary's planted hint that President Bryson was behind Sara's crash and working with the Angolan rebels behind the scenes would only add to the appearance of guilt.

He smiled and sighed. The trap was set. If he was lucky, the vice-president would be installed once President Bryson was impeached and, against the weaker cog, Gary had a very good chance of winning.

And the sympathy votes he would get… He closed his

eyes and drew in a deep breath, relishing the sweet scent of victory.

Within minutes the podium and the microphones were ready and soon-to-be president Gary Parker stepped onto the platform, his shoulders slumped, eyes wet and red-rimmed. He gazed out at the bevy of reporters and camera crews and dragged a visibly shaking hand through his hair as he approached the microphones.

Placing his notes on the podium, he gripped the wooden surface and began.

"My fellow Americans, I have today learned of a tragedy that has hit at the heart of who I am as a citizen, as a husband…" He paused and sucked in a painful breath. "…and as a future father.

"As you know, my wife was killed three months ago during a medical relief trip to Angola. Her plane crashed and all the staff onboard, including my wife, perished." Blinking rapidly a few times, he let the crowd filter through their memories of the event, including the public memorial they'd all been invited to.

No one moved. All eyes remained fastened on him, not even a pen scratching across notepads broke the silence.

"But there are some things you didn't know at the time of my wife's death. Things I couldn't bear to reveal until I knew for sure it was safe to do so."

The sun filtered across the group, the bright heat of the day a strange contrast to the mood he was trying to set. Why couldn't the weather have played along with him just this once? He gave an internal shrug and continued.

"My wife and I were expecting a child at the time of her death."

Murmurs rippled through the crowd, and Gary waited for the reporters to settle back down. This was news to all of them.

"Sara couldn't carry a pregnancy to term because of a physical ailment, so her sister, Dr. Calista Nascimento, offered to carry a child, *our* child for her. In other words, she offered to be a surrogate for us."

He paused to let the additional information sink in. "When Sara died, Callie was one month along. Too soon to let anyone know our good news. Then, after my wife's death…I just couldn't see past my grief to share the news with anyone."

Taking a handkerchief from the inside pocket of his jacket, he dabbed the corners of his eyes, staring at his notes for a long, dramatic moment.

"I got word today that my sister-in-law, along with Sara's and my unborn child were…were…" Again he stopped and shut his eyes, turning his face heavenward. "They were murdered yesterday by terrorist extremists in Angola."

The crowd reacted just as he'd hoped. A mishmash of whispers and indrawn breaths filtered through the group, growing and changing as the mood turned from shock to outrage.

"You'll understand why I'm not up to answering any questions today, but I wanted you to know the truth, along with the rest of the world." He raised a hand and held it out in supplication to the crowd. "As devastating as the news is, it pales beside what I've recently learned."

He allowed the reporters to settle back down in their seats. "I discovered there was a military operation that had evacuated the American personnel from our embassy in Angola. That operation was a complete success, but my sister-in-law was unfortunately captured by the terrorists during the raid. The same military personnel began planning a rescue mission to get Callie out. I stayed in close contact with General Richard Markesan, commander of one of our military's Special Forces units, who was to head up the mission. But before they could succeed, the order was given to abort.

"I couldn't believe the news when I heard it. So I went to the source of the order...President Bryson. I'd like to play you a recording of our conversation and see if you come to the same conclusion I did."

Cameramen pushed and juggled vying for a better spot. Reporters began writing furiously on notepads as Gary set a small tape recorder on the podium and pressed the play button.

By the time the recording reached its end, he stood tall and dignified at the podium, knowing he'd succeeded in his task.

The president was finished.

TWENTY-FIVE

CALLIE GASPED. "He's testifying *for* Gary?"

Cole's tongue-lashing from General Markesan hadn't been as severe as he'd expected. Knowing they were safely on their way to the American embassy in Zambia, where they would catch another flight back to the States had tempered his superior's ire. But then Markesan had shared the news that he'd been subpoenaed to appear in front of congress.

"Not specifically for him, no. He's testifying as to the conversation he had with the president. About the order to abort the rescue mission."

"But Gary will twist the comments to fit his scheme. You've already heard what he's capable of."

"But we have the truth." Cole pulled out the DVD containing that final conversation between José and Senator Parker. They'd also questioned José at length and recorded his answers. The evidence was damning. The rebel had even provided the data for the wire transfers. Maybe the right person could trace them back to Parker. Who knew. Even if they couldn't, there was still plenty of evidence pointing at the senator.

Callie lifted her head and glanced at the woman sleeping in the window seat next to hers. She'd been adamant about not leaving Amanda Silva, the victim of the rebel leader's vicious attack. He'd heard her invite the woman to spend the next several weeks at her home until she recovered.

He lowered his voice. "You up to facing him? You could let Moss and I handle it. The DVD should be enough."

"I want to face him. He killed my sister. Deprived her child of its mother."

"The baby will have you."

Callie stared at him and touched her stomach. Then she turned away and looked straight ahead. "Yes," she said softly. "He'll have me."

Cole sensed something behind the words, but with Moss and Amanda present, he didn't feel comfortable airing his personal junk. It could wait. Besides, he needed to clear up some issues first. So he kept his thoughts to himself and pulled back into his seat.

As soon as they landed, Cole spotted an expatriate newspaper in the airport. The headline caught him up short: American President Accused of Aiding Angolan Rebels.

How had they gotten wind of the scandal so fast?

Senator Parker hadn't let a single blade of grass grow under his feet, evidently. As soon as the man thought Callie's death was confirmed, he'd gone into action.

And they had only days to prevent more heartache for a lot of people.

CALLIE HUNG BACK ONCE they hit the Zambian airport, staying next to Amanda and avoiding Cole.

She'd bared her soul, had told him she loved him, and he'd responded with…well, nothing. Even when she'd said something about Micah being motherless, there'd been no hint of "we" only "he'll have you."

It was heartbreaking. Despite their differences, she'd thought…hoped he might care about her, or at least want to see her again once they got home. Evidently, he didn't.

In fact, if he'd cared about her at all, she'd have expected him to blurt it out, or impulsively act on it, especially after what he'd told her about his childhood. But Cole was in full control of himself.

She shook herself free of her thoughts and touched Amanda's hand. "Are you okay? You're awfully quiet."

The other woman turned her head, the large dark glasses they'd purchased doing a good job of covering her black eyes. "Just thinking about Seth."

"Your bodyguard?"

"Yes. He was a good man. He didn't deserve what happened to him."

"Neither did you. But you can't blame yourself, either. The blame lies entirely with the man who killed him."

Quick fingers went to her face, wiping away a drop of moisture that appeared below her glasses. "I cared about him. And I-I hoped he felt the same way about me."

Callie could definitely relate to the woman's words. "He was there with you. I'm sure he cared."

"Do you think so?"

Feeling like a fraud, she nodded. How could she possibly know that, when she couldn't even sort out her own relationships? "Is there someone you'd like us to call once we get to the embassy?"

"My mother. My brother." Amanda went silent for close to a minute. When her voice came back, it shook. "I don't want them to know what happened back there."

"You don't have to tell anyone you don't want to tell."

Moss came beside them. "Everything okay here?"

Callie glanced at him. "We're coming. Just stopping to catch our breath."

"Okay. We're almost to the luggage area."

Amanda laughed, a keening, hysterical sound. "I don't want my luggage."

Moss frowned. "What?"

"I don't want it. Any of it. I'd rather just leave it behind. With Seth's stuff."

Callie touched Moss's hand. "We'll leave it here. She can

claim the luggage later if she decides she wants it." They'd
made arrangements for Seth's body to be shipped to his family in the States, a heartbreaking task for Amanda, who'd
cried silent tears all the way through the process.

"Why don't you go on ahead," she said to Moss.

He glanced once more at Amanda and trotted forward to
catch up with Cole who was a ways ahead. Moss said something, then Cole nodded. They turned to the left, moving in
the opposite direction of the arrow for baggage claim, and
Callie smiled for the first time since they left Angola.

SHE STOOD OUTSIDE the Senate chambers twisting her hands
together.

"You sure you're up to this?" Cole's voice came from
beside her.

"I don't have a choice. I have to look him in the face,
knowing what he did to Sara, what he tried to do to us."

He put his arm around her and tucked her next to him.
"Did I ever tell you how proud I am of you, Cal?"

Cal?

She tilted her head to look at him. First he avoided touching her and barely spoke to her. Now he was calling her "Cal"
and putting his arm around her? She was so confused, and
she didn't like it.

Maybe Cole was a little confused himself.

He'd surprised her several times today, already. She'd
tried to brush him off and come to the Senate Investigations
Committee alone, but he'd insisted on accompanying her.

He was still looking at her, and she realized she hadn't
answered his question.

"Thank you," she said.

"You're going to do great in there. I can't wait to see the
look on that bastard's face when he realizes you're alive."

Callie gave a small smile. "Me too."

Desperately wanting to say something that was personal, that would follow up on the sudden intimacy lying between them, she could think of nothing. She glanced around the hallway, looking for a topic that would segue into something more meaningful. Again…nothing. Her time with him was coming to an end and unless she could get through to him, he would soon be a distant memory.

And Micah, his tiny namesake, might never even know who his savior was. Surely not. Cole would want to follow the important milestones in the baby's life. So, at least she'd maintain some kind of contact with him. Would that be enough to satisfy her? Not hardly.

She could have kicked herself. Why would he stay in touch? He hadn't even wanted her to give Micah his name in the first place.

But remember why?

The voices played back in her head.

"Don't give him my name, Callie. I don't want him going through life saddled with what it represents."

She'd seen his heart, his deep-rooted insecurities. He'd laid himself bare emotionally.

So, instead of talking, she wrapped her arms around his waist and leaned her head against him. Something brushed across her hair. Had he just kissed her?

Hope welled up in her chest.

One of the double doors opened, and Moss, in a formal blue uniform, slid through them. "General Markesan has just started addressing the committee. Are you ready?"

Callie sucked in a quick breath. "Is my brother-in-law in there?"

"Pacing back and forth, every ounce the heartbroken widower."

"He's a good actor. Even my sister didn't see the truth."

Moss glanced at Cole. "You going in with her, or are you waiting here?"

"I'm going in." He glanced toward one of the side doors. "Maybe you should stay here in case we need you to bring Amanda in to testify."

Moss shifted his weight. "Do you think she can handle it at this point?"

Amanda was at a nearby hotel, ready if they needed her to come. Callie thought the pictures would say enough, though. "I want to avoid that if at all possible."

She looked up at Cole. "Are you ready to go in?"

"Whenever you are."

"I'm ready. Past ready."

Cole pushed the door open and let Callie precede him into the room. General Markesan was speaking through a microphone, recounting a discussion he'd had with the president.

She spotted Gary, who was watching the general. He leaned forward to his microphone and started to ask a question when his eyes met hers. He kept talking for a second or two longer before stumbling, then coming to a halt, staring at her in shocked silence. The rest of the room turned to look, and a series of gasps went through the space.

They'd evidently seen her picture on CNN with the caption Dead beneath it.

Gary's strained voice came through the microphone. "Callie, I—I… Thank God you're alive."

He stood to his feet and strode toward them with a gaping grin as if he were going to embrace her.

Cole stepped in front of her, blocking the man's access. "I wouldn't, if I were you, sir."

Gary stopped, blinked a couple of times then pointed a finger at Cole. His hand was trembling. "Are you threatening a United States senator, soldier?"

"No, sir. I'm protecting an innocent woman from one."

Her brother-in-law's eyes flitted around the room, before coming back to rest on Callie. "I thought you were dead. I mean, I'd heard you were dead. All the reports from Angola—"

Callie stepped from behind Cole. "The reports were wrong, Gary, and your cohort, José Coelho, is out of commission."

The man blanched at the mention of the rebel's name. "I don't know who you're talking about. I only know what I heard through embassy channels."

"The embassy was evacuated, remember? As you can see, I'm not dead." She touched her stomach. "*We're* not dead. And I'm here with the truth—" she turned toward the seated officials, "—if the esteemed senators will hear me."

"This is not the place..." Gary started, but General Markesan stood, interrupting him.

"She's one of my witnesses as to what transpired on the ground in Angola. And I think the rest of the Senate committee will be very interested in hearing what she has to say."

Callie reeled back at the unconcealed hatred in Gary's eyes. But Cole squeezed her hand, giving her the courage she needed to step away from his strong grip and to move toward the table where Markesan sat.

Gary remained standing for a moment or two, before saying "This news is so... I'm feeling a little overwhelmed. I think I'll step outside for a breath of air."

Another elected official stood to his feet. "I think, Senator Parker, you are quite well enough to hear your sister-in-law out. I'm sure you're as anxious as we are to hear how the reports of her death could have been so greatly exaggerated."

Gary swallowed and looked around the room. Finding no allies, he slowly returned to his seat. Once there, he sank into it, burying his face in his hands.

Callie sat next to the general and watched as he adjusted

the microphone, then covered it with his hand. Leaning toward her, he whispered, "Go ahead, Dr. Nascimento, nail the bastard."

She glanced to the side and caught Cole still standing, his eyes on her face. He nodded, giving her an encouraging wink.

In that second, she loved him more than life itself. She could only hope he was still around when she finished testifying, so she could tell him so.

Out loud, this time.

Taking a deep breath, she glanced at the rows of people entrusted with looking after the best interests of her country. "Thank you, senators, for allowing me the opportunity to speak to you this afternoon. I'm here to talk about a very special woman, who had a heart bigger than this entire room. My beloved sister, Sara." She paused to clear the lump out of her throat. "As you know, she died in a tragic plane crash. I'm here to tell you that what happened was not, as you may have heard, the result of our nation's president, but the work of a despicable and power-hungry man. It is my hope that being here today will bring this man to justice and help right a terrible wrong. And that it will help my sister finally rest in peace, knowing her child will never have to endure what she did, all in the name of winning a presidential election."

TWENTY-SIX

COLE STEERED HER through the clumps of shouting journalists waiting outside the Capitol building. Her pale face told him to get her out of there, so he pushed through the sea of microphones and flashing cameras. When they got to the bottom of the steps, he pulled up short.

Parker was there, blocking their path.

"Move aside, Senator." He tensed, ready for anything.

Callie put her hand up. "It's okay." She turned toward her brother-in-law. "What do you want, Gary?"

"I wanted to tell you that your sister…she…" His head bowed. "I loved her very much, but things just spiraled out of control. She started moving away from my political position, becoming more and more vocal against the key issues I needed to win the election. I tried to talk to her, to ask her to think about what was best for the country, but she wouldn't listen." His eyes came up and focused on her.

There was misery in his face, but Cole couldn't tell if it was an act or if he was truly sorry for what he'd done.

Callie didn't say anything for a minute, then she stood taller. "And your baby? Did he move away from your political position as well? Is that why you wanted him dead?"

"No, I didn't order the rebel to—"

"To what? Kill the baby? You'll forgive me if I don't believe you. I was there, remember? I heard your conversation. I heard what you said to the killer once you thought he'd succeeded. You said, 'Finally.'"

He shook his head. "This election is the most important one in a hundred years, you and I both know it's true."

Callie held up a hand. "And you see yourself as what, this country's savior?"

"They need a strong leader. Someone who'll move the country back onto the right path."

"That's for the voters to decide." She took a step forward until she was inches away from Parker. "And they deserve a fair and honest portrayal of the candidates, not manipulated emotions."

"You don't understand."

"No, I don't, Gary."

"Once the baby's born, I'll make it up to him."

Cole spotted several reporters edging closer, microphones extended, as well as an approaching group of senators, but neither Callie nor Parker seemed to notice, caught in a war of stares.

"How can you possibly make up for his mother's death at your own hand?" she asked.

"I'll make sure he's brought up knowing how loving she was."

Callie nodded. "You're right, he will know about Sara. But it won't come from you. I doubt any court in this country would allow a child to be raised by someone who plotted his death."

"You can't prove any of that."

"You don't think so? There are witnesses. Tapes, evidence."

"Circumstantial, all of it." Gary straightened, looking down his nose at her.

Several senators came forward and an elderly one spoke up. "The Investigations Committee has some questions for you, Senator Parker. If you would please accompany us back inside the building."

Gary shook his head. "I'm sorry, but I have a prior commitment."

"How about the commitment to the truth? You owe your constituents an accounting of your actions. You'll either come back with us, or you'll be escorted by a member of the National Security team. The president himself would like to speak with you."

Gary's mouth went slack, the color bleeding from his face. "Surely you can't believe what this woman has said. She's crazy. Sick with grief over her sister's death. You heard my side of the story. It was the *president* who ordered the mission to be aborted. Not me."

He allowed the group to encircle him and lead him back up the steps, but his voice kept growing until it was loud enough to be heard by everyone standing in the area. "This is ridiculous. No one can prove any of this. My lawyers will have a heyday with these proceedings!"

Once they disappeared inside, the reporters scurried back toward Callie, but it was too late. Moss had gotten the car and pulled it up as close as he could without running over anyone's foot. Cole moved toward it, towing Callie by the arm.

"No comment," he shouted, as a hailstorm of questions pelted them from behind.

Finally, he had them both in the car. "Get us out of here, Moss."

"I aim to please."

Within minutes, they were speeding away from the reporters and the nightmare of the last week-and-a-half.

"Thank you," said Callie.

"You're welcome."

"I talked to General Markesan. As soon as you're not

needed here anymore, he's arranged for a military plane to fly you back to…" Moss's brows went up. "Where do you live anyway?"

Callie laughed. "New York."

Cole turned toward her, surprised. "Really? That's where I grew up."

"I didn't know that. Is your mother still there?"

"She moved to Florida where it's quieter." He hesitated. "I'm stationed in D.C. at the moment."

Callie licked her lips. "I see. Ever make it to New York?"

"I haven't in a while, but I'm due for a visit."

"Really?"

Did that mean she wanted him to visit? Or that she was horrified by the thought.

"That is, I've thought about going back to take in the sights and all, but…" Hell, he was terrible at this. Why had he ever thought he could smoothly transition into a relationship little by little? He was messing everything up.

"But what?"

Great. Now what did he say?

"But I don't know anyone there, anymore and…"

"You know me."

Was she trying to help him out? Shit, he could only hope so.

"Yeah. I guess I do." Maybe he should bring up the whole feelings thing. He glanced up at the front seat and caught Moss's glance and raised brow. Naw, he'd be ribbed endlessly by his team if they knew the truth. He had to get her alone. "Do you want to, uh, maybe go out to dinner, tonight?"

"With you?"

His jaw tightened. "Yes."

"What about Amanda?"

Moss glanced again in the rearview mirror, his ears tuned

into their conversation just like Cole had feared. "I could stay with her, if you want," he offered.

Callie hesitated. "I think that would be all right. Do you mind if I check with her, first? After what she's been through…"

Moss's eyes went back to the road. "I can see where it might be difficult being in a room with a strange man."

Cursing at his insensitivity for forgetting about the other woman, Cole grimaced. "Never mind. I don't know what I was thinking."

Callie touched his hand. "I'm not saying no. I just want to check with Amanda. I'd like to go out with you, if that's okay?"

His heart lifted just a little. "Great."

"But first, I need to buy a new outfit." She glanced down at the business suit she'd grabbed off a rack as she'd headed to the Capitol building. "Can we stop on the way to the restaurant?"

He'd love nothing more than to stop on the way. But it had nothing to do with buying clothes and everything to do with shedding them.

"Hey," said Moss, yanking his attention back and making him wonder if his friend had read his thoughts. "There's a little complication I just remembered."

"What's that?"

"Dr. Nascimento has a doctor's appointment."

"I do?"

"Yes. General Markesan wants you to head straight from here to Walter Reed and let the docs look you over."

"That's really nice of him. I'm sure everything's okay, though."

Cole shook his head. "I think it's a good idea. You've just spent a week marching through the jungle."

"So our dinner date is off?"

"Well…" What was he supposed to say? "We could go afterward if you want."

Moss glanced at them through the mirror. "I'll drop you off."

"I'd still like to talk to Amanda, so could we go by there, first? I could take a taxi to the medical center afterward."

Now was his chance. Cole could talk to her on the way. "I could go with you, if you want."

"I do." Her fingers slid through his. "Thanks."

He smiled. Life was good.

COLE HELD HER HAND while the technician squirted gel over the growing bulge on her tummy. Her muscles rippled at the icy sensation, and Micah twisted inside of her, making her smile.

"What?" Cole asked.

She wasn't sure he'd want to be in the examination room with her, but he hadn't balked when she'd asked. Maybe if he saw the baby on the ultrasound, she could get some idea of how he felt about them both.

"I think even the baby feels how cold this is. What did you want to talk to me about anyway?"

Cole glanced at the technician. "It can wait."

She wished she knew what he was thinking, but military men were pros at keeping their emotions wrapped up tight. It still made her uncomfortable, but she knew now that Cole was nothing like her stepfather. Maybe she should tell him about her background, so he'd understand how it made her feel. The man had kept his face empty and emotionless, even when spanking them to within an inch of their lives. It made her more afraid than if he'd burst into a rage. She'd often wondered if he could kill her, using just that blank stare.

Callie shuddered.

"Okay, hon?" the technician asked.

She forced a smile. "Fine."

"I'm going to start the scan now."

Cole's hand tightened on hers as the image appeared on the screen.

"There's his spine. Bladder. His…uh, do you already know the sex?"

Callie nodded. "It's a boy."

"That's right. He's got all the equipment in all the right places." The woman's teasing glance went to Cole as if he'd fathered the child. Callie wished more than anything that were true. But she wouldn't change things, even if she could. This was her sister's baby, part of her.

The technician moved the wand to another area of Callie's abdomen. "The baby's still in the head-up position, but that's normal at this point."

Callie turned her head to see if Cole was as amazed as she was. The baby had grown in the month since her last appointment. He was so well formed. Perfect.

"There's his heart," the technician went on, changing the angle of the scanner. "His head. Oh, he's sucking his thumb. He's a little doll."

Callie's eyes suddenly welled up and spilled over. She turned her head to the side, away from the screen and her shoulders shook, rattling the paper liner beneath her.

"Cal? What's wrong?"

The technician rubbed her arm. "The baby's just fine, hon. Nothing to worry about."

Callie nodded, unable to say anything. Her hand tightened around Cole's until she was clinging to him for dear life. He leaned over, sliding his cheek against hers. "It's going to be okay, sweetheart. Your sister would be so happy that you fought for her baby's survival, that he has someone like you to defend him once he comes into this world."

He understood. Oh God, he understood why she was crying. The realization made the tears come harder, and she gripped his neck, pulling him down to her level and holding him close.

She heard a door close somewhere in the distance, but ignored everything but the man stroking gentle fingers across her forehead, down her temples.

Taking a deep shaky breath, she struggled for control and found it at last. "Thank you. I-I'm okay now."

He leaned back and looked into her face. "You sure?"

"Maybe not on the outside, but inside where it counts." She swiped at the tears, embarrassed for him to see her blubbering like this. "After all we've been through, *now* I cry."

He bent close and kissed her. "You deserve to cry. Especially now."

She glanced around and laughed. "I think I scared the technician away."

"She wanted to give you some privacy." He picked up a piece of paper. "She printed this off for you to take with you, though."

It was Micah's face, in beautiful 3-D, his thumb popped in his mouth, eyelids tightly fastened in sleep. He looked so snuggly and warm and…safe. "He's safe now, isn't he?"

"He is. We'll make sure he stays that way."

We? Callie wanted to say the word aloud. Wanted to ask him what he meant by it. She'd agonized over the you, you, you for the last two days. But she needed to be patient and see where this went.

Cole helped her sit up, and she noticed all the gunk still smeared over her stomach. "Can you hand me a paper towel, please?"

He ripped three from the dispenser, but instead of giving them to her, he cleared away the gel himself, rubbing in tiny circles. The room heated as she watched his hands sliding over her with such gentleness. Almost like…

Cole stopped. "Am I hurting you?"

"No." Her voice had lowered an octave, coming out in a husky rasp.

He ran his fingers across her belly, checking to see if he'd missed any spots, all the while watching her eyes.

Putting her hand over his, she said, "I think you'd better stop."

Cole pulled her white shirt over her stomach and handed her the suit jacket hung behind the door. "I'm sorry."

"For what?"

He dragged his hands through his hair. "Hell, I don't know. You act like you can't stand me touching you."

"I can't."

His eyes went from confused to stricken. But when he went to turn away, she reached out and stopped him.

"I can't stand you touching me, because it makes me want what I can't have."

"Which is?"

Callie slid off the exam table and laid her palms on either side of his face. "You. I want you."

He dragged her to him so fast that the wind rushed out of her lungs. His lips were on hers, and the next thing she knew she was pressed against the bed in the examining room wondering if he was going to take her right there. She didn't care. He could. When she wrapped her arms around his neck, he pulled away. "Let's get the hell out of here."

She shook her head, struggling to catch her breath. "There's a problem with that plan."

"What?" His face stilled.

"We both have roommates."

"Oh."

"Yeah. Oh."

His look of disappointment was so complete that she couldn't help stepping next to him and running her fingers down his chest until they hooked into his waist-band. She pulled him closer. "You do realize, Cole, that there are always other hotels...other rooms."

"Lead the way, woman."

Callie shrugged into her jacket and picked up her new purse. As she started toward the door, Cole stopped her with a look. "Aren't you forgetting something?"

"What?"

He picked up the image of the sonogram and handed it to her. "The baby."

She patted her stomach. "Don't worry. I've got him right here. He's not going anywhere for now."

Hand in hand they headed for the door.

TWENTY-SEVEN

COLE PROPPED HIMSELF up with his elbow and stroked his fingers down the long straight line of Callie's naked spine as he listened to her sigh in her sleep. He'd have to wake her before long. Moss and Amanda assumed they were on their way to dinner somewhere.

How did a man tell a woman he loved her when he was scared to death that he wasn't good enough for her? Scratch that. When he *knew* he was nowhere near good enough. When he knew he would eventually screw up big time and dreaded seeing the disappointment settle in her eyes?

How?

Cole didn't know. He hadn't meant to wind up in bed with her again until after he'd talked to her. But here he was.

Scalini *Manic*-ini strikes again. He could hear the kids chanting the nickname in his head.

Callie might think he was a hero right now. But how long before that shiny spray-on finish wore off and revealed the pitted reality beneath? But she was a psychiatrist. Surely she'd already seen everything there was to see—she'd certainly pegged him in almost every way.

Except one—her view of military men.

He reached down and kissed the warm joint between her neck and her shoulder.

"Ummm," she murmured. "Keep that up, and I'll never let you out of this room."

Cole laughed, before turning serious. "Hey. I need to talk to you."

Rolling onto her back, she didn't bother pulling the sheet over herself, just looked up into his eyes. "Okay."

"Tell me about your stepfather." If the man really was just a typical GI, then Callie would never be happy with someone like him. He'd seen the flash of anger in her eyes the few times she'd mentioned the man.

Callie sat up, her eyes cooling. "My stepfather? Why?"

"Because I'm trying to understand where you're coming from." He sat up as well.

She licked her lips. "I wouldn't even know where to begin."

"What kind of man was he?"

Her laugh was harsh. "He wasn't like you, that's for sure."

"In what way?"

"He's dead, Cole. Do we really need to do this?"

He brushed a strand of hair away from her eyes. "I want to know what makes you tick. Let's start there. How did he die?"

"Suicide."

He took a moment to digest that. Coming out of the service was tough, especially if you'd faced combat situations.

"You didn't consider him a good parent."

"No."

"You mentioned he was cold and unfeeling."

She turned and looked him in the face. "He was controlling. Violent, when he drank."

Violent.

Anger rolled up his gut and lodged behind his eyes when he saw where this was going. "He hit you?"

"And my sister."

"Shit." He cupped her chin. "You think I'm like that?"

Closing her eyes she wrapped her arms around his neck and laid her cheek against his. The soft sound of her breathing filled his ear…his heart. "No, Cole. I don't. Like I said. You're nothing like him."

He smiled and leaned down to kiss her. "My turn to tell you something." As his lips met hers again, he decided now wasn't the time. "No, I think I'll wait until you get home. I want to surprise you."

"Mmm," she whispered as her hand wandered down his body and found its target, which was already hard and waiting. "You want to surprise me? I think you already have."

CALLIE ARRIVED AT her apartment, exhausted from her day at her practice. It was hard to believe that three weeks ago she'd been pushing her way through a landmine-strewn country. She kicked off her black pumps and went to the window, looking down on the city. Her high-rise was surrounded by nothing wilder than pigeons and notoriously sneaky squirrels.

Thank heavens. She'd take the pigeons and the squirrels over snakes and landmines any day.

Amanda had flown home to Los Angeles yesterday, feeling strong enough to face her family and continue counseling with a professional Callie had located in her area. With time, she should recover from her ordeal, though some emotional scars would never completely heal.

Callie sighed and leaned a shoulder against the glass pane. Moss had been so protective of her while in Washington that she'd expected him to call and ask about her, but the phone had remained silent.

That bothered her too. She'd been waiting for Cole to call and set up his visit. He said he had something to tell her.

Maybe he was on another assignment. She thought about trying to track him down, but how desperate would that look?

Very.

She crinkled her nose and watched the lights of the city

pop on one by one. She didn't understand it. They'd spent two wonderful days in Washington, sneaking away to the extra hotel room they'd rented so Moss and Amanda wouldn't get suspicious. They'd talked about everything under the sun, including their childhoods.

Callie had been surprised when he asked about her stepfather. The abuse was hard to share, but she'd forced herself to tell him everything. She would never forget Cole's face as he'd stared down at her, his brows drawn together in anger.

"Do you think I would treat a child that way? That I would treat *you* that way?"

She'd shaken her head, relieved the tiny niggling fear was off her chest and out of her mind. She'd seen the truth in his eyes. But those words were as close to a commitment as she'd gotten from him.

The L-word had not been mentioned again. By either of them. Besides, she'd already said it once. She couldn't bear to say it again, until Cole made up his mind.

She went to the kitchen and flipped the switch on her electric kettle. She remembered her stepfather drinking coffee by the bucket load. Callie drank tea. Only tea. She realized it was an irrational reaction, but that was okay. Some childhood associations were better left behind.

Dunking her bag of Lady Grey, she took the cup and saucer into the living room, annoyed when the inter-apartment phone in the kitchen rang as soon as she sat down. Sighing, she padded back into tiny space and picked up the handset.

"Yes?"

"Callie, it's Jean, dear. I'm at the main door. There's a handsome young man here who wishes to speak with you."

Her elderly neighbor, bless her heart, had taken it upon herself to screen Callie's visitors whenever she happened to be at the main door to the building. Which was most of the time, since she loved nothing better than to drag her folding chair into the entryway and watch the comings and goings of everyone in the building.

"Who is it, Jean?" Callie knew better than try to speak directly to the person in question. Besides, she thought the woman's protectiveness was quirky and sweet.

"What's your name, young man?" Callie heard her ask.

"Cole, Cole Scalini, ma'am," said a deep masculine voice directly into the intercom. Callie's heart leaped and took off running. Evidently Cole had no compunction about bypassing the middleman—or woman.

"He says his name is Cole Scampi, dear. Do you know him?"

She laughed. *Scampi?* An easy enough mistake, since Cole *was* one scrumptious man.

Jean's voice came back through before she had time to say anything. "Do you know him, dear?"

Did she? Oh God, she hoped so.

"Yes, I know him. You can let him up, Jean, thank you."

"You're welcome, dear." The voice faded as the woman evidently turned her head to speak to Cole. "She said you were okay, so that's good enough for me."

Callie hung up the handset and flew into the bathroom, fluffing her hair the best she could. She settled for slapping some clear gloss on her lips and flicking on a quick coat of mascara. She curled her lip and made a face, before laughing again and hugging her expanding belly.

"Oh, Micah, he came. He actually came!"

By the time the elevator arrived on her floor, she'd gone through a couple sets of Lamaze rapid panting exercises and had regained her composure.

Until she opened the door.

His crooked grin hit her between the eyes and she stood there, mouth hanging open.

"Hi," he said.

"Hi." Her mouth snapped shut.

He stood there for a moment. "You gonna ask me in? Or do I have to go through Jean for that too?"

She smiled and moved to one side to let him pass. "Sorry about that."

"No problem. Nice to know you have someone down there to rough up the undesirables."

Callie shut the door. "Jean can hold her own, believe me. She holds a second degree black belt in Taekwondo."

"You're kidding."

"Nope. She has a rainbow assortment of belts hanging on a wall, along with pictures of herself earning each one."

"But she must be…"

"Up there," Callie finished. "She's spunky. I wouldn't want to mess with her."

"Thanks for letting me know. I'll be sure not to cross her."

They both went silent for several long minutes before he spoke again. "I would have come sooner, but you had company."

She smiled. So he *had* been keeping track of her. The lack of phone calls she'd stressed over? Forgiven. "Amanda left yesterday."

"I'm glad she had you on her side." Cole's gaze landed on her stomach. "You're growing. Everything okay?"

She blinked at him, and he rolled his eyes. "Oh hell, I didn't mean it like that. I meant you look healthy. Good." He reached for her hands and held them in his. "Beautiful."

"Thank you."

He reeled her in slowly. "Can I touch him?"

Callie nodded, unable to speak. This couldn't be happening. Cole couldn't be standing in her living room, asking to lay his hands on her stomach.

When he touched her, it was almost a religious experience. His fingers explored inch by inch, and before long, their mouths followed suit. When she pulled him toward the bedroom, there were no more words at all for a long time.

"THERE'S MY BUILDING, just pull in." Callie had to work today, as much as she didn't want to. But Cole was going to wait for her at the apartment. They'd talk later. Last night there'd been no opportunity.

He turned the wheel and pulled into the parking lot of the large professional complex, finding a space in front of the marquis. Squinting he leaned forward. "Is your name on there?"

"Um-hmm," she said, rummaging in her purse for her key card, "the third one from the bottom, left hand side."

"Third one…left hand side, there, I found…" His voice trailed away, and Callie lifted her head to find him staring at the sign. His Adam's apple took a quick dive, his eyes closing for several long seconds as if he were coming to terms with something.

Dread began building inside her chest. "Cole?"

He glanced over at her and then down at his watch. "Look, do you mind if we cut this visit a little short? I've got to catch a flight this afternoon before I ship out. I need to get some sleep beforehand, since I didn't get any last—"

"You're leaving this afternoon?" Why hadn't he said anything last night?

"Yes, you knew I wasn't here for good. I have a job too. Just like you do." His tone was a little sharper than necessary.

"But you just got here." She heard the slight whine in her voice, but couldn't stop it. Something wasn't right. Something besides her voice. "Cole, what's wrong?"

A butterfly hit the windshield and bounced off. Cole flinched, before drawing in a deep breath and running his hand over his face. "Why the hell didn't you come clean with me about what you did for a living?"

"I did tell you."

"You didn't tell me you worked on little kids."

She frowned. "Worked on? That's a strange way to put it."

"Is it? It's not like they have any choice in the matter."

Suddenly, Callie understood. He'd been dragged from therapist to therapist as a kid. He'd grown up not trusting them. Evidently those childhood memories still held some sway.

It hit her. Oh God, she'd made tea just yesterday with the thought that some childhood associations were better left behind. Would that be how it was with Cole? He'd choose tea over coffee? Someone else over her?

Because of his own childhood demons?

Desperate, she said the first thing that came to mind. "Why don't you come inside and see my office?" Maybe if he could face his fears, he'd see how irrational they were.

Yeah, and maybe she could learn to drink coffee. She was willing to try.

Or was it that Cole simply disagreed with child psychiatric work all together?

He eyed her. "I don't think so. Like I said, I need to get some shuteye before my flight."

"I'll drive you to the airport, then."

"No need. I've got the rental car. I'll be gone before you get home this afternoon."

And so this was where they left it. He was leaving, and Callie could see by his face he wouldn't be back. Her heart screamed in protest at the thought, but begging him would do no good.

She believed in closure, no matter how hard the process of shutting the door was. She needed the words. The finality. "So this is goodbye, isn't it? For good."

Cole turned and looked at her. "I'm sorry. It evidently

wasn't meant to be. Between my screwed up childhood and your screwed up stepfather, we'd never make it."

"Evidently not." She popped open the door and stepped out onto the asphalt surface. The morning sun, already hot, shimmered off the black surface, giving it the look of spun glass. For once, the sight didn't fascinate her. Instead, she stood frozen in place, looking into the car. This was the last time she would ever see Cole's rugged face. Pain rolled over her in a series of cascading waves, eroding away portions of her heart.

"Need me to walk you up?" His words roused her back to reality, but she realized they were a mere formality. A way to escape, since he'd made no move to open his door.

Callie shook her head. "No. There's a doorman, he'll make sure I get in."

"Okay. I'll see you, then." Her brows lifted, and he altered his phrase. "I wish you well in all your future endeavors."

A short laugh erupted from her throat. Well, how was that for stilted? "Since my endeavors involve 'working on little kids' maybe you'd better not wish me too much success."

Cole's face suffused with red, but he said nothing, just waited as she shut the car door and stepped away from the vehicle. He then pulled out of the spot and stopped for a child who was crossing the lot with her mother.

Not one of her patients, but Cole wouldn't know that. The building was full of different pediatric specialties. She started her trek across the parking lot.

He wouldn't care, even if he knew.

Maybe he was right. It was better this way.

But in Callie's heart of hearts, she knew she was telling the worst kind of lie. It wasn't better.

But it was over.

HALF-CROUCHING, Cole sprinted from the helipad. His three-week assignment of observing troops on the field was almost over. In reality, he'd run away. But it hadn't done him a lick of good. Callie was still first and foremost on his mind.

He stared across the endless stretch of desert sand.

Knuckles rapping on the side of his helmet brought his attention back.

"Knock, knock…anyone home?"

Cole shoved Moss's hand away. "Cut it out."

His friend's brows went up. "You going to keep mooning over her for the last three days of our tour? Or are you going to actually get some work done?"

"You sayin' I'm not carrying my share of the load?"

"I'm saying you're itching for a fight, and I'm not looking to be the target."

Cole sighed. "You're right. Sorry."

"You need to have whatever this is out with her before it eats you alive."

"There's nothing to—"

"Like hell. You've got the heebie-jeebies for her something bad, even I can see that."

"Heebie-jeebies? You sure you got the right word?"

"Oh yeah." His friend gave a mock shudder. "I get the heebie-jeebies every time I see that cow-eyed expression come over your face."

Cole laughed despite himself. "That bad, huh?"

"Yes. And if you don't do something about it, I'm going to request some psychiatric leave time, because you're driving me up the wall."

Cole tensed, then realized his friend wasn't poking fun at him. He couldn't because Cole had never told anyone about his childhood problem.

Except Callie.

She'd somehow mind-melded it out of him, just like Spock on the old *Star Trek* series. And somehow telling her *had* lifted some of the hurt away. Maybe she really was magic.

But she worked on kids. How could he get past that? "Hey! There you go again." Moss snapped his fingers in front of his eyes.

"Shit, I'm sorry. I'm not very good company."

"You need to go home and deal with whatever cobwebs are clogging up the pipes in your head. I don't trust you watching my back right now, old buddy. Good thing we're in friendly territory."

Moss was right not to trust him. He'd be useless on a real mission. He was going to have to resolve this somehow. And soon.

Why don't you come up and see my office?

Maybe he should have taken her up on the offer. He could have seen for himself what the sight of those kids— all desperately seeking some sort of normalcy...some sort of acceptance—did to him.

"Cole! Come on man."

He glanced at Moss. "You're right. Absolutely, fucking right. I need to go home."

His friend slapped him on the back. "Now you're talking. Don't come back until you're dragging your old spastic, jump-into-deep-shit-with-both-feet self back with you. That's the Cole we all count on."

Cole smiled. His old jump-into-deep-shit self. Maybe he wasn't so abnormal after all. He knew a hundred other guys who routinely jumped in the deep end of that particular substance, before they realized what it was made of. In his line of work, they were all in the same boat.

"I'm going. And you'll rue the day you asked for the old Cole back again."

"I know I will." Moss shook his head. "But right now, I miss him."

COLE STARED AT THE nameplate on the doorway.

Calista Maribela Nascimento, M.D., Ph.D. Maribela. Pretty middle name. He paused at the abbreviations at the end of the plate. But the poster of a sunglass-clad beagle proclaiming Please Come In, I've Been Woofing For You said it all. His lips curved. He didn't remember any of his doctors sporting cutesy signs like that. Just dark forbidding omens of doom.

Or maybe his memories were just screwed up.

Okay, asshole, enough stalling.

His gut twisted in rebellion when he touched the door handle, but in standard Marine Corps fashion, he sucked it up and pushed through the fear. He passed through the doorway and stopped short. The door clipped his arm as it closed, and he growled a curse word under his breath.

A giggle came from somewhere to his right. "Ummmm… Mommy, we should make him put a dollar in the naughty jar."

Cole turned toward the voice and spotted two pairs of eyes regarding him with interest. One, a girl about six or seven years old, and the other, a young woman who must be her mother. The girl was on her feet, hands on her tiny hips, glaring at him.

"Sorry," said the woman, "her dad has the same…uh, problem, and we decided he should receive a fine for each transgression."

He nodded, and then blinked at the girl, who was still looking at him expectantly. "Well, I guess I owe you a dollar, then."

"You don't have to," said the mother. She turned to her daughter and started to explain, but Cole stopped her.

"I screw…ah, I transgressed. So I should have to pay."

He pulled out his wallet and flipped it open, his glance taking in the rest of the room to make sure there weren't twenty more kids each expecting a piece of him. This girl and her mom appeared to be the only ones waiting. When he thumbed through the bills in search of a dollar, he encountered a leftover Kwanza note he'd forgotten to turn in. His heart blipped, and he bypassed the bill, still hunting for the correct currency. When he found it, he handed it to the mother, over the girl's protests.

"I said something I shouldn't have. I'll trust your mom to put this in your jar at home."

The mom nodded and smiled up at him. "Thank you." The girl plopped her bottom back onto her chair. "Why are you here anyway? Do you have a kid?"

This was one nosey little girl. "No, no kids."

"Aunt Callie won't like that. She doesn't care what grownups say, she only listens to kids." The child crossed her arms over her chest with a *so there!* attitude that made him smile again. Her feet were constantly on the move, kicking the chair beneath her with staccato movements.

"So she doesn't listen to grownups?" he asked.

"No, 'cause kids are more 'portant."

"I'm so sorry," her mother began, but Cole recognized a kindred spirit when he saw one.

He knelt in front of the child and met her eyes. "That's because your Aunt Callie is a very special lady."

"Yes, she—" The girl jumped up from her seat. "Aunt Callie, Aunt Callie!" She ran to the doorway, where the object of her adoration stood with shocked eyes fastened on him. He rose on shaky legs as he gazed back at her.

The child's arms went around Callie's knees and she glanced down, before kneeling in front of the girl and hugging her. "How's my petunia, today?"

"My name's not Petunia, silly, it's Grace."

"See? I need your help to keep all my patients straight."

"Is he a patient too? 'Cause he didn't tell me his name. He only said a bad word." The girl's mother sighed and hurried over to her. "We made him give us a dollar to put in the naughty jar. Is that why he's here…because he says bad words?"

Callie mouth smiled, but her eyes remained cool and impassive.

"I'm here to…to…" He couldn't think past those words.

"He's a friend of mine, he's here to visit," Callie finished. "Now let's get you inside, so I can hear about all the exciting things you've done this week."

She opened the door, and the kid and her mother walked through it. Cole thought Callie was going to simply disappear from sight without saying a word to him. But at the very last second, she turned, her un-smiling face regarding him. "You. Sit down and stay put." Then the door closed behind her.

What kind of greeting was that?

She certainly didn't seem to have Moss's heebie-jeebies for him. Or maybe she'd written him off after that stunt he'd pulled in the parking lot.

Sighing, he went to one of the couches and sat down. He felt ridiculous. The purple curvy furniture was lopsided, as if taken right out of *Alice in Wonderland.* He actually had to brace his body a bit to keep from sliding toward the shorter legged end.

His eyes took in the décor. Cheery flowers in varying shades of purple marched along the walls, accompanied by vibrant lime bees and long-lashed butterflies. All cartoonish figures, all zany and cheerful. Very different from what he remembered from his childhood. But the waiting room wasn't completely frou-frou. On the other side of the room, the décor changed, as if someone had taken a huge hacksaw and cut two spaces down the middle and rejoined them with the wrong halves. The other side was a Lego-themed space with table after table of bright chunky blocks scattered helter-skelter, many on the floor.

The furniture on that side was made of PVC and vinyl in bold primary colors that were...hmmm, *un*-tilted and normal sized. Maybe he'd sat on the wrong side. Hard to look dignified with your knees pulled up to your chest.

But he wasn't about to move. Callie had told him to stay put. And he was all for doing anything that would put him back in the lady's good graces.

He checked his watch. These appointments were normally twenty minutes on the dot. He could remember the doctors he visited checking their watches. Discreetly, but he knew they wanted him out of there. He'd learned a valuable lesson. Grownups couldn't fool children as easily as they thought.

Twenty minutes later, he frowned. No sign of Callie or the pushy kid. And the waiting room was still empty. A mysterious textured window on the other side of the space should house a receptionist, but the glass was shut, not even a peek from anyone behind the slider.

At forty-five minutes, he sat with one leg over his knee, searching the room for a magazine. Nothing. What kind of doctor's office didn't at least have a magazine to occupy the time?

At an hour on the dot, the girl skipped through the door, followed by her mother and Callie. The child stopped right in front of him and looked him in the eye. "Do you owe us any more dollars?"

Did thinking curse words count?

"I didn't say anything else bad, so no."

"Aunt Callie has a hidden camera, you know. She can tell if you're lying."

"Grace Elizabeth," her mother exclaimed.

Was that true? Had she watched him squirm as he sat

here? But no, the little girl didn't look as if she'd been ignored while her doctor spied on him.

He felt ridiculous and small sitting hunched over on the crooked couch, but he joked it off. "I think Aunt Callie would know if I were lying, even without the camera."

"She's not your aunt."

Okay, so maybe he'd have a change of heart about medicating kids after all. This one could use a hefty dose of something strong.

"No, she's my friend." Cole had to grit his teeth to get the words out. They weren't friends. And those were the last words he wanted to hear come out of her mouth.

The girl's mom intervened. "Come on, Grace. You've got soccer practice in an hour. You've still got to change into your uniform."

Grace beamed. "Soccer is great. Aunt Callie helped me get on a team."

Her mom glanced back at Callie. "Yes, and it was the best thing we ever did. We'll see you next month, okay?"

Callie nodded. "Kick a good one for me, you hear?"

"I will. Bye." The girl turned toward Cole one last time. "And no more cussin'."

"I'll try, promise."

With that, the pair slid out the door. And he was alone with Callie. He went to stand up, only to find his feet had fallen asleep from spending an hour on that godda—er, that strange couch.

Great. The pushy kid was rubbing off.

He had two choices: stay where he was and look like a complete idiot, or move toward her on numb feet and fall flat on his face…and look like a complete idiot.

"Well?" Her voice made the choice for him.

He sucked in a quick breath and looked for a cue as to

what she was thinking. But her eyes were dark, the normally warm irises cool.

"I came to apologize," he said, forcing himself off the couch.

"For?"

"Making blanket statements about your work." He motioned to the room. "This is so far-removed from what I experienced as a kid, that...well, I can't even compare it."

"I see."

She didn't. He wondered if he'd made the trip for nothing. "Look, I'm not sure what you want me to say here."

"'I'm happy to see you' would be a good start."

Cole blinked. "Of course I am."

"Then say it."

"I...I..." He shook his head. "That's not what I came here to say."

"Okay." Moving over to a side table, she motioned to two carafes. "Do you want coffee or tea? I'm having coffee."

He frowned. Was this a trick question, to see how much he remembered about her? He remembered everything. Every freckle, the sound of every sigh. This was one test he should be able to pass. "You told me you don't drink coffee."

"I didn't, but I'm learning." A tiny smile played about her lips as she poured herself a cup. "It's not nearly as bad as I remembered."

He got it. "Your stepfather drank coffee."

"And I decided I would never touch a cup of it for as long as I lived. I drank tea. Only tea, couldn't even stand the scent of coffee."

"Like me and psychiatry."

She motioned to the waiting room. "Is it as bad as you remembered? Does it make you feel the things you felt as a child?" She paused. "If you can't get past this room, you'd better pick up and head back to Washington, because I can't give this up. I truly believe in it. Believe it can make a difference in children's lives."

Cole looked inside of himself. Yes, a vague uneasiness still rolled around inside him, but it wasn't as strong as when he'd pulled into the parking lot almost three weeks ago. Maybe because he'd finally realized how much he stood to lose. "Did you shudder when you took that first sip of coffee?"

She nodded. "I thought I'd never get past the smell of the grounds. But I did. I'm working through it. One step at a time."

"I saw what you did for that little girl."

"She's come a long way. She's the reason I do what I do."

"She plays soccer."

"Yes."

"Part of her treatment?"

"I can't talk about it. Sorry." She bit her lip. "It's something else you'd have to accept. You'd have to trust me, trust that I know what I'm doing, because I won't be able to allay your fears about any of the children I treat. Ever."

"She seems happy."

"Yes." Callie took a sip of her coffee, squinching her nose a bit.

"It still gets to you, though, doesn't it? The memories."

She held a cup out to him. "Sometimes, but it's easier each day."

He shook his head. "I don't want the coffee, Cal. I want you. I was wrong to run out of here like I did. I hope you can forgive me for being such an assho…stupid." His mouth went dry, but he had to finish it once and for all. He had to say the words. "I love you."

Setting her cup on the side table, she studied him. "Are you sure?"

Was he sure?

"Oh yeah. Very." He fished in his pocket and took out a

little box. "It's not a ring. I want you to make sure you can put up with me before I press you for a commitment."

Callie laughed. "Too late."

His chest tightened. *Oh shit, here it comes.*

Moving toward him, she laid her palms on his chest. "I committed to you that day in Angola, when you dragged me away from that landmine. When we made love for the very first time. I didn't realize it then…but I do now."

His mouth opened, but nothing came out. Callie took the box from his hands and smiled up at him before she opened it. He tried to gauge her reaction as she stared with wide eyes at the silver bracelet and its dangling serpent charm. The creature's tiny emerald eyes glittered up at them.

"I know it's lame," he said, wondering if she would even get the reference. "But I just thought—"

"It's not lame." She lifted the bracelet and set the charm into motion with a flick of her finger. Looking up, she smiled. "It's perfect. In fact…it looks like chicken."

EPILOGUE

"DON'T PUSH YET, CAL, breathe through it. One, two, three, four—"

"Don't touch me, you bastard!" Her head swiveled toward him as she gripped her knees. "You're the one who did this to me, remember?"

Nervous giggles filled the chilly hospital room. Cole leaned next to her ear and whispered, "You're laying it on a little thick, don't you think?"

She kept panting in rapid sequence. "The instructor... *hoo, hoo, hee, hee*...said she wanted...*hoo, hoo, hee, hee*...realism."

Cole rolled his eyes, but kept playing his part. "The contraction's at its peak. Keep panting, my darling." He grinned down at her. "So is this how you're planning to treat me in the delivery room?"

"*Hoo, hoo, hee, hee*... Did I treat you this way last time?" Her panting continued, unabated.

Cole glanced up at the other Lamaze students. "Do I have to answer that question in a public setting?" More laughing commenced. "Okay, the contraction's over. For the moment."

He gave an evil laugh and looked around the room. "But take my word for it, things get ugly in the real delivery room, really ugly."

The instructor stood, her eyes glinting. "Okay, I think we've gotten the idea, guys. Thanks for volunteering."

Cole straightened up and reached a hand down to Callie. She angled her body and looked longingly at her toes one last time, before swinging her legs over the bed and climbing to her feet. "We're happy to help," she said to the instructor. "We're old hands at this."

The woman's brows went up as if afraid to ask. "And this makes how many for you?"

"Just our second. But the first one took us on a trip around the world."

Callie laced her fingers through Cole's as they went back to their seats in the cramped room.

Yes, Micah Cole Nascimento Scalini had survived with everything intact and was safe at home with his Nana Scalini. At age two, he was a bundle of unrestrained energy, but neither Callie nor Cole would change him, even if they could. Nor would his grandmother, who'd flown in from Florida to help before the new baby's arrival. Micah was the spitting image of Sara. For that Callie would be eternally grateful.

Her brother-in-law had been stripped of his Senate seat, but thanks to the work of some tricky lawyers, he'd avoided jail time. Cole had been furious with the verdict. But, Callie knew life wasn't always fair. Besides, the televised trial had given the world an opportunity to render its own judgment as to his innocence or guilt. And that was justice enough for Callie, a fact which she and Cole had agreed to disagree on.

In the end, Gary hadn't lifted a finger to fight for custody of Micah. That had tempered a lot of Callie's residual anger. And two good things had come of the man's destructive actions. She'd met a wonderful, caring man and had given birth to her sister's sweet, sweet baby boy.

The class went on for a few minutes longer, then the professor let them out with the admonishment to practice at home before next week's session.

Callie stood up and stretched her aching back, the charm on her bracelet jingling as she did. Suddenly her eyes widened. "Uh oh. I did say we were old hands at this, right?"

"Yeah, why?"

"Our class participation seems to have come to an un-timely end."

He frowned at her. "Why's that?"

"Because, my dear husband, my water just broke."

* * * * *

REQUEST YOUR FREE BOOKS!

2 FREE NOVELS
PLUS 2 FREE GIFTS!

WORLDWIDE LIBRARY®

Your Partner in Crime

YES! Please send me 2 FREE novels from the Worldwide Library® series and my 2 FREE gifts (gifts are worth about $10). After receiving them, if I don't wish to receive any more books, I can return the shipping statement marked "cancel." If I don't cancel, I will receive 4 brand-new novels every month and be billed just $5.24 per book in the U.S. or $6.24 per book in Canada. That's a savings of at least 34% off the cover price. It's quite a bargain! Shipping and handling is just 50¢ per book in the U.S. and 75¢ per book in Canada.* I understand that accepting the 2 free books and gifts places me under no obligation to buy anything. I can always return a shipment and cancel at any time. Even if I never buy another book, the two free books and gifts are mine to keep forever.

414/424 WDN FVUV

Name	(PLEASE PRINT)
Address	Apt. #
City	State/Prov.	Zip/Postal Code

Signature (if under 18, a parent or guardian must sign)

Mail to the Harlequin® Reader Service:
IN U.S.A.: P.O. Box 1867, Buffalo, NY 14240-1867
IN CANADA: P.O. Box 609, Fort Erie, Ontario L2A 5X3

Want to try two free books from another line?
Call 1-800-873-8635 or visit www.ReaderService.com.

* Terms and prices subject to change without notice. Prices do not include applicable taxes. Sales tax applicable in N.Y. Canadian residents will be charged applicable taxes. Offer not valid in Quebec. This offer is limited to one order per household. Not valid for current subscribers to the Worldwide Library series. All orders subject to credit approval. Credit or debit balances in a customer's account(s) may be offset by any other outstanding balance owed by or to the customer. Please allow 4 to 6 weeks for delivery. Offer available while quantities last.

Your Privacy—The Harlequin® Reader Service is committed to protecting your privacy. Our Privacy Policy is available online at www.ReaderService.com or upon request from the Harlequin Reader Service.

We make a portion of our mailing list available to reputable third parties that offer products we believe may interest you. If you prefer that we not exchange your name with third parties, or if you wish to clarify or modify your communication preferences, please visit us at www.ReaderService.com/consumerchoice or write to us at Harlequin Reader Service Preference Service, P.O. Box 9062, Buffalo, NY 14269. Include your complete name and address.

WWLI3

REQUEST YOUR FREE BOOKS!
2 FREE NOVELS PLUS 2 FREE GIFTS!

♦HARLEQUIN®

INTRIGUE®

BREATHTAKING ROMANTIC SUSPENSE

YES! Please send me 2 FREE Harlequin Intrigue® novels and my 2 FREE gifts (gifts are worth about $10). After receiving them, if I don't wish to receive any more books, I can return the shipping statement marked "cancel." If I don't cancel, I will receive 6 brand-new novels every month and be billed just $4.49 per book in the U.S. or $5.24 per book in Canada. That's a savings of at least 14% off the cover price! It's quite a bargain! Shipping and handling is just 50¢ per book in the U.S. and 75¢ per book in Canada.* I understand that accepting the 2 free books and gifts places me under no obligation to buy anything. I can always return a shipment and cancel at any time. Even if I never buy another book, the two free books and gifts are mine to keep forever.

182/382 HDN FV5V

Name	(PLEASE PRINT)	
Address		Apt. #
City	State/Prov.	Zip/Postal Code

Signature (if under 18, a parent or guardian must sign)

Mail to the **Harlequin® Reader Service:**
IN U.S.A.: P.O. Box 1867, Buffalo, NY 14240-1867
IN CANADA: P.O. Box 609, Fort Erie, Ontario L2A 5X3

Are you a subscriber to Harlequin Intrigue books
and want to receive the larger-print edition?
Call 1-800-873-8635 or visit www.ReaderService.com.

* Terms and prices subject to change without notice. Prices do not include applicable taxes. Sales tax applicable in N.Y. Canadian residents will be charged applicable taxes. Offer not valid in Quebec. This offer is limited to one order per household. Not valid for current subscribers to Harlequin Intrigue books. All orders subject to credit approval. Credit or debit balances in a customer's account(s) may be offset by any other outstanding balance owed by or to the customer. Please allow 4 to 6 weeks for delivery. Offer available while quantities last.

Your Privacy—The Harlequin® Reader Service is committed to protecting your privacy. Our Privacy Policy is available online at www.ReaderService.com or upon request from the Harlequin Reader Service.

We make a portion of our mailing list available to reputable third parties that offer products we believe may interest you. If you prefer that we not exchange your name with third parties, or if you wish to clarify or modify your communication preferences, please visit us at www.ReaderService.com/consumerschoice or write to us at Harlequin Reader Service Preference Service, P.O. Box 9062, Buffalo, NY 14269. Include your complete name and address.

HIDIR13

ReaderService.com

Manage your account online!

- Review your order history
- Manage your payments
- Update your address

Enjoy all the features!

- Reader excerpts from any series
- Respond to mailings and special monthly offers
- Discover new series available to you
- Browse the Bonus Bucks catalog
- Share your feedback

Visit us at:
ReaderService.com